advance reader copy

This is an uncorrected proof and text may change before final publication. Please verify with author or publisher before quoting directly from this text.

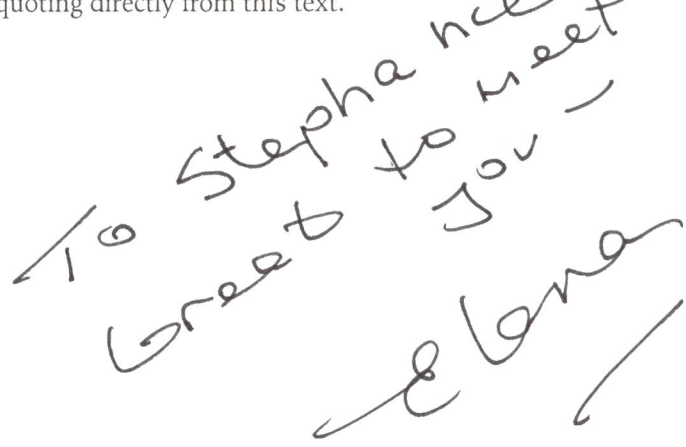

part of the solution

To Abie, Adara, Ace, Violet, Taliya, and Monte, the six young spirits in my life for whom 1978 was unimaginably long ago, and, as ever, to Penny.

PART OF THE SOLUTION

Elana Michelson

Torchflame Books

Vista, CA

Copyright © 2025 by Elana Michelson
All rights reserved. Torchflame Books supports copyright. Copyright fuels creativity, encourages diverse voices, promotes free speech, and creates a vibrant culture. Thank you for buying an authorized edition of this book and for complying with copyright laws by not reproducing, scanning, or distributing any part of it in any form without permission, except by a reviewer who wishes to quote brief passages in connection with a review written for insertion in a magazine, newspaper, broadcast, website, blog or other outlet. You are supporting independent publishing and allowing Torchflame Books to publish books for all readers.

NO AI TRAINING: Without in any way limiting the author's [and publisher's] exclusive rights under copyright, any use of this publication to "train" generative artificial intelligence (AI) technologies to generate text is expressly prohibited. The author reserves all rights to license uses of this work for generative AI training and development of machine learning language models.

ISBN: 978-1-61153-604-1 (paperback)
ISBN: 978-1-61153-605-8 (ebook)
ISBN: 978-1-61153-606-5 (large print)
Library of Congress Control Number: 2025903830

Part of the Solution is published by: Torchflame Books, an imprint of Top Reads Publishing, LLC, 1035 E. Vista Way, Suite 205, Vista, CA 92084, USA

"The Devil and Daniel Webster" by Stephen Vincent Benet. Copyright © 1936 by Stephen Vincent Benet. Copyright renewed © 1964 by Thomas C. Benet, Stephanie B. Mahin and Rachel Benet Lewis. Used by permission of Brandt & Hochman Literary Agents, Inc. Any copying or distribution of this text is expressly forbidden. All rights reserved.

"Absolutely Sweet Marie," Words and Music by Bob Dylan. Copyright © 1966 UNIVERSAL TUNES. Copyright Renewed. All Rights Reserved Used by Permission. Reprinted by Permission of Hal Leonard LLC.

"Desolation Row," Words and Music by Bob Dylan. Copyright © 1965 UNIVERSAL TUNES. Copyright Renewed. All Rights Reserved Used by Permission. Reprinted by Permission of Hal Leonard LLC.

"All Along The Watchtower," Words and Music by Bob Dylan. Copyright © 1968, 1985 UNIVERSAL TUNES. Copyright Renewed. All Rights Reserved Used by Permission. Reprinted by Permission of Hal Leonard LLC.

"The Ballad of Frankie Lee And Judas Priest," Words and Music by Bob Dylan. Copyright 1968, 1996 UNIVERSAL TUNES. Copyright Renewed. All Rights Reserved Used by Permission. Reprinted by Permission of Hal Leonard LLC.

"Mr. Tambourine Man," Words and Music by Bob Dylan. Copyright © 1964, 1965 UNIVERSAL TUNES. Copyright Renewed. All Rights Reserved Used by Permission. Reprinted by Permission of Hal Leonard LLC.

"If You See Her, Say Hello," Words and Music by Bob Dylan. Copyright 1976 UNIVERSAL TUNES. Copyright Renewed. All Rights Reserved Used by Permission. Reprinted by Permission of Hal Leonard LLC.

"Sisters Of Mercy," Words and Music by Leonard Cohen. Copyright © 1967 Sony Music Publishing (US) LLC. Copyright Renewed. All Rights Administered by Sony Music Publishing (US) LLC, 424 Church Street, Suite 1200, Nashville, TN 37219. International Copyright Secured All Rights Reserved. Reprinted by Permission of Hal Leonard LLC.

Cover design and interior layout: Jori Hanna
The publisher is not responsible for websites or social media accounts (or their content) that are not owned by the publisher.
This is a work of fiction. Names, characters, places, and incidents are either the product of the author's imagination or used fictitiously, and any resemblance to actual persons, living or dead, business establishments, events, or locales is entirely coincidental.

prologue

Professor Jennifer Morgan nudged her luggage a few inches closer to the hotel reception desk and placed her book back in her briefcase. She was much too disgusted and sweaty to read standing up. It was years since she'd been in Massachusetts, but instead of wandering the Berkshires, instead of wending her memories back across innocence and other time-worn American dreams, here she was in the lobby of Boston's Regency Plaza, in a nightmare of conferences and packaged tours. On either side, identical lines of people loaded down with luggage and annoyance crept forward toward the check-in clerks, the promise of a shower, and a badly needed drink at the bar.

How could so much time have passed since she had last crossed the border into Massachusetts? It was, after all, just up the interstate from her professorship in New York City and her apartment in the West Village. Still, it had been so very long. Then an invitation had come to give the keynote on a subject close to her heart, the colonialism that ran like tainted blood through the Victorian novel. This was a conference she attended dutifully each year, and this year it was being held in Boston. So

1

here she was, and the line of conference-goers checking into the hotel was not getting appreciably shorter.

Out of boredom, she read through a list of conventions masquerading as a welcome sign. *The Annual Meeting of the American Urological Association. Law Enforcement for Social Justice. Class, Race, and Gender in the Nineteenth-Century Novel.* The sign, Jennifer decided, was the management's attempt to cut down on the number of jet-lagged travelers who would inevitably take fifteen minutes of a desk clerk's time before acknowledging, reluctantly and with nary an apology, that they were in the wrong hotel. At least she, if the list was to be trusted, had come to the right place.

Jennifer's own contribution to the conference lay in the luggage at her feet, as did her laptop, the morning's *New York Times*, and the overpriced bohemian-academic-chic clothing that she had indulged in for this year's presentation. Her new outfit made her look thin, understated, and, at least in her own mind, sublimely self-possessed, but the compulsion to buy it was not something of which she was proud. Who would care, anyway? She'd have the usual meals with the group of Victorianists she always met at this conference, the ones who, like her, could laugh at their own tendency to mistake literary criticism for the politics of middle-class outrage, who could be counted on to order decent wine with dinner, and who made it a point of honor—no matter how hard at work on their latest article—to value teaching over scholarship.

Finally, the line seemed to be moving forward. She drew next to a man who, in noticing her, would no doubt curse his fate for choosing the slowest-moving line. Somewhat guiltily, she glanced over at him and smiled.

"Damn," he said, catching her glance. "I don't even have time to check in. I couldn't get out of the office."

"This hotel hosts a million conferences a year. You'd think they'd have the staffing down by now."

But then, simultaneously, each of them was staring at the other, squinting through the years.

Yes, she thought. The same broad face, the same strong body, give or take forty years. The same sandy hair, now mostly grey. And there was no mistaking the amazement with which he now regarded her. Nostalgia incarnate, in the person of Ford McDermott, was staring at her with astonished eyes.

"Hey, Cisco," she said softly.

"Jen? What are you doing here?"

"The nineteenth-century novel," she admitted. "And you?" Her eyes went back to the list of conferences by the door. Law Enforcement for Social Justice. "Well, I'll be damned. Good for you."

They stood, grinning at each other.

"Look," he said. "I don't even know where to start, and I really am late for this meeting. Could we . . ." He pulled up the sleeve of his suit jacket and glanced at his watch. "The bar at seven o'clock?"

"And miss the senile ramblings of the out-going editor of the *Journal of Victorian Studies*? In a heartbeat. Ford, I can't believe it."

"Do you know how often . . . ?"

"Yes," she said. "Yes, I do."

Ford McDermott picked up his overnight case, visibly reflected on the possibility of hugging her, wove his way through the crowded lobby, and disappeared.

About time, Jennifer thought as she turned the handle on the door to her room. She threw her bags on the bed and went immediately to the mirror. Four decades of feminism, thirty years, minus the occasional sabbatical, of Constructions of Gender in the Victorian Novel, a modest but respectable scholarly reputation, and all she could think, she noted ruefully, was, How do I look? A little the worse for wear, she decided, after a lifetime and a four-hour train ride from Penn Station. But she would do. A well-tended sixty-something met her gaze, the never-quite-beautiful face, the grey-green eyes above the long nose and generous cheekbones. The passionate, earnest twenty-eight-year-old whom Ford McDermott had loved had mellowed, or was it hardened, into a grey-haired woman who could laugh at herself and who had learned that kindness was the better part of valor. What would she tell him about the intervening years? A briefly happy marriage. A career that had gratified, if not inspired. A not-unhappy life of serial monogamy, of intelligent if often self-absorbed men—and women—who had shared the vicissitudes of academe, the slow march of political disappointment, and her bed.

And what of him? She had noted, as he raised his hand to check his watch, the wedding ring on his finger. What would she hear about Detective Ford McDermott's journey from her half-joking lessons in sixties politics to Law Enforcement for Social Justice? She was surprised, as she stepped away from the mirror, to note how much she cared. That his life had been happy. That he remembered her with fondness. That, she shook her head and smiled, she had spent a week's salary on a fabulous new outfit that made her look thin, understated, and sublimely self-possessed.

She settled herself into the nondescript hotel room, her open bags on one queen-sized bed and herself on the other. I should practice the keynote, she thought. Or finish reading the new book on the Brontës everyone will be talking about. But she would, she knew, spend the intervening two hours waiting for it to be seven o'clock. She drew the pillow more comfortably behind her back and settled into remembering.

The circumstances that had brought her and Ford together had started her fourth year in graduate school as she struggled with her dissertation. The literature review was complete, the outline approved by her advisor, the introduction and first chapter in a neat stack next to the typewriter in her room, but then, suddenly, she had stopped, frozen in a sense that her dissertation represented only a failure of imagination. Graduate school had followed college because, as she acknowledged at the time, she couldn't imagine a life outside of a university. She had been happy in the sixties, loving its passionate politics and its unarticulated faith in the efficacy of words. But all through the early seventies, old friends had continued to leave the city for back-to-the-land dreams of purposeful simplicity. Or else they were in law school, determined to use the law's weapons to defend women, prisoners, and the poor. Only she had remained, tethered to what had begun to feel like a second-hand life. On the day the last American troops left Saigon, she had impulsively taken a leave of absence, a minuscule inheritance, and an even smaller stash of determination, and headed up to New England to look for a life outside of academe.

And she had found it. Flanders was a small hamlet on the outskirts of Williamstown, Massachusetts. Williamstown itself was a college town of prim Puritan heritage, but Flanders had been invaded by an opinionated, motley collection of sixties refugees. In 1967, the Episcopalian priest had retired, and the new shepherd of Flanders' collective soul preached liberation theology and wore white sneakers with his Sunday robes. Stone-ground barley appeared in the new health-food co-op, whose manager had bought a run-down organic farm and agitated for consumer protections. A devotee of astrology and the Tarot renovated a ramshackle old guesthouse and opened a café. Throughout the land, the don't-trust-anyone-over-thirty generation was slowly approaching thirty, but the citizens of Flanders, Commonwealth of Massachusetts, were far too preoccupied to notice.

Grandpa Isaac's tiny legacy had been just what the café

needed. Jennifer bought a half-ownership, a few gallons of paint, and a space to settle into what George Eliot would have called a knowable community. Wendy Scholes, her Tarot card-reading co-owner, was an inspired incompetent, endearingly—most of the time—unable to keep the books or order the correct amount of flour. But once freed into the kitchen by Jennifer's better math skills, Wendy made an art of carrot cake and rosemary muffins. The Café Galadriel gathered a clientele of earnest coffee-drinking intellectuals and equally earnest coffee-hating hippies, many of whom, Jennifer noted, were professors and students from Williams College. She had indeed found a life outside of academe, but not, she could acknowledge at this distance, very far.

In her hotel room, Jennifer curled up more snugly into the pillows. It was at the café that the whole awful business had started, the disaster that had brought Ford into her life, broken apart her idyll in the countryside, and sent her back to graduate school, no longer believing that she was cut out for life as a hippie entrepreneur. She could even identify the evening when, in retrospect, it all began. Jimmy Carter was president. *Desire* and *Hotel California* were on the record player. She counted back on her fingers: September 1978.

part one

one

Jennifer surveyed the café with satisfied proprietary eyes. The freshmen at the two corner tables were an excellent sign. Having arrived in Williamstown the day before, having unpacked their carefully faded blue jeans and dispatched their carefully dry-eyed parents, having found their way to the registrar's office and the bookstore with barely concealed terror, they had, no doubt, asked whomever they could find where, you know, *it* was happening. And they had been sent straight to Café Galadriel to nurse their bludgeoned intellects and wounded sexuality on Jennifer's coffee for the next four years.

Around them, the unmatched wooden chairs and tables of the café held the usual Monday afternoon crowd. Brownley (Philosophy) and Krasner (Sociology) sat over a game of chess. The Western Massachusetts Women's Anti-Violence Task Force occupied the round table in the center of the room. Samir Molchev, self-styled seeker of truth, was alone at a corner table reading Suzuki's *The Field of Zen*. On the salmon walls, a pre-Raphaelite poster of the Lady of Shallot hung beside a poster of Che Guevara. *It will be a great day,* read the sign above Wendy's bakery display case, *when schools get all the money they need and the*

Air Force has to hold a bake sale to buy a bomber. A tattered sofa occupied one wall of the room, the coffee table in front of it piled with backgammon sets and old copies of *Ramparts* magazine. A Bob Marley tape played on the stereo.

It was the moment of the year when the café was moving into autumn, away from its summer tourist mode. Behind the cash register, Wendy was packing away the pitchers that had held iced tea and cold cider. Her summer uniform of paisley sun dresses had given way to long sleeves and flowing, ankle-length dresses. Short, with a rounded body and small face, Wendy's size was belied by clothes that began at her shoulders and fell draping to the floor. Her curly, dark red hair followed the same line, rippling down her back and ending just above her waist. Jennifer, whose knowledge of poetry had outlasted work on her dissertation, would have occasion to wonder in the coming weeks if Wendy hadn't modeled herself on the Tennyson heroine behind her on the wall.

Jennifer herself was at her usual spot, the table by the Vermont Castings wood stove that, in the winter months, would reduce heating bills while contributing to what she thought of as the café's fake authenticity. She was dressed, as usual, in dungarees, Indian cotton, and the sandals she insisted on wearing until the snow fell, but her short summer haircut was growing out, and her thick brown hair was starting to take on its haphazard winter unruliness.

"I remember you guys," Jennifer was saying. "You were all practicing to be Leon Trotsky, and you polished your rhetoric and your steely gaze on girls like me who were stuffing envelopes for the cause."

Beside her, Zachery Lerner grimaced.

"We weren't really that bad. We were just showing off for each other."

"Well, you could have fooled me. But anyway, I think it's

amazing that Williams College actually hired you to teach the impressionable young."

Zach's reputation had preceded him, not only at Williams but among anyone who remembered the decade just past: Berkeley in the late sixties, a first book on working class resistance to the war, three years in Leavenworth for refusing induction. Jennifer had recognized him, both by reputation and by the studious features that reminded her of all the budding revolutionaries she had always figured she would marry. His curly hair, already a premature salt-and-pepper, circled a rounded face with deep-set brown eyes and broad features. The lumberjack clothes that covered his burly frame would clearly win no friends among the board of trustees. His face, under horn-rimmed glasses, was that of a Russian Jewish revolutionary, which, at several generations removed, he was.

The front door of the café opened with a loud kick. Annie McGantry, Flanders' organic farmer and herbalist, wedged the door with her shoulder and pulled a trolley topped by a large, covered barrel through the doorway and into the room. She spotted Jennifer and made her way to the table. She eased the barrel off the trolley, made sure that both the trolley and the barrel were standing safely upright, and threw herself into an empty chair.

"Goddamn. Can you believe I ran out of barrels?" she greeted them. "You should see the Kirby cukes this year—it's like they don't want to quit. I tell them, 'Come on, how many pickles do we need? I need to finish canning the tomatoes, so stop putting out, you little sluts, and save some energy for next year.' I've already brought four barrels to the co-op. I can't start selling them for a week—they won't be fit for eating. But at least they're out of my hair. Anyway, here's your barrel. I put them on your September bill."

Jennifer groaned. "You brought them here when I can't sell

them for a week? Do you know how much we've got piled up in the kitchen already? Susan Broady delivered all the—"

"I promise you you're not as crowded as the co-op is. I'm, like, buried. You know, I peed on the seeds before I planted them," she reflected. "I think that's why everything's doing so well."

Jennifer grimaced. "Don't tell me what you put in the brine, okay?"

Zach regarded Annie with curiosity. Annie was pretty, with strong, if currently grimy features, and she looked to Zach's urban eyes to be precisely the kind of unwashed earth mother he would have expected to find in the Berkshires. He glanced briefly at the blue jeans stuffed into Wellington boots, the small breasts and narrow hips, the muscled forearms and dirty fingernails. He found himself impressed by the uncompromising look in her light grey eyes.

"Annie manages the co-op." Jennifer turned to Zach. "She has a back room filled with medicinal herbs, so watch out if you get a rash in her vicinity. Three hundred years ago, she would have been burned as a witch."

"So," Zach indicated the pickles. "Tell *me* what you put in the brine. I love pickles. Or is it a secret old family recipe?"

"My family? Shit. My mother's only old family recipe was for spoon bread."

"Well, my grandmother bought pickles in barrels on the Lower East Side. So, what's in the brine?"

"Salt, of course. Pickling spices. Apple cider vinegar."

"My bubbe would have been horrified at pickles made with apple cider vinegar. She would have put them in the same category as whole wheat bagels."

Annie eyed him, suspecting that he was only half teasing her and not entirely clear about what was wrong with whole wheat bagels. Still, she liked his solidity, and she had always been partial to curly hair. He looked utterly unmovable. Annie took it as a challenge.

"She never tried my pickles, then," Annie drawled. Her voice took on a Southern mountain twang that did not seem quite in keeping with the ANIMALS ARE PEOPLE TOO bumper sticker on her pick-up truck. But it had, Jennifer knew, been her mother tongue. Annie was the offspring of a hard-drinking truck farmer and a deaconess in the Bethel Baptist Church, her small soul the preferred battle ground of her parents' adversarial marriage. In the end, her father had won. Annie had scraped the mud of Mount Haven, Arkansas, off her first pair of Birkenstocks, hitchhiked to San Francisco for the Summer of Love, and sworn she would never set foot in a church again.

"Honey, you come over one night, and I'll teach you the art of making pickles, Annie-style. Hell, you can harvest the rest of the damned cucumbers while you're at it. I could use the help, and you," she regarded the intellectual paleness of his skin, "could use some time in the great outdoors."

There was movement at the corner table. Samir Molchev rose from his chair and placed his book in a cloth satchel embossed with Indian appliqué. Jennifer watched him come toward them, his tall body graceful in jeans and a long, white, collarless shirt.

There really was such a thing, Jennifer decided, as being too good-looking for your own good. Or anyone else's, for that matter. It was as if Samir knew that his body was perfect: broad, graceful shoulders, a soft swirl of hair just visible through his open collar. Soft black hair fell to his shoulders, framing pronounced cheekbones and black, slightly slanted Tartan eyes. All he needed, she thought, was a gold leaf halo and scarlet robes, and the resemblance to a Byzantine icon would be complete.

Beside her, Annie stiffened. "It's late," she announced. "I have to get back." Annie rose, strode across the room and into the café kitchen, and returned with a ladle and an empty mason jar. She raised the lip on the barrel, extracted half a dozen pickles with her fingers, and placed them in the jar. She ladled brine over them, screwed the top onto the jar, and set the jar in front of Zach on the table. "Here you are. A sample. Let it sit for a week before you open it."

Samir came up behind her. "Peace, all." He raised his hands in greeting and eyed Zach with curiosity.

Annie ignored him. Zach reached out a hand.

"I'm Zach Lerner. Good to meet you."

"Zachary Lerner?" Samir asked slowly. The black eyes blinked.

"Yes, *that* Zachary Lerner," Jennifer put in. "Williams has stolen him away from Berkeley."

"And you should hear the Eisenhower Professor of American Democracy on the subject," Zach smiled. "'Just what we need, another draft dodger on the faculty!'"

Samir regarded Zach in silence.

Annie stirred impatiently. "Jen, I gotta go. Where should I put the barrel?"

Samir pulled his eyes away from Zach. "Let me get that into the kitchen for you."

Annie narrowed her eyes. "Don't bother."

"Peace, sister. I'm just trying to help you."

"I'm not your sister, and I don't need your help."

"Just leave it, Annie," Jennifer said hurriedly. "I'll get someone to help me with it later."

Annie turned back to Jennifer as if the exchange with Samir had never happened. "Thanks," she drawled. "I've got chickens wanting their dinner." She nodded to Zach. "Remember, don't eat those pickles for a week."

The three of them watched her has she grabbed onto the trolley and wheeled it purposefully out the door. None of them had any reason to suspect that forty-eight hours later one of them would be dead.

two

"It never fails," one of the weavers was fuming. "If men do it, it's an art. If women do it, it's a craft." Ginger, the new waitress in wire-rim glasses and cut-off jeans, poured a refill of coffee into her cup. Wendy stood over them serving dessert, her long, red curls hanging dangerously close to the baklava.

The café door swung open, and Annie McGantry stormed into the room. She looked around for Jennifer and then headed directly for the counter, behind which Jennifer stood on a stepladder, setting jars of honey on the shelf.

"Damn it, Jen, I'm really getting spooked. I don't want him near me, you hear me?"

Jennifer grimaced. "Yeah, Annie. Everyone hears you."

"Well, are you going to do it then?"

"Do what?"

"Keep him out of my face."

"Who are you talking about?"

"Bullshit. You know who I'm talking about."

Jennifer stepped down, set the ladder aside, and gestured for Annie to follow her into the café kitchen. She propped herself up on the counter as Annie leaned against the refrigerator door.

Part of the Solution

"So I was trying to close up the co-op, right, and the place is really crowded. It's like, what gives? Did everyone run out of tahini at exactly the same moment? Greg had already gone home, I'm frantically dealing with the cash register, and everyone wants to know stuff like whether the new brand of tofu sausage is made with organic cumin, and meanwhile, Samir is walking around like he fucking owns the place."

"Actually, Annie, as a member of the co-op, he does own it."

"Him and eighty-two others. So what? And of course, as usual, the minute he appears, he's pounced on by some woman who's thinking with her groin. This time, it was Dolores. You know, from the law collective. She's a *lawyer*, damn it. She ought to be able to recognize a phony when she sees one."

Annie glanced up in time to see Wendy looking in on them through the open door, her small face registering alarm. "Shit," she swore under her breath. "Speaking of Samir's peanut gallery." She regarded Wendy defiantly until Wendy dropped her gaze and retreated back to her customers.

"So anyway." Annie turned back to Jennifer. "Everyone else is finally gone, and I say, 'Excuse me. Can I help you?' He looks up from where Dolores is practically licking his sandals and says, 'No, thank you. Everything is fine.' I say, 'No, actually, Everything isn't fine. I'm trying to close up,' and he says something to Dolores that makes them both laugh. I say, 'Don't you fucking laugh at me,' and he raises his hand like he's blessing me and says, in that above-it-all voice he gets sometimes, 'It's not me who's laughing. It's the laughter of the immortals.'" Annie paused. "The what?"

"It's from a Hermann Hesse novel. *Steppenwolf*."

"Immortals, hell. He doesn't fool me with his holy-man crap —I was raised around the best of them, and I know that when someone starts talking about immortality, it's time to go check that the money's still under the mattress. I say, 'We're closing. Buy something or leave.' Dolores buys enough granola for an army, as if that's going to make it better, and Samir finally saunters out of there as if he's shown me a thing or two. I mean it, Jen. Keep Mr. Buddha-man out of my face. Out of the co-op. I don't want him anywhere near me."

Jennifer shook her head. Here we go again, she thought. Annie on another crusade. Only this time, it wouldn't be an upstanding political crusade, boycotting grapes for the United Farm Workers or buying coffee from a peasants' collective in Peru.

"Look, I don't know what you want me to do."

"I told you already. Keep him out of the co-op."

"But I can't."

Annie righted herself and turned toward the door, having finished what she'd come to say. "Oh, yes, you can. He's your damn roommate."

"Now wait a minute. Three things, okay? Number one, he's not my roommate. He just lives in the same house. You got that distinction? Number two, he's not the only one who lives in my house. Will and Wendy also live in my house." Jennifer took her hands from her head, the better to gesticulate. "And the four of us have this nice little wheel hanging over the stove, right?" Jennifer placed her hands so that her thumbs and index fingers came together to form a circle. "And every week, we give the wheel a nice little turn, and sometimes the wheel says it's my turn to do the shopping, and sometimes it's Will's, and sometimes it's Wendy's, and sometimes, every four weeks, well, what do you know, it's Samir's. Number three, Samir is a member of the co-op, and you may be the manager of the co-op, but you have no authority to ban anyone, let alone any member, from shopping there. Samir also owes the co-op the same four hours a month that all the members owe. Come on, Annie." Jennifer sat back again, waving her hands in exasperation. "You know all that. You wrote the rules yourself."

"Yes, I wrote them," Annie pounced. "And I know that, as

manager, I can call a meeting of the entire membership to discuss a problem any time I want."

Jennifer looked across at her. "Hey, kid. I'm your friend, remember? This is me, Jennifer. Remember? Friend?"

"One more time and I'll do it," Annie insisted, and headed out the open kitchen door.

Wendy restacked the last of the dishes, left the café through the back entrance, and made her way through the garden to the side door. She mounted the staircase into the two floors of living space that served as home to her, Will, Jennifer, and Samir. She brewed herself a cup of mint tea and carried it to the upstairs bedroom she shared with Will. She sat herself on the bed and took up her deck of Tarot cards.

She would sit here and wait for Jennifer. She had made this place into a home, and it was hers. She had first moved in while a senior at Bennington, happy to be living away from a campus of women who preferred Sylvia Plath to J. R. R. Tolkien and told her she should read Walter Benjamin when all she wanted to do was paint. After graduation, she broke down the wall on the first floor between the dining room and the original living room, painted the walls salmon, bought a second-hand coffee urn at a yard sale, and opened what she duly named the Café Galadriel. Will had come the following year, walking into the café one evening to order the vegetarian moussaka and ask if she knew of a room to rent. He was a carpenter and woodworker, he said, and he was planning to open a craft shop. She had stared down at his long, tapered fingers and the crevices between the bones in his wrists and calmly reached for the Tarot deck behind the counter. She turned over a card: the four of wands. She said, "One hundred fifty dollars a month, and do you think you could help me strip the wainscoting?" He moved into the house and, a month later, started spending his nights in her room.

Then Jennifer had come and, finally, Samir, who had appeared one evening and talked to her about war as an imbalance of spiritual forces. She had told him about the suit of swords, how rashness and violence did less harm in the end than the frozen wasteland of the intellect. The next day, Samir went for a walk with Will, and Will came back saying, "I think we should let him live here." Jennifer hadn't liked it, but for once, she had been overruled.

Jennifer spat the last of the toothpaste into the sink, decided strategically not to flush the toilet, and fervently hoped she would make it to her room without Wendy realizing she was home. She had spent the early evening avoiding Wendy's eyes, paying doting attention to the customers, hissing orders from the doorway to avoid being cornered in the kitchen. All for naught. As she tiptoed across the hall, she found herself ambushed in the hallway.

There was one more tactic left.

"Good night," she asserted heartily.

"Jen?"

"God, I'm tired. See you tomorrow."

"Aw, Jen!"

Jennifer looked across. The bright blue eyes were anxious. The rounded body had taken on the hunched shoulders and folded hands that were Wendy at her most vulnerable, the posture that, about half of the time, made Jennifer want to hug her, baby her, and put her to bed in flannel pajamas with feet. The other half of the time, it made Jennifer want to throw her down the stairs.

"All right," she sighed. Leaning her back against the wall, she bent her knees and slid down until she was sitting on the floor. "Apparently Samir was being really provocative, strutting his stuff around the co-op, and Annie decided he was doing it just to annoy her. Frankly, I think she's probably right. She wants us to keep him out of the co-op completely from now on, or else she threatened to call a membership meeting about it. Now you know as much as I do."

"I'll talk to her tomorrow."

"That won't help. You know Annie in this kind of mood. Talking to her will just send her to the membership faster."

"But we've got to do something," Wendy insisted.

"Yeah, right. But who's 'we' and what's 'something'?"

Wendy's eyes expressed a disconcerting faith that Jennifer would think of something. Seduced again, she tried.

Annie's outrage, she knew, had less to do with Samir's presence at the co-op than a weekend the two of them had spent together shortly after his arrival. Her continued hostility was puzzling. Annie had worked her way cheerfully through half the Williams Geology department and more than one of the editors of *Mother Earth News* with never a hurt feeling on either side. She had now gone on to a relationship with David Sullivan, Flanders' resident poet and keeper of illegal substances, but for once, she was holding a grudge. The basis for her publicly proclaimed contempt was, for a while, a hotly debated item, but Annie would only frown when asked and proclaim, "Never mind. *He* knows."

"Look, maybe we should let her have her way," Jennifer suggested. "The truth is that, whatever happened that weekend, Samir really should stay clear of her. Let's just tell Samir that Annie's mad at him, which is hardly going to come as news, and that I'll do his share of the shopping."

"But it's not fair."

"So it's not fair! Wendy, you know the mess that Annie can make at a membership meeting over something like this. She'll curse a blue streak and some guy from that Jesus freak commune will quit on the spot. Then someone will make a speech about how the purpose of a co-op is to provide food for the people and that barring anyone is incipient fascism."

"It's the principle of the thing," Wendy pouted.

"Well, my principles and I are going to smoke half a joint, get into bed, and not speak to each other until morning." Jennifer pulled herself up from the floor.

"I'm going to talk to Will."

"Who will tell you not to sweat the small stuff and refuse to discuss it further." Jennifer made her way into her room.

"The problem is that Annie's a Sagittarius," Wendy called out after her.

The problem, thought Jennifer, is that you think Annie's the problem. She reached for the jar of grass.

three

Will Hampton stirred what may have been the only grits in New England and repeated, "If Annie and Samir have a problem, then Annie and Samir have to resolve it themselves."

"Stop saying that," Wendy protested. "You said that a million times last night."

"Then why did you think I'd say anything else this morning?"

"Because you're wrong. You're his friend, Will, and—"

"And friends are for when you really need them, not for every stray piece of bullshit that comes floating down."

"Oh, Will."

Wendy sat, miserable at the kitchen table, watching Will at the stove. She was dressed in a flowing purple dress and embroidered scarf, their deep colors at odds with the bright red cabinets that circled the big, yellow room.

Will turned away from his grits at the sudden sound of sniffles. His chiseled face had taken on one of its most characteristic expressions, a steadiness that Wendy regularly mistook for patience but that Jennifer knew to be stubbornness.

Will was of medium height but gave the appearance of being taller; Jennifer was always surprised, when she stood facing him, to note that he was no taller than she. His thick, wide bones were somehow too substantial for the amount of weight he carried, as if he was slightly too large for his own flesh. It gave him a look of power and energy when he moved. At rest and in his usual stance of studied gentleness, he made Jennifer think of marble: gentle, soft, but—to Jennifer, at least—utterly unyielding.

"Baby," Will's big hands cradled Wendy's face. "Do you think Samir was purposefully causing trouble?"

"No."

"And do you think we can convince Annie of that?"

"I guess not."

Well, then, what do you think we're supposed to do about it?"

"But Jen says—"

"I'm sure she does. This is just the situation to make Jennifer crazy." Will released her and turned back to his grits, the argument, he clearly felt, closed.

"Crazy, huh?" said Jennifer from the doorway. "Nah. I just need a cup of coffee."

"Sorry," Will said sheepishly.

"I bet you are." She moved to the Chemex coffee pot and poured a large cup, then settled herself at the kitchen table. Wendy turned away from Will at the stove and looked imploringly at Jen.

"Jen, he won't do anything," she complained.

"Of course he won't. Wendy, how long have you been living with that man? And you still haven't figured him out?"

Jennifer stole a glance at Will, who set down the spoon with which he was stirring the grits, picked up a butter knife, and scooped a dab of butter into a frying pan.

"Fried eggs, anyone?" he inquired innocently.

Wendy stuck out her chin. "Annie can't make up new rules just because she's mad at Samir. It's going to cause a lot of problems. I just know it. I've got a feeling."

"Based on anything in particular?" Jen asked.

"Not really."

"Tarot cards?"

"No, not Tarot cards, for your information! The *I Ching*. And listen, I know you two don't take it very seriously, but it was bad, you know, all movement and change and turmoil. It was like a warning, I mean it. Like something bad was going to happen."

"That's great," said Jennifer. "Any idea to whom?"

Samir walked barefoot across the floor of his attic bedroom, drew on a pair of faded jeans, and moved toward the staircase. He heard voices in the kitchen and leaned over the banister to listen. "Annie can't make up new rules just because she's mad at Samir." With a small smile, he headed down the stairs.

"Annie," Jennifer was saying, "will never understand the fine points of collective ownership, but she can tell the difference at twenty paces between Algerian and Lebanese couscous and all kinds of other stuff I don't want to have to worry about. Sorry, Wendy. I'm with Will on this one. I'm not taking it on."

Jennifer heard Samir's steps in the hall and hurried to change the subject. "Oh, and by the way, I thought I'd invite Zach Lerner to dinner tonight. It's the only night this week none of us is working late. What do you think? Will?"

"Sure. I have some re-varnishing to do after the shop closes, but that won't take long."

"Wendy?"

"It's not fair," she said one last time as Samir appeared at the kitchen door.

Will's disinclination to "do something" was not the result of an unwillingness to become involved. He had been weaned on stories of chivalry and sacrifice, tales of the Underground Railroad from his father and tales of the Old South from his maternal grandmother, a gentle dowager who was elegant of carriage, pleasant to the servants, and racist to the core. According to Will's grandmother, his father was a rabble-rouser who had crossed the tracks of Monroe, Virginia, with no sense of deference for class and blood and with lies on his lips about the Scottsboro boys. George Hampton believed in unions. He called the kitchen girl ma'am. And he won her daughter's heart with talk of the New South that would rise when poor Blacks and Whites made common cause. Of course Lorraine couldn't marry him.

Lorraine was already pregnant with Will when she and George eloped, moved to Richmond, and joined the NAACP. They dutifully returned to Monroe each year to share a Christmas of extravagant presents, cornbread-stuffed pork loin, and the unspoken agreement on everyone's part not to mention Martin Luther King. George and Lorraine sent Will, their only son, to his grandmother each summer, but they raised him to believe in the sanctity of friendship and the brotherhood of man.

Will's first talk with Samir had convinced him that here was a man who badly needed a friend. Samir had just arrived in Flanders and wanted to learn his way around the mountains. Will had taken him along an old Housatonic path to the Hope Mountain fire tower. Afterward, they had stopped for a beer. Samir hadn't talked much at first—years of dissembling, he told Will, had taught him to be careful—but slowly, as they sat there, his story had emerged. The man needed a roof over his head.

Samir entered the kitchen, bringing with him the scent of nag champa incense. He crossed the room and assembled a bowl of granola from the grains and seeds that stood in mason jars along the counter.

"What's not fair?" he inquired, opening the refrigerator and kneeling down to dig through the shelves. Wendy's eyes registered panic.

"The alumni association at Williams," Jennifer said. "You know, about divestment from South Africa." She blinked at Wendy, silently complimenting herself on the quickness of the lie.

Samir retrieved a tub of yogurt from the refrigerator.

"Yeah," Wendy seized upon Jennifer's story. "So there's going to be a letter-writing campaign." She paused. "You want to help?"

"I can't." His tone suggested regret. He fished for a spoon in the terra cotta pitcher that held the silverware and spooned yogurt into his bowl. "The ANC hasn't denounced violence as a tactic."

"What do you expect them to do?" Jennifer hated herself for rising to the bait. "Fight Apartheid with a hunger strike?"

"They could."

"That's hard to do when you're already starving."

Samir set the remaining yogurt down on the counter, licked the spoon, and used it to dribble honey into his bowl. "Politics is just another form of violence," he said sententiously.

What a load of crap, thought Jennifer. The next thing we'll hear is that the ANC should overthrow Apartheid by putting peyote into the water supply.

Samir turned to them and inclined his head slightly. "*Namaste.*" He carried the bowl out of the room.

"Namaste, my ass," Jennifer sputtered. "The light in me honors the light in you, but couldn't you put away the yogurt?"

Wendy jumped up, ostentatiously returned the yogurt to the refrigerator, and stomped from the room. Jennifer stared after her, more than a little dismayed. There was a crack forming in what had been the smooth veneer of her chosen life, and Jennifer didn't like it. In the days to come, she would like it even less.

four

"Don't hand me that crap," David Sullivan was saying over the Outlaws tape on the café stereo. "So what if it didn't grow in the ground? I don't understand you at all, you know." He peered across the table at Annie. "You can't get enough of those little green weeds that dry up and look like parsley—"

"And that *grow*."

"All right, that grow. You'd plant the north forty in psilocybin mushrooms if you thought you could get away with it—"

"That's right. I'd *plant*."

"And," his voice rising against Annie's interruptions, "after the revolution, you're planning to be the minister of hashish. But let anything be so much as breathed on by a Bunsen burner, and you won't get within fifty feet of it."

"That's right," said Annie firmly. "So you see, you *do* understand."

David, the self-pronounced poet laureate of Flanders, threw up his hands theatrically. He was dressed, as usual, all in black, thus acknowledging his debt to the Symbolists and the Beats and, less sublimely perhaps, making the most of his black hair and blue eyes. He was seated, as usual, at the carved maple table where he held court on the weekends with other poets, invariably male, almost as invariably in matching goatees. They would drink Jennifer's wine late into the night, regaling each other with stories of drunken evenings at Polly McGuire's in Paris and that funky old bar—no one remembered the name— off the Spanish Steps in Rome. Jennifer was convinced they made most of the stories up—overcompensating, she told Wendy, for being born too late and missing Kerouac and Cassidy by a decade.

Less well-known, except by a privileged few, were David's organic and inorganic contributions to the well-being of his community. He prided himself on being a connoisseur, on knowing the precise combination of weed and pill that would quench Wendy's thirst for illumination, send Jennifer out to the back porch for communion with the Goddess, and set Annie to smiling beneficently at her well-tended rows of vegetables. His life rested firmly on two treasured principles: the impeccable tastefulness of his drug supply and the poetic superiority of William Butler Yeats, and he had never been known to concede a point on either.

David regarded Annie through wireless eyeglasses. They had been a desultory item for the past year, a relationship, from what Jennifer could tell, three parts friendly mutual scolding to one part casual sex. "Now the virtue of this particular substance," he intoned, "is precisely that it did not grow in the ground. It is the masterpiece of centuries of European science, the culmination of Swedish engineering, the true elixir of life."

"What's an elixir, big shot, and stop using words I don't know."

"The elixir, my dear illiterate, was the object of the alchemists' search, the secret of the life force, the power that would turn lead into gold, prose into poetry—"

"And bullshit into reality," she interrupted him again. She

sat back, staring down at her dirty fingernails. "Did they ever find it?" she asked after a pause.

"Did they ever find what?"

"The elixir."

"Of course they never found it! How the hell could they have found it? How could anyone turn lead into gold?"

"Don't ask me," she shrugged, rising from the table. "You're the one who's supposed to be the chemical genius."

"Where are you going?"

"*To move,*" she quoted his latest poem, "*my rage-stiffened, sorrow-loosened bowels.*"

"Well, my God, woman," he hollered at her back. "Don't just waste it. How can you bear to deprive the cabbages of lunch?"

David took the opportunity of Annie's absence to stroll over to the counter, where Jennifer was decanting a vat of balsamic vinegar into jars.

"Hey there," she greeted him.

"Any idea where Will is?"

"Pittsfield."

"Damn. My plumbing's all screwed up again," he said accusingly. "I mean, stuff backs up into the bathtub every time I flush the toilet. Will said he fixed it, but it's not fixed."

"Really, David. I would think that was the stuff of bracing metaphor."

"At this point, I'd rather have a bath."

Jennifer eyed David carefully and promised to pass the message on to Will. It was in her interest to have David looking fetchingly bohemian, and the patently unwashed ponytail did little to heighten the effect. David's role in the café's profitability was considerable. The monthly poetry readings he had started were beginning to take off, and he certainly brought in the college crowd. It was amazing, Jennifer often thought, how many beers could be consumed by a group of aspiring post-adolescent poets in a single afternoon.

From her post in the oven-warmed café kitchen, Wendy saw Annie go by and made a sudden decision. She quickly checked the Viennese rolls, put the tenth spinach quiche of the day in the oven, and followed Annie down the hall.

The women's room was distinguished from the men's by the picture of Galadriel on the door. Wendy pushed it open and peered down at the mud-caked Wellington boots visible behind the closed door of the stall.

"Annie? That's you, isn't it? I've got to talk to you."

"Goddamn it," came Annie's voice. "Can't anyone even take a shit around here in peace?"

Wendy perched herself on the counter beside the sink, her short legs dangling beneath her. "I'll wait till you're finished."

"Oh, hell, don't bother. Only, don't mention that bastard's name to me, you hear?"

Wendy fought back the sense of defeat already gathering.

"Oh, Annie," she appealed to her, "why do you hate him so much?"

"After that scene in the co-op the other day? You gotta ask?"

"But you hated him before that. You hated him ever since that weekend. You're just using that as an excuse."

The seated figure in the stall was silent.

"So, it's not fair to take some private thing out on him like this and out on all the rest of us. Look, that weekend . . ." Faced with the opportunity, she had to ask. "I don't want to pry, but—"

"The hell you don't."

"Well, all right, then. What happened? Please. I need to know."

Annie shook her head in disapproval behind the locked door of the stall. She sat silent for a moment, then grumbled, "Okay. Everything was fine, right? We'd had a good time. I mean, let's face it, he's a very pretty man, and a lamb got born and he was really sweet about it. He did a ritual that sort of welcomed it to the world. But then on Sunday afternoon, I'm trying to get some weeding done because the Virginia creeper is about to devour the basil, and he wants to get it on again. I say, 'Not now, man, I can't. Basil waits for no woman,' and he gets totally weird on me. I mean, he wouldn't take no for an answer. He kept staring at me with this kind of weird expression, saying stuff about how saying no to sex was like draining love out of the universe. Maybe he thought it was a way to talk me back into the sack, but then he started actually putting his hands on me and pushing me toward the house and freaking me out. Finally, I just ran out and got into the truck and left. That son of a bitch is gonna lose it one of these days, and I don't want to be anywhere nearby when he does."

Wendy stared wordlessly at the William Morris wallpaper that decorated the door of the stall.

"Well, now you know about me and your good buddy, Samir," Annie's voice came at her. Then the metal lock moved and the door swung back, and Annie sat staring up at her.

"Tell me something, kid. Why did you need to know so bad?"

Wendy blushed. "Oh, no," she mumbled. "It's not what you think."

"Hey, I don't think anything. But I don't have to. I mean, there's something going on in your house, and whatever it is, you can see it halfway across town."

"It's not . . ."

"No? Hey, it's none of my business. But you want a piece of advice?"

Wendy nodded, still frightened.

"Will Hampton's the best man in Massachusetts, you lucky bitch. That's my personal opinion." The door swung shut again. "Now do me a favor and get out of here. I'm about to lose the urge."

five

Zach Lerner set out at twenty minutes to eight to have time to walk into Flanders. The thing he couldn't get used to about rural living was the necessity of using a car to go everywhere. Even now, when the crickets no longer kept him awake, when the scuttle of mice in the attic no longer made him nervous, he would regularly walk out of the house and get as far as the road before remembering he had to drive. Flanders was a mile down the road, the college seven. He had chosen to live in this place with his eyes open and his priorities clear. But he didn't like needing a car all the time.

A New York City kid to his fingernails, Zach was still feeling unsure of the decision that had brought him to what could hardly even be called the village of Flanders. He had been flattered, in spite of himself, to be offered the professorship at Williams. He was ready to leave Berkeley, and he wanted to be back on the East Coast, closer to what still felt like home. But the nagging voice in his head told him that he should instead be applying for a job teaching poor people's children. A community college, perhaps, or an urban public university.

Williamstown itself had appalled him, with its Federalist

brick and the complacent faces of men his age who walked down the street wearing khakis and blue blazers. He first went to look for housing in post-industrial, working-class North Adams. If New England, he told himself, was Deerfield Academy and Lord Geoffrey Amherst killing Iroquois for the king, it was also Mother Jones and Big Bill Hayward and the striking workers at the Lawrence textile mill. The industry gone south to a non-union environment, those workers' children's children now grew old among the closed, looming factory buildings. Zach would live among them. It would offset the betrayal of teaching the school-smart children of privilege. Perhaps his next book would be an oral history.

But then he had come upon Flanders. Its short main street was like a dollhouse-sized version of Pacific Avenue in Berkeley. A café with a poster of Che on the wall. A food co-op the only grocery in town. Even the prim, white clapboard church, which looked from the outside like a Cotton Mather caricature, had a mimeographed schedule of social action where the times of the services once would have been. Except for the church and the large grey house that contained the café, the few buildings were modest. Their historic New England tints had been enlivened with pink and purple shutters, the requisite wind chimes on front porches, and morning glories scrambling up the walls. The buildings all hugged the narrow street, but the trees between the houses had grown tall and together, so that when he walked down the street, the dappled sunlight fell on his arms. He passed a sign posted on the wall of the co-op declaring Flanders a nuclear-free zone, and he decided that, however much he railed against the peace-and-love inanities of the sixties, the optimism appealed to him. And Flanders was just run-down enough to suggest a compromise between the colonial digs of Williamstown and the dead faces of the North Adams factories. He rented a small house a few miles from campus on a back road that looped through

Flanders. The road ended in a T-junction: the campus to the west, the factories to the east. He decided that it was a metaphor he could live with, phoned Berkeley to let them know where to send his boxes of books, and bought a second-hand Chevrolet.

Following Jennifer's instructions, Zach followed the flagstones past the door of the café to the side door of the house. Jennifer met him at the top of the stairs and led him through the living room. In one corner of the spacious room, a rattan chair hung from a hook. Resembling a bird cage cut in half, it had been painted a high-gloss enamel green and filled with needle-point cushions. On a diagonal facing the chair, an oversized sofa echoed the rich color, as did three armchairs upholstered in a variety of patched brocade.

For Zach, what brought the room to life was the meticulously crafted wood furniture in contrast to the motley grouping of sofas and chairs. Six antique pharmacy drawers of varied sizes had been used as a focus for a series of bookshelves. Cabinets made of the same polished oak were set on either side of the sofa and mounted on antique brass legs. The large rectangular coffee table in the center of the room, half-hidden in a jigsaw puzzle of Van Gogh's sunflowers, had been made from an old pine door overlaid with a piece of thick glass. Will's handiwork, he guessed correctly. Zach was impressed with both the aesthetics and the craftsmanship.

Will was chopping garlic at the sink when Jennifer led Zach through the open door of the kitchen. Wendy, at the stove, waved to him with a wooden spoon. The kitchen, Zach noted, had none of the motley graciousness of the living room. The tiles were bright yellow; the cabinets red. The walls held non-representational watercolors, again in bright colors, labeled as the houses of the Zodiac. Multicolored dipped candles, already lit, were set into wine bottles on the table. A different sensibility had designed this room.

"Hey, man. Have a seat," Will greeted him, nodding toward the rough pine table.

"Can I help?"

"We got it covered. There's some not-half-bad wine open. Or would you rather have a cold one?"

"Yes, thanks. I'd love a beer."

Samir entered the kitchen just as Will was passing around the eggplant for second helpings. He wiped his hands on a dish towel and joined them, helping himself to salad.

"I don't know," Will said, "if you guys have met."

"Yes, at the café the other day." Zach took in the tall figure in a white shirt and jeans. "Good to see you."

"Samir's on a spiritual and political journey," Wendy offered. "He's studied with Thich Nhat Hanh, a Vietnamese monk who teaches about peace. Samir—"

"Hey, even I know about Thich Nhat Hanh," Zach said, spooning salad onto his plate from the bowl that Jennifer held out to him. "I don't buy the free-your-mind-instead business, but Thich Nhat Hanh more than paid his dues opposing the war."

"He is a great spirit," Samir intoned.

"True enough," Zach agreed. "He spoke on campus one term, and I made all my students go hear him. So, where did you study with him?"

"Around," Samir shrugged. "He travels, you know. I made a lot of the arrangements, helped connect him up with the local spiritual scene."

"That's not all you did," Wendy put in. "You did silent meditation retreats with him."

"Well, yeah. Hey, it's what you do."

Zach felt a familiar annoyance coming on. A so-called spiritual retreat taking people away from the world just when they should have been standing firm. Still, he was a guest at their house.

"I guess I believe in speaking truth to power," Zach said carefully. "You can't do that at a silent retreat."

Samir put down his fork and raised his palms. "It's like this. You sit in meditation, and after a few weeks of silence you sort of start to see the aura around everyone, the light, the God within every human person. And the only way we'll stop war is for everyone to learn to see that aura because when you know you'd be killing God, you can't do it. You just have to throw down your weapons."

Zach sat for a minute, disappointed in the way the conversation was going. "I don't buy it," he said finally. "I just don't think it's helpful to talk in these terms. I think that power is power, right here in the world, and that resistance has to be social and political and that means material as well. Using a religious metaphor is a distraction."

"The opium of the people?" Jennifer smiled.

"No," Zach smiled back at her. "Sports are the opium of the people. But religion is a little bit too much a free ride. I don't mean the Black church or the Quakers or the Catholic Workers. They've been deeply into religious forms of resistance for generations. But for people who have not ever really been political, who've just been doing a lot of drugs, this new spirituality is just a way to, just what the word means, retreat."

Across the table, Samir reached into his pocket and retrieved a joint. He lit it from one of the candles, inhaled deeply, and held it out to Zach.

Zach shook his head and looked around him.

"I'm sorry. Actually, I'm still on parole for my draft resistance sentence, and the terms of parole are very clear about being around technically criminal activity." He stood. "I'll take off. I don't want to spoil the party. I really thank you for dinner."

Will reached out, took hold of the joint, and patted it out in the ashtray. "It's okay. We don't need to smoke right now." He carried the ashtray out of the room and returned quickly, his hands empty.

"All gone," he said. "You never saw it. Please stay."

"I'll come back another time when I can honestly swear that I didn't know there were illegal drugs in the house. But thank you for dinner. Really. It's been great."

"You're very welcome," Will replied.

Zach stood and looked around at them, grateful and a bit embarrassed. He wanted so badly to like them all. It freed him into honesty.

"I don't want you to think I'm some kind of rigid ideologue. I'm not. I don't like the self-righteousness of a lot of movement people who think that smoking marijuana means that you're a bourgeois degenerate. But I didn't like to be around drugs even before I was on parole." He took a breath. "I had a sister who died because of drugs. Becky. She'd come to visit me in Berkeley, and she died out there during a bad acid trip. There was a dealer going around campus selling really bad stuff. Calling my parents was the hardest thing I've ever done."

"I can't imagine." Jennifer leaned forward toward him. "I'm so sorry."

"Yeah. Thanks." He shook himself.

"Sorry, man," Will put in. "I'm really sorry to hear."

Zach paused at the door of the living room, unwilling to leave the evening with what they might call a downer and struck again by the beauty of the hand-crafted wood furniture.

"Did you make all this furniture?" he asked Will.

"Yup."

"It's beautiful."

"Thanks. Wood's my thing. Most of it is oak, except for

that," he indicated the coffee table, "which I made from an old pine door. I've got this whole collection of antique pine."

"Enough to make me a bookshelf? I'll pay you for it."

"Sure, man. I'd be glad to. But I don't need money. Are you around tomorrow night? I can come by and do the measuring."

Zach nodded a thank you, shyly hugged Jennifer and Wendy, shook hands with Samir and Will, and headed down the steps.

six

The next day, Wednesday, dawned bright and sunny, with nothing to indicate that one of them would be dead by the following morning. Wendy kneaded the sourdough and rolled it into loaves as the church bells across the street tolled once for eight fifteen, twice for eight thirty, and once again for eight forty-five. Annie, who refused on principle to tell time by the clock, saw the sun come over the far corner of the barn and left to open the co-op. Jennifer, with a fresh cup of their product in her hand, called the Columbia Coffee Company and insisted that when she said *java* she didn't mean *mocha* and that of course she could tell the difference, couldn't they?

David Sullivan, the last to begin the day, awoke to the sound of Will manhandling pipes in the bathroom. He greeted Will with profuse expressions of gratitude, relieved his morning bladder from off the back porch, and swallowed ten milligrams of valium with a quart of orange juice. Leaving Will to fix what David referred to as the household entrails, he returned to his bedroom to revise a poem tentatively entitled "Orestes at Midnight" and was again sleeping soundly when Samir showed up unexpectedly at a quarter to twelve.

When Samir entered, David's living room was in its usual state of chaos. An Oriental rug and twin Edwardian lamps had been meant to give the room an air of elegance, but the rug was half hidden under piles of books and clothing, and both lamps needed bulbs. The couch, once a deep maroon, was occupied by the remains of last night's dinner. The fireplace, seemingly in use as a cupboard, was filled with a haphazard collection of andirons, a dustpan, screwdrivers, and an electric typewriter without a cord.

Will looked up from the length of pipe he was replacing. "Hey, man."

"Got a minute?"

"Sure."

"Is David here?"

"Yeah, but he's asleep. I just heard him snoring."

Samir stepped carefully over a mound of dirty socks, a stack of the *New York Review of Books,* and several classics of Victorian pornography. He seated himself on the painted wood floor, crossed his legs in a half-lotus, and placed his hands on his knees.

"It's about dinner last night," he began. "Zach Lerner. Wheels within wheels, you know. Lerner was out there when it all went down."

Will eased a new length of pipe into the drain of the claw foot tub. "Sorry, man. I didn't realize."

"It's not that Lerner recognized me. He wouldn't. It's just . . ." Samir leaned against the wall and raised his hands, palms outward. "There's no such thing as coincidence," he pronounced. "That explosion somehow connected with my path this time around and not just because I got framed. That's what Lerner's arrival is saying—that I'm not finished with it all."

"As far as I can tell, man, you've got nothing to worry about."

"When I got set up, a lot of people turned against me. Lerner would have believed them like everyone else. One of the things he was best known for back then was his rap against the Weather Underground, about how violence against ordinary people made the underground no better than the pigs. Well, if he thought I was part of that . . ."

"Why should he?"

"But if he does, man? All he'd have to do is make a phone call."

Will picked up his spanner and tightened the fitting between the new pipe and the old. "There's no way Zachary Lerner would call the cops on anyone. Leave it be."

Samir's response was cut short by a loud yawn followed by the sound of David's footsteps. He appeared at the door, picked his way through the clutter, and sat down naked on the closed toilet lid. "How's it coming?"

"Just about finished."

"Far out."

Taking a pair of clippers from the top of the sink, David placed one foot on the opposite knee and leaned forward over his toenails. He launched into an extended story of the previous evening and a Bennington senior by the name of Sally.

"I'm sure you've seen her at the café. Long hair, hangs around with the American Studies crowd. Has a serious addiction to Whitman. Anyway, I was having a beer at Riley's, and she was sitting at a table with this preppy kid. She kept talking about how mountains were holy places where you could be with nature and touch the gods, and he kept saying, no, skiing's the thing. It's about the speed; it's about the power. I decided it was time to rescue maiden virtue from this supercilious scion of privilege, so I leaned across the bar. I said, *For know I bear the soul befitting me—I too have consciousness, identity, And all the rocks and mountains have.* And she was mine."

Will and Samir were both silent.

"Whitman," David offered in explanation. "'Song of the Redwood Tree.'"

Will took one final tug at the bolt holding the new length of pipe.

"I may actually be better off with Sally than Annie," David continued thoughtfully. "Annie thinks of a mountain as a place to herd goats. So, what's the deal?" he asked as Will sat up, placed the spanner in his toolbox, and got to his feet.

"I replaced the washer, but the pipe was so corroded I went and replaced that, too."

"You're a fucking genius, man. What do I owe you?"

"Forget it."

"When you've single-handedly salvaged my fastidious personal habits? What would you say to a lid of Mexican gold?"

"I wouldn't say no."

"Sit tight, then. No, really. I mean it, stay here. I've got a secret little stash. I won't be a minute, my pretties."

David retreated into the living room, his thin back to the bathroom, unaware that, from his position on the bathroom floor, Samir could see him bend over the fireplace and unscrew the fluted bulb of one of the andirons.

Annie closed the register and made her way back to the storeroom of the co-op, determined to take on the new supply of barley. She switched on the radio to a country music station, helped herself to a carrot in lieu of dinner, and cleared a space on the shelf between the wild rice and the organic bulgur wheat.

She was measuring barley into one-pound bags when she heard the front door of the co-op bang.

"We're closed," she called, and then, hearing no answer, switched off the music and returned to the front.

"Well, I'll be goddamned. I said we're closed."

The man standing in the co-op was Samir.

"Hey, come on," he said, with an uncharacteristically pleading gesture. "How do you know you're supposed to be closed? You always say you don't believe in clocks. How do you know you shouldn't be open?"

"Because it's September and it's dusk. And because I'm busy in the back."

"Look." Samir held up his hands. "I just want to bring us back into balance. Peace, okay? Friends?"

"I already got friends."

Samir took a deep breath. "Anger spirals outward. I get that now. I've been blaming you, and that's bullshit. I was meditating today, and I realized that your anger is just a reflection of my own." He looked at Annie expectantly.

"So?"

"So what I need to do is put that right. It's the karma thing. I owe you four hours of work this month. It's a start."

"A start of what?"

"Of making it right. Of cleaning up a psychic confusion."

Annie could read the self-effacement in the bend of Samir's broad shoulders, and while she didn't for a moment believe his change of heart, she knew he had her cornered. She had to let co-op members put in their hours. She had to keep the terms of membership consistent. She could hear Jennifer on the subject now.

She turned and let Samir follow her back into the storeroom. "I've been putting *that* barley," she pointed, "into *those* bags, weighing them against *that* one-pound weight, and putting them on *that* shelf. You want to do it, go ahead." She watched him set his satchel and jacket on the floor, then lean down and pick up the plastic scoop. She opened the back door and whistled. Gaia, her border collie, bounded into the room.

She took Gaia with her into the front room and sat, cross-legged and hostile on a chair, adding up the day's receipts. She had almost finished when she heard the church bell ring across the way.

"I need some help," she heard Samir call out. Reluctantly, she pulled herself to her feet and walked back into the storeroom.

"I got my hands full," Samir said, in the act of pouring barley into a bag. "My watch is in my jacket pocket over by the corner. See what time it is for me?"

"Do it yourself. I don't like watches and you know it."

"C'mon. I've got to be someplace."

"That's not my problem."

Samir slammed down the bag he was holding, crossed the room, and grabbed his jacket from the floor. He pulled a watch out of his pocket and, the self-effacement entirely vanished, held it up to her face.

"Look," he taunted. "It's a quarter to seven. Got that? And in California, it's a quarter to four."

"I thought you had to put some hours in to mend some fucking tear in the universe. And now you gotta be someplace? You're weird."

Samir stomped through the store, ran to his car, got in, and drove away. Annie stared out after him. Then, quickly, she reached for her keys, locked up the co-op, and started up the truck.

In retrospect, there had been nothing to indicate that one of them would be dead by the following morning. Jennifer and Wendy dropped Will off at Zach's house and drove into Williamstown. David took a long, stoned bath. But when Jennifer entered Will's workroom early Thursday morning in pursuit of a can of fire-retardant paint, she found Samir lying under the table, dead.

part two

seven

Officer Ford McDermott fingered a much-maligned straw-colored mustache and looked down at Detective Johns. Johns' knobby features typically wore an easy-going scowl, but this morning he adopted a posture of officiousness that Officer McDermott knew better than to trust. Allard Johns was a short man of fifty, strong and hearty despite a growing paunch. His short-cropped hair had not yet begun to grey. Usually at this hour, he was on the phone, perched on a corner of his metal desk, a Styrofoam cup of coffee getting cold in his hand. He would be getting the latest about some poor bastard who had fallen asleep at the wheel the night before or griping about Springfield dragging its feet with the new fire regulations. But the news of a murder had inspired in him an uncharacteristic bureaucratic dignity, which expressed itself in an upright position in the office chair behind the desk.

"Samir Molchev is dead all right, sir," McDermott told him. "Bob McBride says it looks to have happened sometime late afternoon or early evening. Cause of death seems to have been a blow to the base of his cranium. We found an andiron near the body. It has a heavy brass top and three iron legs. The PM will have to verify whether it matches the wound, but Bob says that it could well be the murder weapon."

"Well, get it sent in."

"We've already done it, sir."

"And get the team in to dust for fingerprints."

"They're on their way."

"Have you cordoned off the crime scene?"

"Yes, sir."

"Then find out what you can about Molchev's movements."

"I have, sir. The folks he lives with say he left the house around five-thirty and never came home. It was one of them who found him, a girl named," McDermott consulted a notebook in his hand, "Jennifer Morgan. Then, Annie McGantry—she's the girl who runs their food co-op—says Molchev came by for a while last night and left at a quarter to seven."

"Pretty sure of the times, aren't they?"

"Well, one of the roommates who runs the café says that Molchev ate the leftovers from the lunch special, which they stop serving at five o'clock, and that they went upstairs—they live above the café—a little after five. Both café owners say that Molchev came upstairs a few minutes later and left almost immediately. Annie McGantry says she heard the church bell ring and saw Molchev's watch. She says he took off in a hurry."

"Where was he going?"

"None of them seem to know."

"I want to see them over here today. All of them. Get it set up."

"Yes, sir."

"Anything else?"

"Yes, sir," he said again. "The girl who found him, Jennifer Morgan, says that the door to the workshop was locked. I looked at the lock. It's an old one. It can only be locked with a key and only from the outside. So I asked her who had keys to the place and she said only Will Hampton—the workroom is the back room of his craft shop—had his own key, but that there was a key always kept under the window ledge. We checked it for prints. It was wiped clean. She figures that all of them knew where it was."

"Who's all of them?"

Ford consulted his notebook. "Jennifer Morgan," he read, "Wendy Scholes. The two of them run the café. Graham Marlow—the minister of the church they've got there. And Joan Marlow, his wife, but she's in divinity school this year. In Chicago. Annie McGantry. David Sullivan. And maybe Zachary Lerner, but probably not. He's only been in town a few weeks. As far as she knows, that's it."

"Well, send the key over for testing, too. And listen, call in the list. See if there's a sheet on anyone. I want all their criminal records in front of me before I interview them. I'll get over to the crime scene in the meantime."

Ford McDermott remained where he was. His earnest face was respectful, but the broad-shouldered body beneath it moved only at its owner's request.

"Excuse me, sir, but I think we should also be looking elsewhere."

"Come again?"

"The window ledge with the key on it faces the road. Anyone just driving through could have seen one of them get the key or put it back. And I saw most of them this morning, and their shock and horror seemed sincere. I don't think we should assume that one of them killed Molchev."

"Sincere, huh? Just call in the list."

Ford McDermott turned and left the cluttered little office. He did not say, "Yes, sir" before he went.

Allard Johns was tired of being told that the counterculture raging around him was anything like sincere. When he'd been young, plenty of people had been sincere, but that meant they worked hard when there was work to be had. He had spent thirty years maintaining his sympathy for the families who, like his own, had worked the North Adams mills for generations. They were mostly unemployed now, some of them fighting the bottle, some of them just fighting, all of them taking it hard as the bottom fell out of their lives. Their sons would never see the inside of the brick dormitories of Williams. Instead, they had gone to Vietnam, and plenty of them had come back to unemployment, or to nightmares, or in a box.

Johns himself had served his country through the invasion of Normandy and then, as a twenty-six-year-old, come home and joined the state police. He was polite to the solid citizens of Williamstown in their white clapboard houses, polite to the alumni and parents who treated him like the tourist office when they weren't treating him like the hired help. "Piece of cake, that crowd," one of his friends had shrugged as Johns set off one Sunday morning to work another Williams graduation. "Everyone fancied up and well-behaved." Johns had growled, "Piece of cake, my ass. Three thousand people, and every one of them thinks they're better than I am."

It all made him angry, but Flanders made him even angrier. North Adams was North Adams, Williamstown was Williamstown, and if neither place was perfect, well, at least everyone knew which was which. There was something in the very distance, something in the security of the border between them, that made both of them acceptable. Even crime had its place, at least what passed for crime, acts that were on the books but were better understood as youthful exuberance, or despair. He was used to college boys veering drunkenly through the streets, up to pranks that would make it into the tales of Williams legacy told around the Thanksgiving turkey. He was used to poor boys just as drunkenly throwing punches and had even, in his time, told a kid to go home and, for Pete's sake, stop breaking into stores at night, and that, trust him, he never wanted to go to prison. Allard Johns believed in law and order, but of the two, he valued order more.

But there was no order in Flanders. They were rich kids, too, at least they talked as if they'd all gone to college, but they dressed in clothes that would have shamed a hobo. They sold junk to tourists at outrageous prices and bought unrecognizable food in vats. Worse, they had filled a fine old church with communist propaganda. Johns had a special loathing for Graham Marlow, supposedly a man of God, who had spent the war helping cowards dodge the draft. How Marlow could look a vet in the eye was more than Allard Johns could fathom. He himself would have been ashamed.

And now there had been a murder, and that also offended his sense of order. Drug busts, sure. That would not have surprised him; they'd been making him feel like a jackass with their "Oh, no, officer, I never touch the stuff" routine for years. And he could imagine them engaged in all sorts of immoral goings-on that ought to be against the law. But murder needed violence, it needed anger, and he'd have thought all that peace-and-love malarkey would have left them too spineless for murder. Too unmanly, in a word. Although maybe, with all that mixing and matching, even manliness didn't apply.

Allard Johns leaned over his desk and reached for the fifteenth cigarette of a still early morning. There he was, by himself, now that Pete had retired, with no one to help him but that dumb kid McDermott with his yes, sirs and the hair on his face. Didn't the kid know that keeping the peace meant that there were lines you just didn't cross? What the hell did he mean, "sincere"?

It was not like Officer Ford McDermott to drive in silence. Playing the radio was against regulations, but if he kept the car windows discretely shut, the music would help keep his heart beating, and the radio would connect him to the world. He could drive down the road, his body strong and alive under the dark blue uniform, his mind on the pounding rhythms. He might still be stuck in North Adams, he might still be awaiting his long-deferred promotion, but somewhere there was dancing in the street and people were born to run.

But this morning, Ford needed quiet. Police officer though he was, he had never seen a murdered corpse before, and he needed a moment to let the feelings settle and get used to the memory. He hadn't made a fool of himself, had studied the medical examiner's casual professionalism and acted accordingly. But now that he was alone, he remembered forcing his hand out to touch Samir Molchev's quiet face, reminding himself that it would be cold. A quiver ran across his broad features, and his wide-set hazel eyes filled with tears.

Hell, he told himself, he should have acted differently. He shouldn't have acted so apologetic and been so nice to everyone. He should have showed up in Flanders that morning, siren on, doing eighty. He should have driven across the well-kept lawn by the café and left the police car tired but triumphant to wait outside the door. He should have assumed that everyone in Flanders was a suspect.

But he couldn't do it. Not in Flanders. Not to them.

Ford had been in high school when Flanders started to change, and he had been less puzzled by the new residents than by his parents' irate reaction to their coming. His mother had complained about "those hippie girls" who wanted to buy wool at her knitting shop. His father had set his jaw and said nothing but soon stopped selling rolling papers in the grocery and once refused to serve a young lady who showed up in bare feet on a Sunday. Ford had said, "Hey, they don't mean anything by it," and had tried to be friendly. But Flanders went its way, asking nothing of a Charles McCann Technical High School senior, and

Ford's own way went through Flanders very seldom, and only on the way to somewhere else.

Only once had he gone there for a specific purpose, and that journey, among the longest of his life, had met with no appreciable result. Two years out of high school and classified 1-A, Ford saw a sign for draft counseling outside Graham Marlow's church. He thought about it for weeks—such things could not actually be talked about—and finally, one night, drove back to Flanders and parked outside the church. He sat in the car for half an hour, turned around, and drove home.

Ford never went back to Flanders. The next day, a drunk driver missed a stop sign and smashed into Ford's car. The accident broke Ford's leg in five places, and by the time he was fully recovered, the draft was no more. A high number in the lottery made the problem moot. But Ford never forgot that, had he asked them, Flanders would have helped him, and he always thought of them with gratitude for the help they never gave.

Besides, he told himself as he turned off Route 2, he approved of their spirit of rebellion. He had learned about justice by reading the Gospels and the Declaration of Independence, and both texts had helped him decide that there were worse things than fighting for a cause. He had always wondered what the lives of the folks in Flanders must be like from the inside, about what it would be like to be them. Now, circumstances were such that he would finally get to know.

You idiot, another voice interrupted the fantasy. They've never liked a cop in their lives, and now that they are all suspects in a murder case, they aren't about to start. Well, then, he would have to solve the murder and prove beyond a shadow of a doubt that it hadn't been one of them.

Ford McDermott turned a corner and drove down the main street of Flanders. He turned off the motor, eased his body out of the car, and, for the first time in his life, headed up the steps of the Flanders Episcopal Church.

eight

Father Graham Marlow eyed the neat piles of paper on his desk with a wholehearted rush of self-hatred. Nuclear Power Plants, read one carefully lettered folder. The B-1 Bomber, read another. Native American Land Claims, read a third. So he was one of those people, after all, whose charity increased geometrically the further it got from home.

Samir Molchev was dead, and for the first time in years, Flanders would need a comforting, reassuring presence. Grief would need to be soothed, fears eased, and the jackhammer blow of authority kept from descending too violently upon them. And here he was, sitting idle and miserable in the office, dreading the hours ahead. Graham pulled himself out of his chair and made his way toward the community room that served as kitchen, meeting room, and refuge. The least he could do was make some coffee.

It appeared, when he entered the kitchen, that he had a visitor already. A curled-up figure sat in one of the overstuffed old armchairs in the back, a large wool blanket over its head. It moved slightly in response to his footsteps. As he peered down, a set of long, tanned toes appeared from under the red and green plaid.

"Jen?" he asked tentatively.

"Yeah." The voice was garbled.

"What are you doing?"

"Hiding."

"Oh. Well, be my guest. You want some coffee?"

Then he remembered. The cops had mentioned it. "You found him, huh?"

The blanket nodded. He placed a hand on what appeared to be the head. "If you come out from under there, you can cry on my shoulder."

The head shook.

"Why not?"

"Because I'm sucking my thumb."

He turned and walked around the circle of folding chairs in the middle of the room to the row of countertops and appliances that constituted the kitchen. "Well, I'm right here if you need a hug."

Water poured into the coffee urn, coffee grounds measured, he came back and sat down beside her.

"Don't be mad at me," she announced. "I've just blown my nose on your blanket."

"I was expecting you to throw up."

"Already did that. It didn't help."

There was a resolute movement, and the head appeared. "Oh, Graham. It was awful."

"Yeah. I know."

"No you don't, so don't give me any platitudes. I really am hiding. You should see my house. The cops are marching up and down the stairs, in and out of Samir's room. Wendy's beside herself, and Will isn't even pretending to do anything except stare stony-eyed at the wall. He sits in one room staring for a while. Then he goes and sits in another room. Wendy moans, 'Oh, my God,' every five seconds. And me—big tough guy, right, always in control, always knowing what do—I'm saying, 'It's okay, Wendy, everything will be all right,' and all I get out of her are these accusing looks out of the corner of her eye when she thinks I'm not looking, as if it's my job to make sure nothing bad ever happens to her, and I've messed up completely. If she calls, I'm not here. I just left for Mars. I swear, I was about to say to her, 'You're absolutely right, Wendy. This is a total and unmitigated disaster, and if you had any imagination, you'd realize that that corpse in there isn't just Samir, it's all of us, it's this whole place and everything we've been doing with our lives.'"

"Jen, look, don't you think you might be—"

"Don't say it. I really hope that I *am* overreacting, because it is my considered judgment that everything we've built here just went down the tubes."

"I think you're wrong."

"Yeah? Would you still think so if I told you that the door was locked?"

"Huh?"

"The door to Will's workroom. It was locked when I got there this morning. And Will's key is in his pocket. Whoever was there with Samir last night locked the door afterward. Whoever did it knew where the key was."

"Well, anyone could have—"

"Yeah, that's what the cop said. What's his name, the young one? And stop looking at me like that. Yes, I told him. I was running at the mouth about how I unlocked the door and walked in, and there Samir was. He picked up on it before I did, and the first thing he wanted was a list of everyone who knew about that key."

Her head disappeared under the blanket again. "Jennifer," she intoned. "Will, Wendy, Graham, Annie . . . Should I go on?"

"No. And for crying out loud, come out of there. I don't believe you think for a minute it was one of us."

"You're right. I don't. But I do think that it doesn't matter a damn if it was or not."

Jennifer stood, blanket still clutched around her, but with her face reappearing just in time to miss tripping over Graham's extended feet. "If it *was* one of us, none of us will ever get over it. If it wasn't, if it was some passing maniac, they'll never find him, and everyone will sit around wondering who's next. And even if no one's next, nobody's going to come to a town with a maniac on the loose. That means no café, no craft shop, no anything."

"Nothing like looking on the bright side."

"Yeah. You always wanted a congregation of welfare recipients."

"Are you through yet?"

"No. Do you realize that people come here in the summer because they think we're cute? Cute! Like the Pennsylvania Dutch or something. We step one foot outside this town, and we're going to realize we're anachronisms already. And I'm not even thirty!"

Graham raised an inquiring eyebrow. She laughed and sat back down. "Okay, okay. What do you want from me? I've spent all morning trying to come up with a little bit of courage, and inflated ranting is the closest I've managed to get."

"You never used to lack courage."

"Yes, I did. I just used to be able to fake it. In the old days, when I thought we had history on our side."

But she was clearly feeling better.

"Listen," he told her. "I'll be right back. I'm going to call the Berkshire Law Collective. We may need some legal advice before this is through."

"Okay, and I meant to tell you, you ought to let me give you a haircut, and I think you should dig into whatever drawer it is that you keep your collars. Johns has been looking for an excuse to mess with us for years, and this is his big chance. You've got to play the respectable, concerned clergyman protecting his flock from the barbarians. Those pigs—hey, stop poking me—those pigs will want to wipe the floor with us, and they're not going to bother about minor details like who's guilty before they do it."

But Graham was looking over Jennifer's head toward the door. Her eyes widening with sudden comprehension, she turned quickly around. Officer Ford McDermott was standing in the doorway.

Graham could see the pain in his eyes. Jennifer was much too flustered to notice. Both of them searched wildly for something to say, but neither Jennifer's glibness nor Graham's internalized lexicon of conciliatory phrases rose to the occasion.

"I'm not a pig," Ford McDermott said, standing large and awkward. "I'm sorry your friend got killed. Detective Johns wants to see all of you at the police station this afternoon. I thought that you, Reverend, could help spread the word. He wants to see everyone I interviewed this morning." Ford consulted his notebook and read out the names. "At three o'clock." He turned to go.

"Wait a minute," Jennifer called out. "I didn't mean you," she blurted. "I meant Johns."

But Ford, already on the steps outside, had discovered anger amid the hurt feelings. "He's not a pig either," he shouted, hurrying to the car.

"All right, no one's a pig." Jennifer ran out the door and appeared on the steps of the church. The car door slammed.

"I thought maybe I could help you," Ford said, more to himself than Jennifer.

"Well, come back then, please," she called to him. "We need all the help we can get."

Ford remained seated in the car, gathering the scattered

pieces of his dignity. Finally, he leaned out the window and looked up.

"No," he said. "I won't come back in. But I'll tell everyone to meet here, at the church, at three o'clock instead of at the police station. Detective Johns won't like it, but it's better for everyone if he has to see you here."

By the time Jennifer remembered to call out a thank you, Ford McDermott was halfway down the street.

nine

Jennifer scarcely had time to pour herself a cup of coffee and mutter, "Well, I really blew that one," before Annie's, "Anybody here?" had sounded from the steps. Annie entered the room without waiting for an answer and announced that she was glad to find somebody to talk to before she went entirely into orbit. Jennifer's attempts at comfort were received with a look that said, "If you can take it, I can," but Graham's offer of a caffeinated beverage, which usually won from Annie a horrified stare, was accepted gratefully. Swinging her leg to sit backward on a folding chair, she hugged the back of the chair and commenced to narrate the events of her day.

"You know, I didn't even know what had happened until this cop shows up at the farm this morning, tells me about Samir as if I might actually care, and wants to know if I know anything. *If I know anything?* I say, 'Hell, no, I don't know anything.' I tell him that when Samir left the co-op last night, he had all his arms and legs on and that I don't know what happened after that. So he gets real interested in all this Perry Mason stuff like what direction did Samir go in, and then it hits me. Maybe he thinks I did it! So I say, 'Listen, I didn't kill him if that's what you're thinking.' 'Oooooh nooo. I don't think that,' he says and that he's sorry my friend is dead. Well, for once, *once*, the McGantry brain is in working order, so I don't say what I'm thinking, which is, Hell, don't waste your sympathy on me because I'm not all that sorry. I hated the bastard. I just say, 'Yeah, heavy shit.' When he leaves, I get to thinking, Oh momma, everyone in town knows I had it in for Samir, and here I've just gone and admitted that he was at the co-op last night. Then I find myself doing stuff like feeding the goats chicken feed, and I figure I better drive into town and come here."

"Wait a minute, Annie," Jennifer put in as soon as Annie gave over her narrative. "Samir was at the co-op last night?"

"Hey, don't you start asking me questions, Jen. I've had enough."

"What time did he . . . ? Oh, hell," she said, remembering that she was talking to someone who insisted on telling time by the sun and moon. "Do you have any idea at all what time he was there?"

"Yeah, I do. He was there about a half an hour, I guess, and he left because he said it was a quarter to seven and that he had to hurry. I mean, I know because he shoved his watch in my face. What I want to know is, why did he come by begging for a chance to fucking repent if he didn't have time to put in his lousy four hours? It was the craziest thing I ever saw. I hate the son of a bitch, and I'm not exactly his favorite person either, and suddenly he shows up, fills a few bags of bulgur wheat, takes off in a mad hurry, and next thing I hear, he's dead."

Annie peered at Jennifer as if expecting an explanation.

"Did he say where he was going?"

"Nope. Just that he had to meet someone. He went off in the direction of Williamstown like I told that cop. Listen, do you really think someone killed him? Couldn't it have been an accident? Or maybe the creep killed his own lousy self."

"I gathered from the cops this morning," Jennifer said, "that it pretty much had to be that someone killed him. Suicide was impossible because of the angle or something, and it couldn't have been an accident since he was lying straight out in a way no one could actually fall."

Annie was silent. When she spoke again, her voice had changed. "Jesus fucking Christ," she said. "I didn't like the guy either, but . . . you mean someone *actually* killed him?"

"It gets worse. The door to Will's workroom was locked when I got there this morning, and the spare key was right where it should have been. It looks very much like whoever killed him knew about the key." But it was awfully hard to take in. When Zach walked into the church a few minutes later, Annie was still shaking her head in disbelief.

Zach settled himself into a chair, barely nodding a hello.

"So, you've heard." Jennifer approached him.

"Yes, I heard. I had an early class, and there was a cop ringing my doorbell when I got home."

"Welcome to Flanders. Picturesque scenery, picturesque culture, picturesque little village murders."

But Zach was in no mood to appreciate Jennifer's irony. He shifted his weight nervously in the chair.

"Look, I don't want to be insensitive. Someone's dead, someone I'm sure you cared about. I'm sorry."

Annie had wandered over while Zach was finishing. "Not me, as you may have noticed."

Zach regarded her but did not attempt to answer. His dark eyes were grim behind his glasses.

Jennifer read in his stolid body language what Zach had been careful not to say. "But this has nothing to do with you, and you're not all that happy to be included in it."

"It's not that." Zach shook his head. "Hey, I'm sorry. I know my problems are the least of it. But I've probably got the fattest FBI file in Western Massachusetts. And I've got a prison record, remember?"

"For murder?" asked Annie. It was the first she had heard of it.

"No, of course not. For draft resistance."

"Yeah, well, to them, that's probably a worse crime." Annie snorted.

The door banged, and David Sullivan, with more energy than they had ever seen him expend, burst into the room.

"It's gone," he gasped.

"What's gone?" Jennifer asked.

"My andiron. It was in the fireplace, and I went to get it this morning, and it's not there. I mean, one of them is there, but the other isn't."

"You'll excuse me," said Jennifer, "if I ask why you took this particular moment to look for your andiron?"

"Because . . . never mind. It's just gone, and I need it."

"In September?" asked Annie.

"Yes, in September. Anyone happen to know where it is?"

"Don't be stupid, David. Why should we know where your andiron is? It's probably somewhere in that stinking mess you call a—"

"Wait a minute, Annie," Jennifer said. "Actually, I do know where it is. David, I'm afraid that you will find your andiron in the police station in North Adams."

"The police station?" David hollered. "What's it doing there?"

"Well, you see—"

"Oh, my God. That's terrible. I mean, that's really terrible. You guys got no idea."

"It's even worse than that," Jennifer said. "I managed to be in the workroom this morning when the cops were there. That's where they found the andiron. The cops think it was used to kill Samir."

"Jen, if you're messing with me . . ."

"Wish I was."

"Oh, my God."

"Hey, David," Annie said, "you didn't kill him, did you?"

David shook his head, half flattered by the suggestion. "No, I didn't kill him. But if they connect me with that andiron, I'm finished."

"Why?" put in Annie.

"What do you mean, why? Why do you think?" David asked incredulously.

"Don't tell me. You've got a stash of something stuffed in there. The . . . what were you going on about the other day? The elixir, that's right. The acid."

"A good twenty tabs of it, among other things. The brass finial at the top screws off. It's hollow, so yeah, it's a good place to stash stuff. What the hell do I do?"

"Call the cops immediately and report it missing," said Jennifer. "Tell them you're sorry to bother them with such a trivial matter at a time like this, but that it's an heirloom and you're really worried."

"Yeah, right."

"I'm serious, David. If you don't want to call them, at least when Johns questions you, volunteer the information. Say something, if you like, about how you're not sure it's important, but he might want to know. I mean, how else are you going to account for your fingerprints?"

"*Fingerprints?*"

"Yes, that's right. Fingerprints. Nice clean ones on a shiny metal surface. On a shiny metal murder weapon. At the 'scene of the crime.' If you don't tell them the andiron's yours, you really will be finished."

David sank into a chair, his head in his hands. "I don't believe this is happening."

Graham was glad when Wendy arrived, although her ravaged face and intermittent tears added to the tension in the room. He was glad because it made him feel less helpless. Having been trained to deal with grief at death, he now had something to do. And he was glad—although he hadn't known Samir well—that at least one person was sorry. Wendy's visible bereavement made him feel less guilty for having no tears of his own.

But it soon became apparent that Wendy needed support rather less than the silent, shaken Will, who entered the room behind her. She was looking wild and desperate, but she quickly found a haven in Jennifer's arms. Will merely seated himself in the farthest chair in the corner. Above the clenched jaw, a slight movement played on his cheek.

"How are you doing?" Graham approached him.

"All right." The jaw stayed closed.

"Want to talk?"

"Nope."

"Anything I can do?"

Will shook his head.

Graham felt a sudden shot of helplessness at the look in Will's stony eyes. Will, he thought, had been Samir's friend and had known Samir's story. He had created a place in the community for Samir and pushed back in his quiet way against Annie's loud dislike. He knew that Will was a loving man in whom stoicism and depth of feeling jostled for the upper hand. Will must be grieving now, deeply. But today, the stoicism was in control.

"Well, if you change your mind, let me know," Graham said. "I'll be around, okay?"

But Graham was not around for the next hour and so never knew if Will had changed his mind. He called Chicago to talk to Joan, his wife. Then he called the law collective and arranged for a meeting the following morning. Taking Jennifer's advice, he lassoed her into trimming his hair, changed into a collar, and replaced his sneakers with leather shoes. By the time he and Jennifer returned to the meeting room, it was three o'clock, and the county police car was parked across the street.

ten

Johns' back was to the door as Jennifer and Graham stepped into the room, and Jennifer took a minute to survey the scene, trying to see it through Johns' eyes. There was nothing reassuring in what she saw. Annie was sitting cross-legged on the armchair closest to the door, staring at Johns through angry grey eyes. Her blonde hair was uncombed, and there was a noticeable split in the inside seam of her jeans. David was on the floor leaning up against her chair, his thin body in its usual black.

Zach, by himself in the armchair opposite Annie's, sat composed and insular. The face with which he had met Johns' entrance was watchful, his body poised to react. On the sofa between the two armchairs, Wendy sat, clutching the hand of a motionless Will. She was dressed in a flowing burgundy robe, and her long red hair, forgotten and unbrushed in the horror of the morning, stood out wild against her small face. Her head was thrown back, tears trickling down her face, a portrait of grief and ruin. *The curse has come upon me,* Jennifer thought fleetingly, *cried the Lady of Shalott.*

What Jennifer didn't know, however, was that Johns was every bit as uncomfortable as her friends so clearly were. He had hoped that, by the time he confronted them all, he would have more in the way of background information. Which of the unfathomable crew in front of him had an arrest record? Had the time of death been further clarified? What was there to know about Samir Molchev? Mary would page him if anything came through, and he could always be in touch by radio.

But meanwhile, he had to question the people who had known the victim, one of whom, he had decided to believe, had murdered him. He had questioned witnesses scores of times, was proud of the ways in which he could match his manner to the situation, draw on a range of behaviors, and treat witnesses —or suspects, for that matter—with the most effective combination of menace, kindness, and officiousness. But to do that, he had to know who he was dealing with, or at least think he knew. Who were these people, anyway? And what did he suspect them of? Immorality, certainly. Maybe even debauchery. Disloyalty to the point of treason. But murder? He hadn't, in his time, investigated many murders. And frankly, as much as he hated to admit it to himself, none of the group in front of him really looked the type.

So here it was again, another boundary broken. Between law-abiding citizens and lawlessness. Between guilt and innocence. And the location made him furious. The questioning of witnesses and suspects should be done at police headquarters, as any wet-eared trainee knew, where the aura of official legality lent a sobering effect. Instead, McDermott, now standing awkwardly beside him, had arranged the meeting at this church, if you could call it that, where all of them felt right at home amid their hippie sacrilege. *Jesus was an outside agitator,* he read on one poster. *Free all political prisoners,* said another. The whole room, and everything in it, was a disgrace.

Well, if he had to admit to himself that none of them looked like murderers, he didn't have to admit it to them. He planted his feet more firmly and set his shoulders as Graham stepped forward.

"Good afternoon, Detective," Graham said, approaching Johns with his hand extended. "We're all very upset about this, as you can imagine, and we'll be glad to give you any help we can."

Johns grunted in Graham's direction and ignored the proffered hand. If he couldn't take on a bunch of unkempt hippies, he told himself, he had no business being an officer of the law. These folks had to know something. Whether or not they were guilty, they were going to be protecting each other with lies, omissions, and shadings of the truth. One by one, even here, he could break down their stories. And he'd start with the redhead who was sniffling on the sofa. She'd be the easiest to bully, and none of them would be sure just what she might have let slip.

"I'll talk to each of you separately," he began. "You got an office, uh, Reverend?"

"Certainly, Detective." Graham pointed to the open door. "Feel free to use the desk, the telephone, anything you need."

"McDermott, you stay here. I don't want anyone talking about the events this morning. You got that? We'll start with, let's see . . . you, over there."

Jennifer looked sharply at Johns. You son of a bitch, she thought. So you do know what you're doing. Wendy let go of Will's hand and followed Johns into Graham's office, visibly terrified. With her red hair flowing down her cowed shoulders, she looked like a pantomime of doom.

"Somebody," Jennifer said, "have a conversation. We can't sit here like this—we'll go crazy." No one had spoken since Wendy's departure ten minutes before. Instead, they had sat silently, all too aware of Ford McDermott's presence. Zach had immediately reached into his cloth briefcase and retrieved a pen and a set of student papers. He sat working his way through the typed pages, head bent, pen raised, making the occasional margin note as a gesture of defiance in the face of his own apprehension. Annie, who could not have sat still even at a far more relaxing moment than this, had restlessly gathered up their used coffee cups and was washing them in the sink. Will sat unmoving, leaning back on the armrest of the sofa, his palms flat against his knees. Graham, as befitted his clerical posture, was quietly pretending to read a book.

At Jennifer's words, David pulled himself up from the floor beside Annie's now-vacant chair. He sauntered with affected ease to where Jennifer sat in the circle of folding chairs.

"How can we have a conversation? Behold the gatekeeper, guardian of authorized speech." David pointed at Ford with his chin.

"Well, then, recite me some poetry. I can't stand the silence."

David grimaced. "Sure thing. How about 'The Ballad of Reading Gaol'?"

Ford, uneasy with the position of monitoring their conversations, had at first meandered around the room, reading the posters and announcements and finally taking up copies of the brochures and pamphlets laid out in the entryway. He had settled himself across from Jennifer on the other side of the circle of folding chairs and had begun to read. He was unwilling to look at them, wishing to indicate without words that he wasn't listening. He hoped they wouldn't whisper to each other. He did not want to be placed in the position of asking them to stop any private conversations. But David had made no attempt to modulate his voice.

Ford chose, correctly, to interpret David's bravado as fear.

"Nobody's going to jail." He looked up. "This is just information-gathering. The clearer we can get individual details, the better, and people tend to remember more accurately if they don't first hear what other witnesses have to say."

"Excuse me, Officer, but that's bullshit."

"David," Jennifer put in quickly. "That's not going to help."

David yielded or, rather, chose to saunter back the way he had come. He stretched back out on the throw rug in front of Annie's chair.

Jennifer remained seated, awkwardly upright on the folding chair. She looked over at Ford, his downcast eyes giving her the opportunity to study him. If the lines of his uniform were to be believed, there was little excess on him, just the muscles left over from high school football or wherever it was one grew that kind of strength in his world. His face was mustached but otherwise carefully shaven, and his light brown hair just barely reached to the collar of his uniform. His features were soft, his eyes wide set above rounded cheeks, and she realized with a start that she found him attractive. He looked, well, maybe just a bit overly wholesome. But at the moment, that beat the hell out of a host of other possibilities.

Having made a decision, she rose and crossed to his side of the circle of chairs.

"*To live outside the law, you must be honest,*" she said.

He looked up at her. "Come again?"

"*To live outside the law, you must be honest,*" she repeated. "It's a Bob Dylan line. It means . . ."

"It's okay," he interrupted her. "I get what it means."

"Good. Because that's us, in a way." She sat down in the chair next to him, speaking in an emphatic near-whisper. "I don't mean to have delusions of grandeur—we don't actually live outside the law in any big way. But I'm afraid your colleague in there," she indicated the office, "is at a total disadvantage because he's never going to be able to distinguish serious, violent criminality from the honest minor illegalities within which we spend our innocent little lives. I'm afraid he doesn't know the difference." She paused. "I think maybe you do."

Ford moved in his chair noncommittally, unwilling to break ranks, no matter how much she had echoed his own concern. "He's the detective. I'm just a cop."

"I guess I don't know the nuances of the hierarchy."

"It's his job to supervise the collecting of evidence, interview witnesses, tap into state and federal resources, and draw conclusions about the case. I'm up for a detective shield, but it hasn't happened yet. He's in charge, not me."

"I understand what you're saying. But can I just talk to you? What I really want to say is that we couldn't be more harmless. Graham's a priest, for crying out loud. David's a poet, a little pretentious, maybe, but that's not a crime, although given his little speech just now, maybe it should be. But David wouldn't know how to kill off a fictional character, let alone a real person. Wendy could have written the manual on how to be a flower child: art, astrology, face paint, free love, Jefferson Airplane. Zach's a professor at Williams. He's a political activist, I grant you, but he's the kind of high-minded idealist who is horrified by the idea of personal violence. And Annie is an organic farmer who doesn't use chemical fertilizer, in part, because she doesn't believe in killing Japanese beetles." She stopped, trying to gauge the effect of her words.

"And him?" Ford asked her, looking over at where Will sat, head in hands, on the sofa.

"Will's an artist—a woodworker and sculptor. He has the craft shop next door." She paused, knowing that wasn't an explanation. "Look," she ventured, "there are three things you should know about Will. One, he's the classic chivalric knight, you know, the ones who supposedly rode around doing noble deeds. Wendy's his lady love. He really loves her, but I think half of it is that she looks the part and is always needing to be rescued." She stopped. "She's my best friend. I can't believe I said that."

Ford allowed himself a slight smile. "You said three things."

"Well, the second thing about Will is that the silent routine is pretty typical. You'll be lucky if you get him to say anything. But number three is, Samir was his friend, and Will has raised personal loyalty to an art form. There is nobody more solid, and nobody I trust more in the world."

Ford put down Graham's pamphlets. He was silent for a moment, looking at Will.

"Who else were his friends?"

"Will's?"

"No. Samir Molchev's."

"I don't know about the others. Graham gets along with everyone. It's in his job description. I don't think that he and Samir were particularly close. Zach just moved here, and I don't think he and Samir had much contact. They had one conversation the other night when I'd invited Zach to dinner and all of us were there. David liked Samir because Samir once compared him publicly to William Blake. Of course, Samir would have had no way of knowing what William Blake looked like, but . . ." She stopped.

"So," Ford said after a moment. "What about the women?"

Jennifer paused. "Well, Samir and Wendy were very close," she said carefully. "You see for yourself how upset she is."

"And you?"

"Me?" She thought a minute. "I wasn't particularly his friend," she ventured, sensing that a flat-out lie would be a mistake. "We lived in the same house, but I can't say we ever really talked very much."

She could see that he didn't believe her.

"And Annie?"

Jennifer cursed herself inwardly. You're an idiot for having started this conversation, she berated herself. And worse, you're a bad liar. You're more transparent than glass. But she could hardly now start blurting out the bad blood between Samir and Annie. Or could she? Chances are, he would hear soon enough.

"I think it's fair to say that they weren't friends."

She felt Ford pull back. He looked at her a little sadly

"To live outside the law, you must be honest," he said.

Jennifer met his eyes. Touché, she thought. So, you are nobody's fool.

eleven

Jennifer was still lecturing herself on her own stupidity when Wendy emerged from the office. Her face looked calmer as she crossed the room and settled in on the sofa next to Will. She curled back up against him. Johns appeared at the office door.

"Jennifer Morgan," he called out, looking around and pointing a questioning finger back and forth between her and Annie. Jennifer raised a hand in acknowledgment.

"I'll talk to you next."

Heart pounding, she followed him.

Johns seated himself in the chair in front of Graham's antique oak desk. He had moved Graham's papers and books to the overflowing bookshelves and staked out the desk as police territory. Spread out across the desk were a walkie-talkie, a spiral notepad, and Johns' hat. What he had not moved were the two framed posters on the wall in front of him, reading *Blessed are the peacemakers* and *Property is theft*.

Jennifer took the chair Johns indicated across the corner of the desk, feeling helpless. Somebody had killed Samir, and that was more harrowing than she wanted to acknowledge. Samir's unknown past, or else a stray piece of miscellaneous violence, had leached into her world. And here was this policeman who hated them all and who hoped, she was sure, that one of them was guilty of murder. He sat there with his tight face, with a look that was accusatory and predatory by turns. I am probably the glibbest person on the planet, she thought. I spend my life with my mouth on automatic pilot and my brain on fog. Now, when anything I say might help find a killer or frame a friend, I am realizing the disadvantage of being able to talk faster than I can think.

Johns' questions established quickly that she had not seen Samir after approximately five the past evening. He had been in the café, and she'd seen Wendy give him the last of the daily lunch special, which they stopped serving at five o'clock. Vegetarian chili, to be exact. Yes, she was absolutely sure that she had not seen him again until she had found him in the workroom that morning, and she had told Officer McDermott all about it. Her voice quivered. She hated to ask Johns a favor. But she had nothing to add and, if it was okay, she'd really like not to talk about that again.

Johns was willing to turn to her own movements and those of Will and Wendy. Into the mix of feelings she was having about him, she did him the justice of adding a small bit of gratitude.

It was clear to her almost immediately, however, that Johns' main interest was to corroborate whatever Wendy had told him about the evening's comings and goings. She could feel the adrenalin every time he tried to disrupt the logic of her memories, but it was all perfectly credible, she told herself, not least because it was true.

"Wendy and I both work all day Wednesday. That way, we can both be off on Wednesday evening and have an evening together each week. We came upstairs a little after five o'clock. The two kids who work Wednesday evening, Mark and Ginger, could probably verify that. They didn't know Samir very well. They're students. They both just started working at the café. Then I went into the living room. Wendy went up to her room."

"How do you know she went to her room?"

"Because she always goes to her room after work. She meditates."

"So, you don't know for a fact that she was in her room, only that she usually goes there."

"I heard her climb the stairs."

"But you didn't see her."

"No, I didn't see her. But it's an old house. You can hear footsteps, and you know where people are. And then I didn't hear anything."

"So, you don't actually know where she was."

"Yes," she insisted, "I do. Meditation means Wendy sits on a pillow and doesn't move for half an hour. I would have heard her if she *hadn't* been meditating. Look," Jennifer broke out. "You're on the wrong track if you're suspecting Wendy. She's the most harmless person in the world, and she cared a lot about Samir. If Samir was murdered, there really is someone dangerous out there, and I swear I would do anything to help you find him. But if you're interrogating us at this level, you're not . . ." She stopped. It was clear that Johns was simply letting her run off at the mouth and that she wasn't getting anywhere.

Johns sat unmoving, his posture of bureaucratic judgment undisturbed, until Jennifer stopped talking. "Can we continue, Miss Morgan?"

Jennifer forced herself back into the rhythm of her narrative and his interruptions. She had just gone into the kitchen when Will came home. What time would that have been? Twenty to seven, she figured. How did she know? Because she was watching *The $25,000 Pyramid*. It started at six thirty, and she'd gone to the kitchen during the first commercial, which always took place about ten minutes into the show. She hadn't talked to Will. She had just seen him pass by the open kitchen door and go directly upstairs. She had heard the shower running.

Then, as arranged, she and Wendy had headed into Williamstown. They were going to the movies. They had dropped Will off at Zach Lerner's house on the way. She wasn't sure what time that was exactly, but the movie had started at a quarter to eight, and they had gotten there just in time. She and Wendy had sat through a Hitchcock classic, shared a popcorn, said hello to five or six people they knew, and yes, she could make a list of them. After the movie they had picked Will up at Zach's and all gone home to bed.

Johns had a few additional questions when she was finished. Why hadn't Will driven himself to Zach's house? Because his car was in the shop. Why hadn't they gone into Zach's house? Because it was late, and Wendy had the breakfast shift this morning at the café. Had either Wendy or Will said anything or acted in any way unusual? Jennifer hesitated, torn once more between frankness and distrust. In the end, she forced a laugh.

"Look, I'm not trying to give you a hard time, but it really depends on what you mean by unusual. Wendy observed on the way to the movies that Mercury was in retrograde and the moon was in Cancer and that she hated that convergence because something bad always happened. Some people would call that unusual, though you've got to admit that, in this instance, she was right. She was certainly herself, if that's what you mean."

"And Will Hampton?"

"Will didn't talk much, as far as I remember. But that's not unusual. He's always quiet."

Jennifer knew, as she said it, that this was not quite the truth. Will had been untalkative, but it had not been the exacting, watchful, loving distance from which Will typically negotiated the world. His silence last evening had had a different quality. Something had been on his mind.

Johns let her go with a last, disapproving nod. He followed her out of the office, and she was not surprised to hear him ask for Will. Will pulled himself up from the sofa, and Jennifer watched him walk to the office, his thick shoulders hunched inward. Wendy, now abandoned, turned in her direction, but Jennifer couldn't bear to return to sitting in that fearful silence, her friends cowed and isolated in the corners of what was usually a boisterously communal room.

She took herself to the steps outside the church and sat, restless, frightened, and wishing that she still smoked cigarettes. I can always go back to graduate school, she thought bitterly. The Victorian novel awaits. She would go back and finish her dissertation, become one more lifetime freeloader off the sumptuousness of Emily Brontë, who had died poor and unhappy at twenty-nine. I study *Wuthering Heights*, she told herself, in order to roam over the moors to the place where I was always meant to be. Middle Earth. Narnia. Never Never Land. Flanders. I came here, she thought, at a moment at which, like Catherine Earnshaw in Brontë's novel, I was about to fall bleeding into adulthood. And now this place is about to be taken away from me.

She was startled out of her train of thought by Ford McDermott emerging from the church and hurrying down the stairs to the police car across the road. She was only a little bit ashamed of herself to have realized that she cared more about keeping Flanders alive than she cared that Samir was dead.

Having worked his way through the list of Flanders witnesses, Allard Johns knew that he had not made a dent. The awareness made him furious. The three who lived with Molchev all had alibis—the two girls had been together, and the guy had been either with them or Zachary Lerner all evening after approximately six forty-five. According to Annie McGantry, Molchev was at the co-op at the time. That appeared to rule Zachary Lerner out as well, unless he had killed Molchev before Will Hampton arrived. The time of death had not yet been pinned down, and in the meantime the medical examiner had guessed that death might have occurred as early as five o'clock. But according to Jennifer Morgan and Wendy Scholes, Molchev was still home at that time. The McGantry girl, meanwhile, looked like she was capable of anything, and it was only her word that Molchev had left the co-op unmolested. The girl was a farmer—she might well have had the strength to bash in someone's head—but he found it hard to believe, not that a woman would commit murder, but that she would do it that way. David Sullivan, whose andiron was a possible murder weapon, claimed to have been home all night and offered to recount the plot of every TV show on ABC. He would have to see what the reports on the andiron showed. The fact of the matter was that apart from the locked door of the workroom and the limited number who knew about the extra key, there was hardly a suggestion that any of them had been involved.

Johns gathered up his papers, intending not to let on that he was anything but satisfied. Let them think they had exposed themselves. What he needed was a handle, a way through their complacency. Meanwhile, he would let them cringe under the most intimidating tone he could muster. The withholding of information was a double-edged sword.

He was just formulating a strategy that would, he hoped, scare them into docility when the pager in his pocket sounded. He headed out the office door.

"McDermott," he barked. "Get on the car radio."

Graham rose quickly to his feet, hoping to end the questioning as cordially as possible. But Johns strode forward, tense and hostile, and it was Graham who stepped back to yield the space to Johns.

"Anything else we can do for you, Detective?" Graham asked.

Johns ignored Graham and peered around at the faces. "Yes, there's something you can do. You can keep in mind that I'm going to get to the bottom of this."

"Detective," Graham began, "I don't think it's necessary to—"

"I'm a church-going man, Reverend, but don't try my patience."

"Look, we all want this solved."

Johns grunted. "Maybe, maybe not. But let's be clear about something. You can save your peace-and-love act for the tourists. There's a corpse in the morgue at North Adams General that didn't get there from peace and love, and I'm going to find out who put him there. You should think again about what you've decided not to tell me, because I'm going to find out what it is, and who's covering up, and why. You got that?"

Ford's reappearance in the room did nothing to relieve the tension. He walked straight toward Johns, turned his back to them, and leaned down to speak directly into Johns' ear. Jennifer entered the room behind him, having watched him speak into the car radio and seen his expression change.

She had just taken a nervous seat when Johns turned back to the group. He had what he needed, a lever with which to pry open their self-righteousness. He addressed himself directly to Zach.

"Lerner," he barked. "You didn't tell me you got a prison record."

Zach slowly set down the papers in his hand, closed his pen, and placed everything back in his briefcase. His movements were deliberate, controlled. This was something he had hoped to avoid, but he had faced down the police in much more frightening moments than this, and he was not, he reminded himself, about to be intimidated by a self-important, small-town bully. He took a breath, uncrossed his legs, and turned to Johns.

"I didn't tell you because you didn't ask me. I'm not required to tell you."

"Not even that you're on parole in my jurisdiction?"

Zach sustained his tone of patient exactitude, more the legalistic scholar than the exposed ex-con.

"In point of fact, Detective, the state parole board should have provided that information when I moved here. You'll have to take it up with them."

Johns stared hard into Zach's impassive face. He had raged helplessly through the anti-war movement, been kept assiduously away from the protesting students by a university that protected its pampered brats no matter how outrageously they broke the peace. They had shouted foul language through bull horns, stopped traffic, and to his mind rebelled against the government. Any North Adams kid would have been jailed for a week for making half as much trouble, or as much noise. And the professors, not only the ones who looked like Zach but the condescending ones in ties and corduroy jackets, had all too often been at the head of the march. So what enraged him most at this moment was the look of defiance in Lerner's eyes, a look that Johns took as personal, as intellectual and social derision, and, ironically, had Zach known it, as class disdain.

"You're damn right I'll take it up with them," he pushed back. "There are terms to your parole, Lerner. I don't know what you thought you could get away with, but not on my watch, you hear that?"

A sardonic smile flitted across Zach's broad features. "I promise you, Detective, I know the terms of parole. I have no desire to go back to prison. Living in a town in which somebody dies doesn't violate the terms of my parole."

"This isn't a town," Johns spat back. "It's a scandal. Illegal drugs aren't the half of it, whatever crap you've been feeding your parole officer. But we'll sort that out at the station. Lerner, you're coming with me."

Zach stood, needing his feet under him. He raised a hand to Graham, who had cleared his throat and appeared about to step in.

"Detective," Zach said firmly, "I went to prison for draft resistance. I hardly did that because I find the taking of human life acceptable. You know perfectly well that whatever happened here has nothing to do with my prison record."

"We'll let your parole officer decide that. And," he added viciously, "your employer."

There was a sudden sound from where Will sat with Wendy on the sofa. Will had gotten to his feet.

"You have no cause to arrest Zach," he said quietly. "He had nothing to do with this."

"What did you say, there?"

"I said you got no cause to arrest Zach. He didn't kill Samir. I did."

"What?"

"I killed Samir, Detective. Leave these good people alone."

Ford McDermott was thinking fast as Johns walked over to Will. The others were too stunned to move.

"Sir," he spoke up quickly. "He's lying. The times don't add up."

"Lying, my ass," Johns spat out. "You mean everyone else is lying. Good thing for the rest of you that this isn't a court of law, or I'd have half of you in jail for perjury."

"Will." Zach went over to him. "You don't need to do this. They can't actually do anything to me."

"The hell I can't," Johns snapped. "I'm calling the parole board first thing in the morning. Meanwhile, Hampton, you're under arrest. You've got the right to an attorney," he launched into Miranda. "You've got the right to remain silent . . ." But

Will was already walking toward the door, with Ford McDermott more following than leading.

"Will," Graham called. "I'll have a lawyer down there before nightfall."

Johns peered at them from the doorway, gratified by the helplessness in their eyes.

part three

twelve

Jennifer and Wendy sat at the kitchen table, Wendy hugging herself and biting her lip in an effort to keep from crying. Her arms were crossed, each hand buried under the opposite arm. She swayed slightly as Jennifer leaned forward yet again.

"He can't have done it," Jennifer repeated. "Just keep remembering that. He was already home by the time Annie says that Samir left the co-op, and you and I or else Zach were with him all night. Steve Davies said he'll have Will out in the morning. He didn't do it, and they can't frame him even if they want to. They have no evidence."

"Then why did he say he'd done it?"

Jennifer let out a frustrated breath. "Hell, I don't know. I love Will a lot, but I've never figured out where he lives inside. Some cockamamie act of chivalry? Who knows?"

On the other side of the table, Wendy's small face crumbled. She raised a hand and held it over her eyes, pressing against both temples and struggling to hold back tears.

"Aw, sweetie," Jennifer came around the table and knelt in

front of Wendy's chair. "He'll be home tomorrow. Really. We just have to get through tonight."

Wendy gave up the struggle not to cry. She took her hand from her face, wrapped her arms around Jennifer, and sobbed.

Jennifer nestled Wendy's head more comfortably onto her shoulder. That crazy son of a bitch, she raged inside, rubbing Wendy's back. Why had he come out with that nonsensical confession? Could he really have thought that he could prevent whatever trouble Johns could cause Zach? Was he protecting the secrets of a dead man by saying he'd killed Samir himself? Will, she knew all too well, was tenacious to the point of stubbornness, and all the manipulative cajoling in the world would go for nothing. He would determine not to tell her. And he never would.

But how, she continued her internal rant, could he do this to Wendy, who, she realized with a start, was not reassured by anything Jennifer said because she couldn't take in the obvious fact that Will hadn't committed murder. Wendy, loyal, innocent, trusting Wendy, was clearly convinced that he had. Wendy, of all people, who trusted in astrology and Tarot cards because she needed to account for causes and effects, because the world was baffling and the reasons for things unclear. Wendy, who trusted Will and Jennifer, the two of them standing guard over her vulnerabilities like a pair of matching bookends. Will did it by being unyielding and exact, she with a verbal and emotional expansiveness that was failing her now just when Wendy needed it most. Jennifer, who thought of herself as taking on the world with whatever weapons were available and who expected to win any fight that could be fought with words.

But this fight, at least, did not seem to be one that could be fought with words.

"There's nothing we can do," she said aloud, as much to herself as Wendy. "We just," she repeated, "have to get through the night."

Wendy roused herself sufficiently to hear Jennifer's frustration. She squeezed her shoulder in sympathy.

"Poor Jen. You hate it when there's nothing you can do."

"Damn right."

Wendy released her, the tears ended for the moment. She reached across the table for a tissue. "You'll think of something, Jen. Don't worry."

"I appreciate the confidence, dear one, but what can I do? I'm not a lawyer. I'm not a cop. I'm an ex-English major, and the only things I know about this stuff I've read in murder mysteries."

Jennifer rose from her crouch and moved back onto her chair as Wendy blew her nose. Wendy looked somehow smaller, shriveled. With the tears gone, Jennifer could see the terror.

"Wendy," she said sternly, "Will didn't do it."

Wendy nodded, pretending to believe her.

"At least I can make you a cup of tea." Jennifer rose. "The classic replacement for usefulness, according to the British novel." She crossed the kitchen, filled the kettle, and set it on the stove. "We'll do the counter-culture version. Chamomile."

The classic British mystery, she remembered her advisor once saying, is the mirror image of the nineteenth-century British novel. In the novel, the ostensible theme is the nature of human beings in society, but the implicit themes underlying that are money and sex. The mystery is the opposite. Murders are committed because of money and sex, but those become the stand-ins for the real nature of human beings in society. That's why the classic British detective is eccentric, celibate, and independently wealthy, or at least two out of the three.

Well, she reasoned as she spooned tea leaves into the pot, it was hard to believe that Samir had been killed for money. He so clearly hadn't had any. And sex? She looked again at Wendy, who was once again fighting tears across the table.

"Sweetie," she said quietly, already knowing the answer. "Did you sleep with Samir?"

It was, Wendy was quick to admit, a relief to have it out in the open. Will, she reminded Jennifer, had taken a booth at a weekend craft fair in Boston. Jennifer had been at a cousin's wedding in New York. She and Samir had meditated together, and Samir had talked afterward about the Buddhist understanding of Nothingness. Nothingness and Nowhere, where souls finally met because there were no longer separate souls. They'd done mushrooms, and Samir had stroked her legs and talked about their higher selves clinging to each other in the human darkness. She didn't believe in monogamy, she said defensively. Will knew that. They had an agreement. And it had never happened again.

Jennifer patted Wendy's hand. You bastard, she thought, to have even tried it. Whatever half-baked notions of free love were floating around in Wendy's head, Will was your friend, and you took the first opportunity when he was out of town to go after Wendy. Only Wendy would not have seen that she was being thoroughly had. And using the oldest line in the countercultural book: the Great Cosmic Fuck. Damn, she thought, I'd like to kill you myself.

But Will was not a man to kill some guy for screwing his girlfriend. Will would go very cold if he knew about it. He would never say a word to Wendy and would make sure that Samir never guessed that he knew. Will would make it a matter of crazy pride to pretend, even to himself, that it wasn't important. Jennifer had known Will Hampton long enough to know that.

Jennifer poured the chamomile tea into mugs and set one on the table in front of Wendy. "You're wrong," she said, "if you think that your sleeping with Samir had anything to do with this. You have to put that out of your head. You'll drive yourself crazy."

"Oh, Jen. I'm so scared."

"Well, if you want to be scared, be scared of what this may end up doing to all of us. That's why I'm scared, and I could use the company. But if you're scared because you think Will, of all people, killed Samir in a fit of jealousy, you really have to let it go. It's some vestige of your Methodist upbringing or something."

Wendy raised the cup to her lips and tested it carefully.

"Presbyterian."

"They're all the same to me."

Zach had driven home from the church and was now settled in an armchair, a dinner of frozen pizza baking in the oven and a beer in his hand. He had put in a call to his lawyer and to his dean at Williams and then tried to put his own situation out of his mind. It was nonsense, his lawyer had assured him. Of course Flanders would have the same low level of illegality as was common to any such community. People smoking dope. The occasional presence of more serious drugs. For that matter, his lawyer had said, people probably jay-walked from time to time. And the university? If anything, Zach knew, they liked the prestige of having on their faculty someone as adept as Zach at seizing the moral high ground. And Zach was famous, for an academic: he had made the six o'clock news.

Besides, his lawyer had reminded him, Zach had been a model prisoner. Having been sentenced to an unheard-of eight years to make draft resistance less attractive to others, he had gone to prison proudly. He had started a high school equivalency program. He had taught math and basic literacy. The exercise yard at Leavenworth, he told a reporter who interviewed him, is an extension of the Ho Chi Minh trail.

Zach had served three years and been paroled. His parole officer was a conservative Republican who hated everything Zach stood for except what mattered most to him: that Zach held down a job, showed up each week, and didn't shoot heroin. He was not likely to give Zach a hard time for living in a town in which someone he had barely known had gotten killed.

So, then, enough worry about himself. More interesting was what to make of Will's sudden confession. Zach was not a man to resist the attractions of a flamboyant act of courage, and Will's noble if pointless gesture had certainly been that. Beyond that, he didn't know what to think. Will had done it to protect Zach, and Zach was uncomfortably poised between gratitude and chagrin. He hadn't needed or asked for Will's help, and now he was beholden. It was a strange thing to have done, he concluded. Well, he thought, people make their stands where they find them. And stands mattered. They made people strong.

David had also been impressed with what he termed Will's misguided Christian martyr routine and was now telling Annie, as they passed a joint back and forth, that he was considering a poem about it. "False Confessions" might be a good title, and a nice allusion might be made at the end to Jesus' despair. Had he felt forsaken, not to die, but to realize at the very end that the sacrifice was pointless, that he had just plain been duped? No, that probably wouldn't do. Why was it that, every time he tried to talk poetry to Annie, he ended up sounding to himself like André Gide?

He took a final toke on the joint and placed it carefully in the ashtray. He turned to Annie, took one of her naked feet in his hands, and put his thumb into the instep. He rubbed, waiting for her sigh of relaxation, then bit each of her toes in turn. He wasn't really in the mood, but one had to take Annie as and when one could find her, and if he knew Annie, she would not be around for long. Sally, his recent Bennington conquest, might make for better intellectual companionship, but there were limits to the compromises one willingly made for one's art.

Graham, as had become his habit, was on the telephone. He called the Law Collective again and talked to Steve Davies. He called Jennifer to find out how Wendy was. He called his wife Joan in Chicago and spent an hour on the phone relating the events of the day.

"So now," he said to her, "what do I do?"

"Did you arrange for a lawyer?"

"Yes."

"Did you ask for additional police protection?"

"Are you kidding? Forget it."

"Well, then, I'm not sure you can do anything else at all."

"But, honey . . ."

"Yes, I know. Well," she said after a pause, "it just might be that one of them is guilty. You might try being the keeper of souls."

The cell was small and bare and very clean. It contained an old iron bed, a stained enamel toilet and sink, and a wood table and chair. Will sat on the bed, staring at the concrete wall.

The clank of metal interfered with the silence. Someone was asking him how he was feeling. He grunted that he was feeling okay. Someone asked him if he was hungry. He grunted again.

Ford McDermott stood in the cell, a dinner tray in his hand. He set it on the table and then remained, waiting for Will to respond to him. Will looked up at him with reluctant interest.

"What do you want?"

"I want to talk to you. I think you meant well this afternoon. I want to help you if I can."

"You don't believe I killed him, do you?"

"No, I don't."

Will reached across, eased the tray off the table, and set it on his lap. His face said plainly that he did not wish to talk anymore.

Ford sat down across from the prisoner who did not want to talk to him, wishing there was something he could do.

thirteen

Allard Johns was at work by seven the next morning. He let himself into the new state police building that had been opened, with much fanfare, only the year before. The outside of the building, of artificial stone and white vinyl siding, had been designed to represent the modernization of staunch old New England. But the inside of Johns' office had been painted the same dull green, and his old metal desk and chair had been moved to his new office with the Commonwealth's taxpayers in mind. On the wall was a picture of Johns shaking hands with the governor, notices of rule changes, and a poster of the FBI's most wanted list. He set down his cup of mini-mart coffee, pulled off the lid, and lit a cigarette. He spread his notes out in front of him on the desk.

He had called Pete as soon as he'd gotten home the night before. His old partner, now retired, had come right over, and the two of them had dissected the day's events over several helpings of his wife Janet's meatloaf. Then, the kitchen table cleared, they had spread out sheets of paper and together made an outline of the evidence. This morning, pulling on his cigarette, Johns figured he had the most likely answer: Hampton had left his girlfriend asleep after eleven at night and gone back out, met the victim under circumstances unknown, and murdered him. Pete wasn't so sure. He thought it might have been a conspiracy.

He and Pete had started with what was known of Molchev's movements. According to Jennifer Morgan and Wendy Scholes, he'd come to the café, had something to eat, gone upstairs to the house they all shared, and then left shortly after five o'clock. It wasn't clear where he had gone after that, but according to Annie McGantry, he had appeared at the co-op and driven away right after the church bells rang at six forty-five. He was found dead at approximately seven the next morning, having died before midnight, Bob McBride thought, pending the autopsy.

Johns and Pete both agreed that Will Hampton was the obvious perpetrator. He'd offered only the briefest answers when Johns interviewed him, saying only that he had closed up the craft shop at half past six, as usual, gone home, and been dropped off at Zachary Lerner's house by the two women a little before eight o'clock. His truck was in the shop. Brake trouble. Ralph's Auto in North Adams, if Johns wanted to check. He'd been picked up at Lerner's at around eleven, been driven home, and gone to sleep. But then he had stood up and confessed to the murder as soon as Johns moved in on Lerner. Part of some plot to confuse the police? Overcome with guilt when someone else was being held accountable? Who knew why these people did what they did.

So, then, they had mapped out the two possibilities. The first assumed that everyone was telling the truth about Hampton's movements. If so, Hampton had an alibi until eleven o'clock, when he went to bed. But Johns was adamant that his alibi after that wasn't real. Sure, he'd been shacking up with Wendy Scholes, but he could have snuck out after she was asleep. Anyone could see the Scholes girl was daffy, and she looked like she slept hard. Killed before midnight was what

McBride said. That would put it on the late side, but it was in range.

There were, of course, a variety of factors that pointed to other possibilities. The andiron, the probable murder weapon, belonged to David Sullivan. Johns would hear this morning, he hoped, about what the lab analysis showed. And Annie McGantry—they only had her word for it that Molchev had left the co-op alive, and even if that part of her story was true, she had no alibi for the rest of the evening. She could have followed him to the workroom and killed him there. Finally, Johns did not like Zachary Lerner, and while there was nothing to tie him to the murder, it was interesting that violence had hit the community so shortly after he had arrived in town.

The other possibility, more likely as far as Pete was concerned, meant two or more of them in it together. If so, Pete had nodded ponderously, this was a difficult and complicated case. Any of Hampton's so-called alibis could be false; any of his pals could be in it with him. Pete's first choice was Zachary Lerner, the only ex-con among them. Could he believe they were hiring professors like that? There was no telling why Will Hampton had tried to take the heat off Lerner. There was, in Pete's experience, no honor among thieves. But perhaps that was part of their plan.

In the clear light of day, as Johns settled in behind his desk, he was not inclined to believe Pete's conspiracy theory. It had made Pete feel important, poor son of a gun, but to Johns' ear, it sounded too sensational. Crimes just didn't happen that way. His bet was that Hampton had committed the murder by himself, sometime right before midnight, or, even more likely, shortly afterward. McBride had put the limit at midnight, but a lot of things could confuse the time of death. He puffed on his cigarette, sipped his coffee, and waited for the day to begin.

His first call, to the coroner's office, came just as Robert McBride was returning to his office from the autopsy room.

"Bob? Allard Johns here. Good morning. Listen, about the time of the murder. We're thinking Molchev died on the late side of what you reckoned yesterday. Maybe midnight, but it could have been one or two o'clock in the morning. What do you think? Hundreds of factors involved in this thing, from what I understand."

"You mean in the progress of rigor?"

"Maybe so."

"I don't know, Al. Check to see if there's an air conditioner in the room. But now that we've done the autopsy, I'm inclined to say earlier rather than later."

"But it's possible?"

"In theory."

"Good. That's what I was figuring." Johns prepared to get off the phone.

"But wait a minute, Al. Something else. Molchev had a meal a couple of hours before he was killed. That boy met his Maker on a full stomach of kidney beans, tomato sauce, vegetables, and brown rice."

Johns swore to himself. It was not the answer he wanted. He consulted his notepad, knowing what he would find.

"Vegetarian chili at around five o'clock?"

"Sounds right to me. In that case, I'd say he died around seven."

"Hell, he could have eaten the leftovers for a midnight snack."

"Could have, sure, Al," McBride said to him. "That's your department, not mine."

So then, Johns thought as he put down the phone, chances are that Pete was right after all. It was a conspiracy. Johns found that deeply unsettling. True enough, he had spent a career not on murder but on burglary, vehicular crimes, and the occasional arson. But he prided himself on his instincts, and he just hadn't pegged that bunch yesterday as co-conspirators. Too in love with their own phony righteousness to expose any criminal leanings to each other. Except Lerner, of course. But it was perfectly clear they thought of him as a hero, not a criminal.

Johns had just lit another cigarette when the intercom sounded and Mary announced that Steve Davies had arrived.

Steve Davies, people's advocate and Director of the Berkshire Law Collective, was a very patient man. In his veins, he was wont to say, ran the blood of Welsh miners, and miners knew how to wait. He walked politely into Allard Johns' office, his black hair and full beard both well-trimmed, his work boots clean, his ex-metalworker's shoulders squeezed into a well-pressed corduroy jacket. He greeted Johns, shook hands, and in an unruffled voice demanded the immediate release of the prisoner.

"Sorry, Mr. Davies. I can't do that."

Davies pulled up a brown metal folding chair, unasked. "But what, Detective," he inquired, "is the case you have against him?"

"I have a confession, that's what I have. That's all I need to hold him."

"A confession," Davies repeated. "Right. Let me see if I understand you. You have no idea as to motive, correct? You have no witnesses. You have no reason to think that Mr. Hampton was in the vicinity at the time of the crime. You do not know, or perhaps I should say you will not tell me, at what time the crime was committed. But you have an unsolicited confession from the prisoner, and on the basis of *that* confession, you wish to keep the prisoner in jail and book him on a charge of first-degree murder."

Johns grunted. "That about sums it up."

"And you'll be bringing him up before the judge on that charge sometime this afternoon?"

"We are still investigating the evidence against him."

"But, Detective." Steven's voice was very reasonable. "You haven't got a case."

Johns drummed his fingers on the desk. "Seems to me that a confession is a good place to start."

Steve Davies continued in his reasonable, maddening tone of voice.

"One other point, Detective. I'm sorry. I should have asked immediately. Had the prisoner been read his rights before he made that confession?"

"He wasn't a suspect at the point he confessed."

"Well, has he been read his rights since?"

Johns leaned forward in his chair, balanced his cigarette on the edge of his ashtray, and rested his forearms on the desk. "Don't start with me, Mr. Davies. Of course he's been read his rights."

"And has he confessed again since?"

"The son of a bitch won't open his mouth except to eat. But I heard him loud and clear, and so did McDermott."

"I don't care who heard him. If he hadn't been read his rights, it doesn't matter what he said."

Johns gritted his teeth. He was not going to lose his temper in front of this self-satisfied bastard. "There was no reason to read him his rights," he said steadily. "He wasn't a suspect, just a witness. You don't read a witness his rights. And then"—his irritation showing in spite of himself—"he just confessed, free as a bird. His own choice, Davies. I didn't ask him. His own damn choice."

Steve Davies stood up, six feet and two hundred pounds off the ground.

"Will Hampton's confession broke up an act of political harassment that stinks from here to Nantucket, Detective. I've got six witnesses willing to swear that for no reason remotely connected with Samir Molchev's murder, you were threatening the freedom of a professor at Williams College. Someone who went to prison because he *didn't* believe in killing. Someone who has paid his debt to society and is a model parolee. You want it said in a court of law that that's your version of law enforcement? Man, I'll have the ACLU down on you so fast you won't know what hit you. You're gonna be famous, Detective. You're gonna make the front page of the *Boston Globe*."

Johns adjusted his posture and set his short body upright in his chair. "Don't threaten me, Davies. You don't make the rules around here. McDermott," he called into the front room. "Hampton's lawyer's here to see him."

Then he sat impassive, watching Steve Davies leave the room.

It was late morning by the time the assistant district attorney arrived, and Johns, forced to wait for him, had tried not to waste time. He read the report on the andiron: two sets of clear prints, one of them Molchev's, neither of them Hampton's. He phoned Springfield and asked for a copy of Zachary Lerner's fingerprints. He phoned Molchev's home and arranged to get access again to his room. That done, he went out for another cup of coffee. He smoked another cigarette. He resented Ford McDermott. He missed Pete.

Finally, Mary announced the arrival of Douglas Phillips Tyringham III, late of St. Paul's, Princeton, and Harvard Law, now paying his blue-blooded dues in the office of the district attorney. Johns had met him once before, though Tyringham wouldn't remember him. Tyringham's father had been considering a run for state attorney general, and he thought it behooved him to invite the Berkshire County police force for some glad-handing and a barbeque at his eighteenth-century estate. Tyringham's father had made a speech: he was a liberal Republican who believed in law enforcement for the benefit of the citizenry. It was clear that, in his view, what was good for the citizenry was best known to his family and their friends.

The Tyringham now sitting in front of him was of medium height and build, a straight nose over thin lips, and light blond hair cut fashionably just at the open collar of his shirt. His linen sports jacket was draped over his arm, and his khaki trousers ended in bare ankles and a pair of loafers that Johns was smart enough to resent. Tyringham looked to Johns as if he could barely be bothered with a little murder in some boondock Berkshire town. But Tyringham, unlike Steve Davies, was supposed to be on his side.

Johns was wrong in believing that Doug Tyringham did not take murder seriously. He had been schooled in the tradition of public service. He was planning an early run for Congress. He had been to law school in the sixties and had debated the nature of the social contract more times than he could count. There was no contradiction, he contended, between equity and criminal justice. One could not have a decent society if people were worried about getting killed, raped, and robbed.

But he would be damned if he would debate the nature of the social contract with the tin god of a detective who was now scowling at him across the desk. Doug, for one, could tell the difference between draft resistance and murder, and he also knew the difference between confessing before and confessing after being Mirandized. He knew that, in the absence of other evidence, they had nothing with which to hold Will Hampton. Hampton's guilt did not appear likely to him, and he saw little to be gained in hanging tough now. He also had a healthy respect for Steve Davies' legal skills, and he knew a pointless cause when he saw one.

Johns adopted his most professional manner in reporting on the facts to the ADA. He made the case for why the murderer was one of the seven people he had interviewed. He explained why, given the confession, they should book Hampton on murder and get on with building a case. If it wasn't Hampton, he reasoned, filling Tyringham in on the factors pointing to David Sullivan and Annie McGantry, the real murderer would become clear soon enough.

"In other words," Doug Tyringham interrupted, "since one of the group you interviewed yesterday had to be the murderer, and since Will Hampton is the one you have in jail, we should keep him there until we can arrest one of the others. As far as I can tell, I'm afraid we don't have any real grounds for suspecting any of them."

"Sure we have grounds." Johns tried laying out the logic again. "Molchev was killed," he repeated, "behind the locked door of the workroom in back of Hampton's shop. Those seven are the only ones who knew where to find the key."

"The key that was wiped clean and has nary a fingerprint on it."

Johns grunted in acknowledgment.

"Those seven," Doug continued, "are the only ones you know about. No defense attorney, let alone Steve Davies, is going to let us get away with that. And the confession is out the window the minute we get into court. We have no motive. As far as we know, we have no murder weapon. And Hampton has alibi after alibi."

"Which won't hold up if this was a conspiracy." Johns fell back on Pete's theory.

"Be reasonable, Detective. The same evidence that suggests a conspiracy suggests that Hampton's innocent. I can't get around that. You want Hampton in prison, find me some evidence. You've given me nothing, Detective. And I have no intention of taking this to court and being made to look like a horse's ass."

Johns shook the hand Doug Tyringham held out to him and was glad when Doug left the office. He'd had more than enough of so-called experts with letters and Roman numerals after their names. They hadn't been there with him and Pete last night, as they sat piecing together the evidence of Samir Molchev's murder. They didn't seem to care that he had a confessed murderer in jail. They couldn't see the forest for the trees.

fourteen

Will sat, ashen but unharmed, on the oversized sofa in the living room. Wendy was curled up tightly beside him, her head in his lap and her eyes closed, her legs hidden under a long patchwork skirt. Jennifer sat facing them, cross-legged in the hanging rattan chair, engaged in something halfway between a panegyric and a harangue.

"You crazy bastard," she scolded him. "I mean, very brave and admirable, and we all love you madly, but you're a maniac. Off to jail to prove some half-cocked point, leaving us too terrified to even be proud of you. You really are. You're a maniac!"

Will glanced up at her, unhappy. He nestled Wendy more closely into his side.

"Shut up, Jen," he said.

"Shut up? Fine. Then you talk. Why'd you say you'd done it?"

"Because I *did* do it," Will said mildly.

"Horseshit."

Will was not about to argue the point.

It was not a terribly inspired speech that followed, and as Will could have told her, it wasn't going to work. A murderer out there. All of them in danger. This wasn't really the right moment for some half-baked stab at being noble. Someone, after all, had actually killed Samir, and maybe she was just speaking for herself, but she was eager to get past this and on with her quiet, unassuming little life. Flanders, their charmed village, needed to be protected because didn't he realize that the world was getting harsher and that the counterculture was going down the tubes? He'd read that Tom Wolfe piece last month—they were now in the "'Me' Decade," for crying out loud. And there was nothing more 'Me' Decade than murder. She stopped, finally, feeling ridiculous.

"Jen, if you're so sure I didn't do it, why do you think I know anything about it?"

"Because you knew more about Samir than the rest of us did. I'm assuming someone killed him for a reason, and that reason just might lie in whatever secrets he told you. I'm not really prying, but Jesus, Will, the guy's dead, and keeping his secrets isn't going to help him now."

"Jen, I promise you, if I thought this had anything to do with Samir's past, I'd tell you about it in a minute. But I don't think it does. If I figure at any point that there's any connection, you'll be the first to know. If not, there's no point talking about it."

"Come on, man. He's dead."

Wendy stirred and opened her eyes. "But don't you want to know, Will? I mean, why Samir is dead? Samir was the last person who should have died from violence."

Oh, no, Jennifer thought. Not Wendy's rap about the St. Samir the Beneficent. She uncrossed her legs and eased herself out of the chair.

"I'm going down to the café. That new guy Mark isn't working out. I want to make sure he isn't putting sugar in the saltshakers." She made her way across the living room and then turned to face Will from the door. She wasn't going to beg him. Or move him. Or break his nose, which at the moment she would have dearly loved to do. But suddenly, she could see him apart from her own irritation, and it pained her that he looked so alone.

"I think," she said slowly, trying to make her voice gentle, "that you weren't just protecting Zach yesterday. I think you know why Samir died. And I know you won't tell me. But we have to get past this."

Will peered back at her from over Wendy's head. He looked crushed, exhausted.

"Please, Jen," he said. "Just let it be."

"I can't. I don't think I have that in me."

"Please," he repeated. "Let it be."

The café was crowded for a Friday afternoon, the room filled with undergraduates. She overheard groans of "Paris in August is the pits, man" and "I'm taking Randolph's Modern Chinese History. I hear he's really tough." An assistant professor of literature was holding forth at the corner table, three earnest young women—two English majors and the editor-in-chief of the literary magazine—hanging on his latest insights into Gabriel García Marquéz.

Jennifer checked in quickly with her two new employees. Ginger, intense as usual behind her granny glasses, was lining up coffee cups and tenaciously steaming milk for cappuccino. Mark, as imperturbable as Ginger was systematic, was languidly serving quiche and salad to two backgammon players at the table by the door. His lanky frame kept time to the Stones song playing on the stereo. Not the best music to think with, she decided. She replaced the tape with an old Joan Baez album, seated herself at her corner table, and took up the week's receipts as an excuse to be alone.

But alone, she soon learned, was too much to expect. The backgammon game was put on hold as the players, two art historians on lunch break from the Clark, came up to her to express their horror. Then the editor-in-chief and one of the undergraduates hurried over for information, interrupting the assistant professor's explication of Colonel Aureliano Buendía as an embodiment of the Latin American revolutionary trajectory.

"There's not much to say," she told the faces around her. "Yes, Samir's dead. Yes, it seems someone killed him. No, Will's not in jail. He's home." This was a small town, she realized as she spoke. The art historians knew Will, the editor's boyfriend did community work with Graham, and the undergraduate had been to the co-op and had had the benefit of Annie's assessment of events, namely, that murder was just too fucking weird. She had just shooed her customers back to their tables when Wendy surprised her by appearing at her side. She had expected Wendy to remain glued to Will.

"Jen," Wendy whispered, dropping into a chair. "What do we do? He wouldn't tell me anything."

"What do you mean, 'what do we do?' We don't do anything. You can't make that man talk. He'll shut up now just to goad us."

"But why did he say he killed Samir? And why won't he tell us?"

"I don't know. I have no idea what to make of any of it."

"Well"—Wendy's loyalty surfaced—"he's just doing what he thinks is right."

Jennifer shrugged. Baez's haunting voice came back into her awareness: *I'll never prove false to the boy I love 'til all these things be done.*

"Okay, but listen. I've figured it out." Wendy pulled her hair back behind her shoulders. "This murder," she pronounced, "is definitely a Scorpio crime."

"Oh, give me a break!"

"No, really. I'm not kidding. It's the only sign that makes any sense. First, I thought it was a Leo crime—Leos, you know, are arrogant and self-centered and can be very irresponsible. But then I thought, no. That would be true of almost any murder, and this one, in particular, is much more . . ."

"Oh, come on. Why don't you go ask the Ouija board for the name of the murderer?"

Wendy was not particularly offended. "Well, I think Ouija boards are silly," she said magnanimously, "but if you really want to, I suppose we can." Then her face fell. She leaned over and rested her head on Jennifer's arm.

"Jen," she whispered. "I want you to do something for me."

"Aw, sweetie. Anything." Jennifer patted the long red curls falling across Wendy's face.

"I want you to figure out who killed Samir."

"You're putting me on."

"No." Wendy sat up. "I'm serious. You're smart, Jen. And you won't be able to stop yourself from thinking about it. I know you think I'm an airhead, but I know you by now."

"I don't think you're an airhead. I love you."

"Yeah, you love me, *and* you think I'm an airhead. But I'm telling you this is going to drive you nuts. It's all in your horoscope."

Jennifer barked a laugh. "You're right. I do think you're an airhead."

"And I think you're an Aries with both your moon and your rising sign in Libra. Listen, Aries are smart, restless, energetic, and the one thing they can't stand is waiting around for something to happen. But then, in conflict with Aries, you've got all that Libra energy, and you need for things to balance. If you don't have balance in your immediate environment, you go bonkers. Come on." Wendy squeezed Jennifer's arm. "You've got to admit that's pretty close."

"I'm not admitting anything of the kind."

Wendy sat back, a slight pout on her face. "You don't realize it, but you're being selfish."

"Why, because I won't use the Zodiac to figure out who killed Samir?"

"No, because you hold this place together, and you're not listening to me."

"I do not."

"You do, Jen. Graham thinks he does, but he doesn't. He's too much of a Pisces."

"Stop it already." Jennifer slapped her hand down on the table. "Look, I know you've had a rotten couple of days—I mean, that's an understatement if I ever heard one—but if you mention one more Zodiac sign, I'm going to knock you upside the head."

Wendy gasped.

"Oh God, I'm sorry. I can't believe I said that. I just want you to stop with the astrology already. And I am not going to try to figure out who killed Samir."

"It's okay." Wendy shook her head hard to push the tears away. "No more astrology." She stood and dug into the deep side pocket of her skirt. She brought out a small stack of Tarot cards and placed them in front of Jennifer on the table. Jennifer let out her first real laugh in two days. "You're unbelievable."

"They're the Major Arcana. Mix them."

"Not a chance."

"For me?"

"Not even. Absolutely not."

Wendy retrieved the cards and walked over to the assistant professor's table.

"Anyone here into Tarot?"

One of the undergraduates nodded. The assistant professor looked at her askance.

"As metaphor," she smiled prettily. "As a form of magical realism."

"Yeah, well, anyway," said Wendy, "if you could just shuffle these." She handed over the stack of cards.

Cards shuffled, and the undergraduate launched on the relationship between Tarot cards and the *Zohar*, Wendy sat back down next to Jennifer. She spread the cards out on the table. "Pick one."

"No."

"Just one card, and I promise to stop."

Jennifer, relenting, turned a card up on the tabletop. The High Priestess looked up at her.

"There," Wendy smiled serenely. "I told you so."

fifteen

Left alone, Jennifer leaned her elbows on the table and placed her chin in her hands. You will not, she lectured herself, make a fool of yourself running around with a magnifying glass in your pocket. You will not ask people stupid questions. You will not fool yourself into believing you could ever figure this out. So, what will I think about instead, another inner voice protested. Finishing my dissertation? Revising my resume? The pile of receipts on the table in front of her no longer promised much distraction. She inclined her head toward the music. *Weep no more, my own true love,* Baez was singing. *I am your long-lost John Riley.*

Baez's voice trailed off, and Jennifer rose to replace the tape with Dylan's *Highway 61 Revisited*. Then she opened the drawer that fitted into the tabletop and retrieved a fresh accounts book. She turned to the first page of columns and lines and grabbed her pen.

It was easy enough to start listing the questions. Was Samir actually killed in the workroom? If so, what was he doing there? If not, how had he ended up there? Was the andiron used to kill him? If so, how was it taken from David's house? If not, what was it doing in the workroom? And what, then, was the weapon? *Weapon?* She shook her head at how quickly she had turned to the language of police procedurals—or Clue. She closed her eyes and saw the workroom as she had found it. Objects lay as Will would have left them on any given evening, his tools all in place, the transistor radio and the electric kettle side by side on the shelf. The re-varnished trunk that he had been restoring that day sat in the center of the room. The room smelled of lacquer and turpentine. But she had nearly tripped on the andiron just on the other side of the door. And then there had been the so-still figure lying next to the wooden trunk, eyes closed, arms at his side, and, when she knelt to touch him, cold as ice.

She shook herself to banish the image. I don't even care if this murder is ever solved, she realized. I just want it to go away, the way Samir has gone away. She shuddered again at the memory, but what came to her was how little of the horror remained. Perhaps it was that, however much she thought about it, it didn't feel as if Samir's death had been evil. It felt more as if Samir himself had been evil, or, rather, that he had been a magnet attracting whatever was small and cruel. Will's gift for loyalty warped into isolation, Annie diminished in her Earth Mother largesse. And Wendy, lovely, open-hearted Wendy. Jennifer knew in her bones that Samir had found the duplicity of their one night together more satisfying than the sex.

They're selling postcards of the hanging, Dylan sang. So be it, she thought. We are not what we were. We are now a small village of overgrown flower children beset by a small village murder. What she cared about, fiercely, was that she would never find out that someone she loved had killed Samir.

The riot squad is restless. She let Dylan draw her into thought. *All hail to Nero's Neptune. The Titanic sails at dawn.*

A late summer sun fell against the salt and pepper shaker on the gingham tablecloth and a patch of salmon wall. Jennifer looked up from her table, nodded at a sculptor who sold her work through Will's craft shop, and waved to two puppeteers who drove down regularly from Bread and Puppet Theater in Vermont. Wendy, she noted, had come on duty and was preparing dinners in the kitchen. Joni Mitchell was on the stereo. Of the afternoon's patrons, only the assistant professor and his acolytes remained.

Annie loomed briefly at the front door, spotted Jennifer, and came directly over to her table. She looked weary, dark circles under her grey eyes, her feathery, dirty blonde hair hanging limp.

"You look like you've just harvested the entire Northeast," Jennifer greeted her. "You really need more help this time of year."

"You got that right. I've been getting up at four, and it doesn't even get light this time of year until six. I've been canning for two hours every morning before getting out in the field, and I've been on duty at the co-op every afternoon. I just got off this minute."

"You should go to work for corporate agriculture. The pay is better, not to mention the hours."

"Yeah." Annie snorted. "Unless you happen to be a migrant worker. But anyway." She looked around. "Is Wendy here?"

"In the kitchen."

"Good. I don't want her to hear me and give me a hard time." She leaned forward, sat on her hands, and put her head closer to Jennifer's. "If I thought Samir, excuse me, I mean our dear co-op brother, the late lamented Samir, was a thorn in my side before he died, you should have been at the co-op this afternoon. I spent half the afternoon hearing from customers about how Samir was *such* a deeply spiritual person and the other half insisting that I throw a memorial service for him."

"Well, I spent the afternoon being told by Wendy that I'm

the High Priestess from the Tarot deck, so that means I'm responsible for figuring out who killed him."

"Hey, you outrank me. I'm only the Queen of Pentacles. That's not even one of the, what does she call them?"

"The Major Arcana?"

"Yeah, that's it. So, anyway, I had to listen to how Samir had believed God was in everyone, was really a pantheist, or even an animist, believed that God was in the corn, and the rain, and probably in the tomato worms, and that every meal was a communion. I mean, are you kidding me? The Holy Trinity, right? Samir, the Buddha, and the baby Jesus. A few people who are members actually proposed that I personally run the memorial service. I know, I know"—she put up her hands—"don't start with me. I know I don't call the shots about whether a co-op member gets a memorial service or not. Brother Vishnu thinks we should do a silent meditation."

"Well, at least then you won't have to make a speech."

"And Jason, you know, the sitar player who likes to pretend he's George Harrison, is in buying his week's worth of fruit and nuts and offers to lead a service about the transient nature of the material world. The transient nature of the material world? Of course Jason thinks the material world is transient—he doesn't get enough Vitamin A to see straight. I don't think he's eaten a vegetable in ten years! But when did everyone get so goddamn spiritual around here? You don't need some medieval religious crap to believe in organic farming. All you have to do is read the labels on the insecticides."

The transient nature of the material world ought to have its uses, Jennifer thought. I really need to talk to Graham.

Zach Lerner, who had driven into town in shy search of Annie, had seen her pick-up truck parked outside the café and entered the room. He sat down beside them, and Annie quickly turned to him as an expert witness in the case against religion. Hadn't these people ever heard of the politics of cancer? Hadn't they ever read Rachel Carson? No wonder the movement was in decline, with everyone joining the God brigade.

Zach turned around to catch Ginger's eye as she circulated among the tables. He ordered a cup of black coffee, then turned back to Annie and shook his head.

"Hey, listen. The God brigade, if you want to call them that, didn't destroy our happy little revolution—we did that ourselves. We picked ourselves up, feeling very smug that the war was over, and began collecting antique coffee grinders, writing novels, and going to therapy."

Annie pulled herself higher in her chair. "And growing organic vegetables?" she said defensively.

Zach smiled at her. "I didn't say that."

"Well, I don't see that going to graduate school like some people is any better," she said, ignoring the fact that Zach had gone not only to graduate school but also to prison.

"I'd be the first one to agree with you," he answered. "I'm just saying, we have no one to blame but ourselves. And a lot of people in the sixties were pretty sophomoric to begin with. 'LSD will free the world.' 'Fight the system—grow your hair.' 'Read Tolkien and end the war.'"

Annie, her exhaustion fading, leaned sideways, jostling Zach softly with her shoulder. She liked the conviction in his face, and she had always found intellectuals sexy. Besides, she was getting bored with David, and she felt somewhat vindicated, having always disapproved of LSD.

"I tasted your pickles," he offered, sensing that her mood had changed.

"What? I told you they weren't ready. You were supposed to wait until next week."

"Yes, but I was having a hamburger. I just took a couple of bites of one, so I could report back to the Lower East Side."

"Report back what? That after three days in brine a pickle isn't worth eating? If they don't already know that, they should stop making pickles. So then, what did you think?"

"Well," he said tentatively, "I only had a bite or two. They were a lot more bitter than I'm used to."

The café door now opened again, and David Sullivan entered, a black T-shirt over black dungarees and a black silk jacket hanging from his thin shoulders. He headed straight for their table, put his hands in his pockets, and leaned against the wall.

"A good evening to you, Professor," he bowed to Zach. Then, he turned to face Annie.

"Well, if it isn't Mother Earth herself," he began. "Gazing in rapture at her latest consort. And about to stand up and recount breathlessly how she's sorry, she just, you know her, lost track of the time. And then Lerner over here will get very embarrassed and say how you were just discussing recycling plants in China, which he'll call the People's Republic of China. And then she'll say how you were just discussing piles of shit, which she'll call organic waste."

Annie peered at him wordlessly. She had, she remembered vaguely, agreed to spend the evening with him, and the full blast of David's rhetoric always left her slightly dazed.

"Okay, man, so I forgot. You wouldn't believe the day I've had."

"I'm sure I wouldn't. The farmer at harvest time, gathering her green and golden offspring in her calloused hands, honest sweat on her nipples and running down between her thighs." He assumed his best mock-epic pose. "And I was going to bathe you in bergamot and ply your sun-cracked lips with kisses. So why don't we just get to the point which is," he raised his voice to pronounce, "if you're moving on to your next man, my love, do it on your own time, and don't keep me sitting home with my cock in my hand waiting for you to show up."

Annie, by now, had recovered and was ready for a fight.

"Well, while you've got it in your hand, I've got fifteen sheep in the pasture."

"*Stop it!*" Wendy stood over them, dishcloth in hand, having run in from the kitchen. "Samir's dead! He's not even buried yet. And you were his friends, and you're being horrible. How can you go on like that," she demanded, the tears rising, "when he's still lying there in the hospital morgue?"

But this evening, not even the dead kept center stage. During Wendy's outburst, Zach had first stiffened and then collapsed slowly onto the floor. "I'm sick," he managed to get out before his teeth clenched. His back and chest muscles convulsed as Annie knelt down beside him. He was still convulsing as the ambulance arrived and as he was lifted onto the stretcher, arms and legs rigid, his eyes wide with terror and pain. He was still convulsing as he was rushed into the emergency room at North Adams General, where the doctors administered phenobarbital, stopping the convulsions just in time.

sixteen

It was hard to convince Annie not to try to keep up with the ambulance. Eighty miles an hour was fine if you had a siren blaring, but not if you were in a ten-year-old pickup truck with a transmission that tended to fall out of fifth gear. Annie sat forward in her seat, hands rigid on the steering wheel, while Jennifer and Wendy sat close together on the other side of the stick shift, Jennifer intent on being a second set of eyes to make sure Annie didn't plow into the local traffic on her way up Route 43.

Nobody spoke until Annie pulled into the parking lot in front of the emergency room. She turned sharply into a parking spot and applied the brakes too quickly, flinging Wendy into Jennifer. Jennifer put her arms around Wendy.

For once, Wendy pushed her away.

"But why Zach?" she demanded.

"Don't even ask that," Jennifer responded. "Personally, I expect to be told that Zach has a perfectly controllable, mild form of epilepsy and that he stupidly forgot to take a pill."

"Yeah, well, personally"—Annie breathed out hard—"I want to crawl into a hole. You heard Zach. He ate one of my pickles."

"You can't think that has anything to do with this!" Jennifer objected.

"Why not? Because you don't want it to? C'mon." Annie switched off the ignition and opened the door of the truck. "Let's go in."

By the time they walked into the emergency room, Zach had been wheeled through the swinging doors of the treatment area. No, said the receptionist behind the glassed-in office, there was no information about him. No, it wasn't clear when there would be. Yes, if they wanted, they could wait.

The waiting room was a monument to disappointment. Five rows of green plastic chairs each ended with a fake wood table bearing stained ashtrays and old magazines. The smell of disinfectant hung in the air. The walls were a dull pale green. The single poster, in contradiction to the ashtrays, was of a lit cigarette atop a coffin.

In the front row, a young boy sat, wheezing rhythmically. His mother, a thin, youngish woman in curlers covered by a scarf, was looking at her watch and sighing dramatically in the direction of the receptionist. Beside her, a very young couple sat, the wife hugely pregnant, the husband hovering, looking thoroughly scared, holding a paper cup of water. In the next row, a baby howled, its mother looking around frantically, and a young girl retched into a paper bag.

"This place is proof that America needs Feng Shui," Wendy observed.

Jennifer snorted. "This place is proof that American needs socialized medicine."

Annie grunted. "I can't take it. Let's go wait outside."

They settled themselves on the cement step outside the door and peered at each other in the dark. Wendy folded her long skirt under her and drew her hands into the sleeves of her blouse. Annie sat with her legs astride, elbows on her knees.

Jennifer crossed her legs in front of her and ran her hands through her hair.

"So what are we dealing with here?" Annie finally began. "Some homicidal maniac who's going to pick us off one-by-one?"

"We're dealing," Jennifer was adamant, "with some kind of seizure."

"And if you keep saying that, will it make it true?"

"I don't get it," Wendy put in. "I know not everyone liked Samir." She glanced over at Annie. "But Zach hasn't been here long enough for anyone to hate."

"David does."

"No, he doesn't." Jennifer waved away Annie's suggestion. "He was just being melodramatic. If he got really mad, he'd throw a shoe at you and then go around saying that he'd been known to beat women. But I really can't imagine him hurting anybody."

"And anyway," Annie noted, "if David wanted to kill someone, it would be much easier for him to give them bad drugs. The cops could never prove he'd done it, and he could tell everyone else that, shucks, he didn't know they were bad. They'd come from a reliable source, so he figured they were terrific."

"What? And ruin his reputation for having the best drugs around?"

"He couldn't have done that with Zach," Wendy said. "Zach never takes drugs, remember? First of all, he's on parole." She turned to Annie. "But even aside from that, he told us when he came to dinner last week that he hates drugs. He said that in Berkeley, a lot of people died from taking bad acid, and one of them was his sister."

"Phew," Annie breathed. "I didn't know that."

"He told us at dinner, right after Samir lit a joint."

The door opened behind them. They scrambled to get out of the way of a nurse pushing an old man in a wheelchair. The man, with a pale, unshaven face, was breathing audibly. Walking behind him was an exhausted-looking, middle-aged woman, her hair hanging against pallid, fleshy cheeks. She turned to address the nurse.

"I'm sorry. I know he's trouble. He got scared. You know how he gets scared."

"That's okay, Jackie. I know. Mr. Mooney," the nurse raised her voice and spoke directly into his ear, "you're fine. The doctor said you're fine. You can go home now."

"I can't breathe." The old man's voice was belligerent.

"C'mon, Dad." His daughter glanced an apology at the nurse. "They said you can go home. We have to go home." She bent down and took his elbow. "Can you walk to the car? I'll help you, Dad."

The old man stood weakly as his daughter took his arm. They crossed the parking lot to an old Pontiac sedan, the old man protesting as his daughter eased him into the car.

"Remind me not to grow old in this country." Jennifer sighed.

They sat for a moment, their thoughts returning to Samir and Zach.

"I suppose," said Jennifer wearily, "that if it turns out that someone has tried to hurt Zach, we will have to figure out who could have done both. You know, once you have two sets of motives, opportunities, and stuff, it's supposed to limit the field. In fact, it probably complicates things so much you need an abacus just to figure out what you've got."

"They don't need an abacus," Annie said glumly. "They've got me, and what I need is a nice little country where they speak English and don't have an extradition treaty."

"Annie, stop that."

"Why should I? You want two sets of opportunities? Here I am."

Part of the Solution

It was two o'clock in the morning before they were told that Zach was out of danger, that no, they couldn't see him, and that visiting hours would begin at noon the next day. Jennifer suggested pointedly to the doctor that they might want to analyze the contents of Zach's stomach, but the doctor only bristled at the uninvited interference. They didn't know that Allard Johns had been contacted at his Friday night poker game or that, as Annie dropped them off and headed home, Ford McDermott was placing police locks on Zach's front and back doors.

Wendy had called Will from the hospital, and they found him at the kitchen table, a beer in front of him and Graham at his side.

"They think he'll be okay," Jennifer assured them.

"What happened?" Graham demanded.

"We don't know."

"Do they think . . . ?"

"Who knows what they think?" Jennifer took a chair. "They certainly weren't about to tell us. Annie's come up with a theory of a rabid crypto-fascist homicidal maniac who won't be happy till he's killed us all."

"How cheerful," Graham offered.

"Well, personally, I find some of the alternatives a lot less cheerful. And don't"—Jennifer put up a finger in warning—"start telling us how you killed Samir."

"But . . ." Will began.

Jennifer cut him off.

"Did you try to kill Zach?"

"No."

"Then you're full of shit, so shut up and stop confusing things."

They sat in silence, thinking. Will took a final swig on his beer.

"Look," he said. "I promised that I'd tell you about Samir if I ever thought his story was relevant. Well, Zach spent ten years in Berkeley, right? Samir was at Berkeley too."

At first, he had been just another pothead, Samir had told him, working in a smoke shop and living in the Haight. He had tried to be part of the anti-war movement, demonstrating and mouthing the slogans. But the activists seemed too angry, too much a mirror image of the militarism they opposed. In the end, he came to the belief that only love could free the world.

The protest, he reasoned, could not be against people. Not soldiers. Not even the government. It would have to be against the machinery of war itself. He schooled himself in the theology of non-violent resistance, followed the Berrigans, read Martin Buber, and when he came upon Thick Nhat Hanh, he knew he had found a spiritual and political mentor.

The plan was to demonstrate against the troop ships. They would sit chanting until they were driven off or arrested. They would shame America as Gandhi had shamed Britain. Peace would triumph simply through their power to endure. And it was, he told Will, working. They were not disrespectful hippies, not hardened radicals, and even the mainstream churches had begun to take notice, even in areas whose economy depended on the military. They had organized among the workers and on the navy base in San Jose. They were effective. That made them dangerous.

He had heard the explosion from two blocks away. He got there in time to see flames pouring out of the windows and stayed to see the black bags that carried the bodies of his friends. The police claimed that the explosion was caused by the cache of explosives in the basement and that the pacifism had been a cynical front. Samir's name—his real name—ended up on the FBI's most wanted list, and Samir became one of the disguised drifters of the urban underground. Job to job, name to name, hide-out to hide-out, and after Nixon was disgraced, Mitchell in jail, and J. Edgar Hoover dead, Samir had come upon

Flanders. Let them find me here, he had decided, if there is anyone left to bother. I cannot run anymore.

He had taken Will into his confidence out of some need that he himself couldn't quite fathom, but he did not want anyone else to know who he was. It was a relief, he had said, to talk about it all, and he had told Will story after story over the table in the workroom. Years on the run had taught him suspicion, but he was sure that Will would never say a word. Slowly he had relaxed into the illusion of normalcy and had begun to feel safe.

What his real name was, Samir had never mentioned. Will had never wanted to know.

"My God," breathed Wendy, half thrilled to be finally hearing the story. "They must have still been looking for him." Her voice grew tearful. "I guess maybe they finally caught him."

"And what?" asked Jennifer. "They figured they might as well try for Zach while they were in the neighborhood?"

"Do you really think so?" Wendy bit her lip.

"No, I don't. Zach isn't dead. Whoever tried to kill him, assuming someone did, blew the job completely. That smacks of rank amateurism to me."

"Besides," Graham put in. "Zach isn't wanted by anyone. The government knows where he is—he's on parole, for crying out loud. And anyway, they tap phones and plant evidence in this country. They don't hit you over the head and poison your food."

"Are you sure about that?" Will asked.

The room was silent. They'd kind of hoped it had been the FBI.

"I've got a question," Graham spoke again. "Did Samir and Zach know each other at Berkeley?"

"No," said Will. "Samir said they'd never met. He knew Zach's name, of course, and Zach knew his, or at least his real name. But they'd never seen each other face to face, and I'm sure that Zach has no idea who Samir was."

It was three-thirty in the morning, and they were all too tired to think. Someone had said something important, but Jennifer tried to wrench her mind into alertness, struggled a bit, and lost. Graham got up to go.

Perhaps Will had not told them all of it, Jennifer thought as she dragged herself upstairs. As it was, there was something about the story that made no sense at all.

seventeen

The police lab agreed to work through the weekend, and their preliminary report lay on the empty passenger seat beside Johns as he turned onto Route 2 on Monday morning. Lerner hadn't eaten much all day, but he had eaten dinner; he had chopped meat, ketchup, some kind of bread, and a bit of pickled cucumber in his stomach, plus a dose of strychnine that easily could have killed him. Lerner was lucky they had gotten him to the hospital. Allard Johns didn't approve of Zachary Lerner, but he approved of poisoning people even less.

There were a number of questions in Johns' mind as he drove into Flanders, and he was determined to answer them systematically, to make sure he could present an air-tight case that even that condescending pup of an ADA would have to take seriously. Chances were extremely good that the strychnine had come from the pickles. Strychnine was soluble in vinegar, he had been told, besides which it would take something as spicy as pickling brine to begin to mask strychnine's bitter taste. That weird café would have to be closed down for a full police investigation. Apparently, there had been some sort of argument right before Lerner keeled over, and he needed to determine what the relationship was between that and Lerner's poisoning. He needed to discover where the pickles had come from and when—not to mention where—Lerner had eaten them.

And he had to figure out how this new crime related to the murder of Samir Molchev. Why had the Flanders bunch suddenly dropped their peace-and-love posturing and started bumping each other off? Their usual doings might be a disgrace, but he had taken their sincerity for granted. What would make a community like that spawn a killer? It was that last question that occupied Johns as he turned off Route 2, drove down the little main street of Flanders with its small houses and overhanging trees, and parked in front of Café Galadriel.

Unnaturalness, for one thing, he decided as he switched off the motor. This bunch was wrong. It simply wasn't true that all you needed was love. You needed stability. You needed parents to worry about and children to raise. You needed a job to go to on all those mornings you would much rather stay in bed. You needed—he would never forgive them for this—to be willing to fight for your country, not only because your country was right but because wars were a part of what it means to be a country, a part that you didn't have the power to overrule. That was it; there had to be some things that couldn't and shouldn't be overruled. And if there weren't any, well, it was a slippery slope, with murder at the bottom. It only took one worm to corrupt the apple in their little hippie Garden of Eden. One snake. One murderer.

Johns was not surprised at what he saw as he entered the café, the dumpy old couch along one pink wall and the assertively unmatched tables and chairs. It had never been clear to him why every hippie hangout had identical posters on the wall. Or how large glass jars filled with food could be considered a form of decoration. In justice, he had to grant that there was a certain tattered hominess about the place, not least in the smell of baking coming from the kitchen. But the jars of food, so visible, made him furious. Did they think they could get away with absolutely anything?

Jennifer and Mark were alone in the café, getting ready to open, Mark doing his hapless best setting the tables, Jennifer laying out fillings for the breakfast burritos and gnawing on fear like a bone. She had awakened with a sense of dread, burrowed into the covers until the last possible moment, and then stood in the shower fighting back tears. She was glad that she was scheduled to open the café this morning rather than Wendy; Wendy was probably less frightened than she was—Wendy, after all, had the comforting belief that Jennifer would save the day. But Wendy was far less likely than she was to be able to fake business as usual.

How reassuring her certainty had been, she thought now, that Samir's death had arisen from something in his past. Not some random act of viciousness by someone cleansing the world of flower children. Not a deliberate act of brutality on the part of anyone she loved. Some piece of the malevolence she sensed in Samir had materialized in Flanders, and if it had taken Samir with it, over time, well, her universe would right itself, better for the fact that Samir was no longer in it. But what, exactly, was she supposed to do? Figure out who had committed these crimes? Save them from the next one? From each other? All she knew about solving crimes were things she had read in murder mysteries. British murder mysteries. With Victorian values and Edwardian panache.

Meanwhile, she had only Mark for company, and she wished that Ginger was on duty instead. Ginger was both tenacious and watchful, a pre-med student on scholarship who studied hard, waited tables for pocket money, and carefully hid her belief that most people were fundamentally stupid. She could handle whatever the day would bring. Mark, on the other hand, was Jennifer's very definition of a space cadet. With a head of dark red hair and a Grateful Dead T-shirt that covered his ungainly body almost every day, Mark resembled a year-old Irish setter beginning to progress from puppy cuteness to adult grace but currently at a stage at which he couldn't be trusted not to upset the furniture.

Mark had, indeed, been accepted into Williams at a moment of transition. He had spent elementary school memorizing the names of galaxies and won prizes in junior high school for recreating early experiments to measure the speed of light. But his senior year of high school was a blur. He tried learning the guitar. He read Isaac Asimov. He took to dropping acid and thinking about the time-space continuum.

It was clear from his first semester that the guys in the Physics department weren't, as he put it, fucking around. He wasn't going to get by comparing Jerry Garcia's ripple in still waters to the second law of thermodynamics. And he sure as hell wasn't going to get laid. The chicks who dug his rap about curved space were all majoring in art history; physics majors, he decided, were preppies whose fathers worked for NASA and who had slide rules for brains.

In three years, Mark had duly gone from physics major through earth science and English to arrive at anthropology. His senior thesis, now in the earliest stages of development, was on the implicit quantum physics of Amerindian cultures. The role of chance in the universe. Coyote. The trickster god who plays dice with the universe after all.

Jennifer only needed to see the police car through the window to know that Zach's seizures had, after all, stemmed from a second attempt at a murder. This one had been blessedly unsuccessful, but that didn't mean that any of them were safe from a murderer or, for that matter, the law. She hoped it would be the young cop, Officer McDermott, who was about to pay them a visit, but she was not surprised to see Detective Johns walking up the flagstones to the front door of the café.

It would probably be easier to get through the next hours if she could muster some version of self-mastery.

"Good morning, Detective. The coffee's almost ready. Can I get you some?"

"No. I take it you were here last evening?"

"Yes, I was."

"I'd like your statement as to what happened."

"Sure. But this is going to take a while, and I need coffee even if you don't."

Johns, ignoring her, helped himself to a chair.

At the coffee urn, her back turned to Johns, Jennifer tried to gather herself. Don't tell him about the fight between Annie and David. Don't tell him Annie and David have been lovers and that Annie has been coming on to Zach. She might think Annie's fears of being accused were groundless, but there was no point giving Johns ammunition. She carried her coffee to the table and seated herself across from Johns.

"Please," she said. "Ask away."

Johns retrieved a pen from his jacket pocket and consulted the notepad already in his hand.

"What time did Mr. Lerner arrive?"

"I'm not exactly sure. It was dusk, so, what would that be? Around seven."

"Who was here?"

She shrugged. "The café was crowded. I'm not sure I even knew everybody."

"How close were you to Mr. Lerner?"

"You mean, were we friends? He just moved here. He—"

"No, I mean how near were you when he fell?"

"Pretty close. We were at the same table."

"Who else was at the table?"

Jennifer stiffened. "Look," she tried, "Zach had only been there about ten minutes. He'd ordered coffee, but it hadn't come. He didn't eat anything. He didn't drink anything. Nobody got close enough to him to even touch him."

"Who else was at the table?" Johns' voice was patient. Jennifer wasn't fooled.

"Annie McGantry was here when Zach came in. David Sullivan had just arrived a minute or two before he got sick. Wendy Scholes had just come from the kitchen."

Johns asked placidly, "What was the fight about?"

"What fight?"

Johns had already determined to drop the politeness at the first sign of anything less than full cooperation. They might have gotten the better of him around Zach Lerner's potential arrest. But his attempted murder was another matter.

"Don't play dumb with me, Miss Morgan. Maybe you think it's okay to have a murderer on the loose, but not on my watch, you got that?"

"I'm sorry, Detective. There was no fight. There was some banter between Annie and David, but it was hardly a fight."

"That's not what I heard."

She fished for a way to turn the conversation. "Look, please tell me. What happened to Zach? Do they know yet?"

"You want information, Miss Morgan, read the newspapers. As far as I'm concerned, you may all be in danger, and you may all *be* the danger. I'm of two minds about all of it. You answer my questions, and we'll take it from there."

"Detective," she shot back, "I own this café. Someone being poisoned here would not be good for business, so if for some bizarre reason I wanted to kill Zach Lerner, I wouldn't do it in a way that had anything to do with food. Meanwhile, I live here. Someone is trying to kill my neighbors, and I'm every bit as frightened as you would expect. I'm telling you, nobody got within two feet of Zach. I was sitting right there."

"So, what was the fight that you say wasn't a fight about?"

"Annie had made a date with David and forgot about it. He was annoyed. It was no big deal."

If she could only leave it there, with no indication that Zach had been the subject of David's wrath, she might, she decided, just survive the morning. Johns appeared to be satisfied. He looked around. Mark, having finished setting tables, was leaning against the counter, his hands picking an invisible guitar.

Johns asked, "What's that guy's name?"

The grass he had smoked before work that morning was the kind that made Mark feel mellow. Under its sway, it didn't bother him that people got upset when he forgot to tell them that the chili of the day was three-star spicy or that he had brought a pot of Earl Grey tea when they had asked for peppermint. He handed out the menus and wrote down the orders, but then he got to talking, and it was cool the way words fell from his mouth; it was always a surprise to see what came out, and by the time he got to the kitchen to place the order, sometimes the order pad was no longer in his hand.

"Yeah, I was here. Sure." Mark sat down dutifully, his skinny shoulders hunched inside the Grateful Dead T-shirt, trying to look attentively at Johns. It dismayed him to be talking to a policeman. The last thing he wanted was to make things worse for anyone. He knew David from his brief days as an English major; it was clear to Mark that underneath David's hipster poet persona was just another kid nobody had picked in sixth-grade softball. But as far as the fight with Annie was concerned, Mark was thoroughly on Annie's side. Annie, with her taut little body and her passion for the microbiology of herbs, was Mark's latest vision of a force of nature. Pure energy. And not as in MC^2. Energy as in sex.

"David was upset, yeah. I mean, he was, like, home waiting for Annie. So he got pissed off and made this scene. It was even kind of funny, actually." He stopped speaking and waited to be let off the hook.

Johns had been a detective long enough to know the virtues of silence. Sit there for enough time, make somebody sufficiently uncomfortable, and they'll cross-examine themselves.

Mark's voice squeaked his sincerity. "And it's, like, just Annie. I mean, her fight with David was nothing special. It wasn't serious or anything."

Johns still said nothing. He leaned forward without moving his eyes from Mark's face, his uniformed forearms at odds with the gingham tablecloth.

"I mean," Mark begged him, "you should have seen some of the scenes about Samir. She could be absolutely furious. And now that he's dead, she's just put it down, like nothing ever happened. It's just, like, people have their feelings. It's no big deal. It's just, like, what is."

There was a small sound in Jennifer's throat. That was it, she fumed, she was firing Mark's ass the minute Johns was out of there, assuming he would ever leave.

"So, there were also fights between Annie McGantry and Samir Molchev?"

Mark watched the words fall from his mouth and hunched his shoulders in resignation. He'd blown it. He couldn't get his thoughts back together, and anyway, it was too late now. Jennifer listened, dismay filling the place where her stomach used to be, as Mark, fed by Johns' questions, recounted Annie's animosity, Samir's sudden appearance at the co-op, and Annie's blow-up at the café. She was dreading the moment when Johns would turn to her and force her to affirm or deny Mark's story.

Part of the Solution

But Johns didn't even bother. Instead, he ran his eyes along the shelves behind the counter. Chutney. Local wildflower honey.

"Tell me something." He turned to Jennifer. "Do you serve pickles?"

"Yes. Why?"

"Where do you get them?"

Jennifer bit her lip. Whatever this was, she didn't like it. But she saw no way out.

"From Annie McGantry. She cans them for the co-op."

"Do they come in jars?"

"No. A barrel."

"Where are they?"

She rose and let him follow her into the kitchen, then she stood and watched as he took latex gloves and a plastic evidence bag from his pocket, pulled on the gloves, and ladled a sample into the bag. He sealed the bag and marked it.

"You weren't planning to open today, were you?"

"Yes, I was."

"Sorry, Miss Morgan. I'm afraid we've got a crime scene here, and we're going to need to cordon it off until we eliminate various possibilities."

"But I've already told you, Detective. Zach had nothing to eat or drink while he was here. He may have taken ill here, but whatever caused it happened someplace else." An unwelcome memory surfaced: Annie handing Zach a jar of pickles, a teasing come-on in her eyes. "You have no reason to close us down."

"I tell you what, Miss Morgan." Johns ostentatiously removed the gloves. "You can wait until I get a court order to close this place, or you can just give yourself a holiday while I get this sample to the police lab. I don't want anybody in here until it's thoroughly searched. So, you can leave and lock the door behind you, or you can let me do it with police tape and some very public notices. Your choice."

He turned and walked out of the kitchen toward the front door. On impulse, she followed him.

"Detective, you know perfectly well that we didn't serve Zach anything to make him sick. He didn't eat anything while he was here. He certainly didn't eat any pickles. And if he had, whatever it was would have had to work so fast that he never would have made it to the hospital alive."

Johns left without replying. She stood, her arms flapping a useless argument, feeling anything but the High Priestess. More like the Fool.

eighteen

The clothes he had slept in for three days were sticky on his back and sides, but the pain in his gut was better—after two days of fasting, the stomach shrinks and you aren't so hungry anymore. The police had gathered, and the streets were noisy with bullhorns and sirens. By that night, the sit-in would be over, and they would all be in jail.

Zach was not frightened of jail, but he knew that between this moment and jail there would be moments of pain and even terror. The police would mount the stairs in riot gear, and the sickening thuds of billy clubs would be followed by screams. His mind followed the moments as his body tensed against them, and then it was happening, step by ineluctable step. Someone was holding his arms, and someone else pounded again and again into his empty, twisted gut.

He opened his eyes to bottles held by metal clamps above his head. He looked around. One arm was wrapped in tape where the IV entered. The other bore a bracelet of hospital plastic, He raised it to his eyes: Zachary Lerner, Dr. Connors, North Adams General. His arm dropped, too hard, onto his stomach, and he slept again.

David walked into the house well-pleased with the previous weekend. He had left the café and driven up to Bennington in pursuit of Sally, who put aside a half-written paper on "Leaves of Grass" to soothe his wounded feelings. On his way home, he had stopped by to see Jennifer and heard that Lerner was on the mend. Annie would be pulling her horny little hair out before he was in any condition to resume their romance, but David could now afford the revenge of disdain. It really was scandalously simple to seduce some women with one's interpretation of "Leda and the Swan." And Annie, after all, had been flat-footed intellectually; it was going be nice to have a woman with the proper appreciation for the well-crafted metaphor.

"Mr. Lerner, you have a visitor."

He opened his eyes. The nurse was standing at his bed, Will Hampton behind her.

"Hey, man. How are you?"

Zach shook his head weakly. "I feel like a half-dead puppy." His voice was raspy.

Will pulled the single chair closer to the bed. "What do they think happened?"

"They say strychnine."

"Damn."

Zach closed his eyes again, not up to the task of talking. And what for, anyway? In his years as a leader of the anti-war movement, he had suffered his share of police violence, but a concussion was as close as he had ever come to dying. Three years in a maximum-security prison, and he'd gotten by without a scratch. Now, when he was trying to live like an ordinary citizen, complete his parole, teach his classes, and maybe make a friend or two, he'd ended up nearly dead. First Samir. Now him. What in the hell was going on?

At least in the movement when someone tried to kill you,

death had a kind of meaning. You were servant to the rhythm of history. He was hardly Joe Hill, killed by the copper bosses and not wanting to be found dead in the state of Utah, but if he was going to die young, at least it should be for something. He thought of his sister, carried to a hospital as he had been carried, dying of a poison she had thought would bring wisdom. He hadn't even been looking for wisdom. He had just been eating! Why?

He kept his eyes closed. "I can't talk," he whispered. "Sorry."

He drifted back to sleep.

"But Jennifer, really, it's got to be a Scorpio, probably with a moon in Aries."

"Don't start, okay?"

"Really, I mean it. I know you think it's stupid, but it's the only sign that fits."

Jennifer groaned.

They were in the living room, at loose ends from the unexpected holiday that Johns had forced on them. Jennifer, desperate for something to do, was hunched on the old sofa working a long-abandoned needlepoint. Wendy was perched across from her on the rattan chair. On the stereo, Billy Holiday was singing "God Bless the Child."

"Scorpios," Wendy began, "have many positive traits."

"Of course they do. Don't you think it's strange that horoscopes never say, 'Everyone born under this sign is pond scum'?"

Wendy ignored her. "They're very emotional and dedicated. And they're, you know, subtle. They can get really careful carrying out a plan. All that is usually positive, but sometimes it all turns negative, and then they get secretive and paranoid."

"That means that Scorpios," she went on, "make very good detectives, or else they make very good crooks. They feel at home in the little secret places in their minds. They can keep things to themselves forever, analyzing them and never needing to say a word. You know those thoughts everyone has sometimes that make you blush just to think them?"

"Only too well."

"Well, that's where negative Scorpios live."

"And the moon in Aquarius?"

"Aries."

"Okay, Aries."

"Well, Scorpio is a water sign, and an Aries moon just intensifies the characteristics of water signs, good or bad. Aries is selfish to begin with, and an Aries moon with a bad Scorpio sun could produce a murderer any time, especially"—Wendy nodded knowingly—"this kind."

"What kind?"

"You know. Sneaky."

"So have you figured out just who in our little circle happens to be a Scorpio?"

"No one is. You're an Aries. Will and I are Libras. Graham's a Pisces, Annie's a Sagittarius, and David's a Capricorn."

Jennifer had to acknowledge to herself—acknowledging it to Wendy was out of the question—that she had just been given a pretty good description of the killer. Someone had planned these crimes and executed them without seeming to leave a trace. Assuming the obvious, that none of her friends was capable of murder, a stranger had crept, unseen, among them. He—could it have been a she?—had killed Samir and nearly killed Zach. And there was no reason to think it was over. Jennifer wished suddenly that she were a Scorpio if they made such good detectives.

The phone in the hall began to ring. Jennifer pulled herself from the sofa.

"Don't worry, Jen," Wendy's voice followed her. "Aries are just as smart as Scorpios."

Jennifer pretended to ignore her. She hated it when Wendy read her mind.

Ford McDermott was not above acknowledging a feeling of satisfaction. He had long suspected that Johns was holding up his promotion to detective, clinging to the myth of his incompetence as a talisman against time and change and doing his damnedest to portray Ford as the dumb kid who might be good for getting kittens out of trees but who had to leave real police work to the grown-ups. Sending Ford to interview Zach Lerner must really be sticking in Johns' craw. Johns, however, had left himself few choices. Having threatened to arrest Zach Lerner as a suspect, Johns would find it awkward to interview him as a victim. Ford parked in the hospital parking lot, grimly aware of a sense of gratification, and sat for a moment, rereading the lab report.

The lab had agreed to spend the weekend on the strychnine-riddled contents that had been pumped from Zach Lerner's stomach. Early that morning, Johns had collected a sample of pickles from the café kitchen and had closed down the café on what Ford believed were shaky grounds. He had then driven over to the co-op, taken a sample of pickle jars from an outraged Annie McGantry, and closed the co-op down as well. The report had come back half an hour previously. Neither sample of pickles contained any trace of poison. A third sample, taken from Zach Lerner's refrigerator, was laced with it.

Ford left the car and walked into the lobby of the hospital, past the vending machines to the elevators. He took the elevator up to the third floor. He identified himself to the duty nurse at the workstation and asked for a quick update. Yes, the doctor had said Mr. Lerner could be questioned. He was lucid and recovering.

Lovely, David thought, settling himself into the hot water and drawing deeply on his hash pipe. A couple of tokes, a nice hot bath, and then perhaps a nap. Sally had kept him up much of the night, and there was nothing like rising from a happy bed to a day of rest, nothing like a morning nap when the sun was shining and his loins were spent. He had charmed Sally with his Irishness, having intuited, on the basis of not a little practice, that she had come from a family who easily paid Bennington's huge tuition and who nodded benignly any time she announced that she was now a Quaker. Or a socialist. He had railed against the banality of the lace-curtain Irish. He exaggerated his working-class origins. His parents, he told her, had taken him to Ireland when he was just a gawky kid, and his father had stood in the old schoolyard, weeping softly in front of a statue of St. Francis. The smallest sparrow. The Holy Spirit. *Set upon a golden bough to sing.*

Still, he thought, taking another toke on the hash pipe, he would remember Annie with fondness. He summoned the memory of stopping by the farm one morning and finding Annie naked, leaning into the goat pen and watching a kid at its mother's teat. He had come up behind her, cupped her breasts, and, when she didn't protest, eased his erection out of his jeans, entered her from behind, and reached forward to stroke her with his fingers. The whole time he was moving inside of her, his eyes had been on the baby's mouth sucking on its mother's teat. He had tried unsuccessfully to write about it—there was no way that feeling could be made into a poem. But he'd never forget it as long as he lived.

The water had nearly filled the tub. Time to turn off the tap. He raised a foot, wrapping pink, wrinkled toes around the faucet and giving a strong, if uncoordinated tug. It was weird, really. Nobody had seemed to notice that Annie was the connecting factor in this odd spate of crimes. Samir. Zach. And now here he was, at home, alone, in perfect health, in the bathtub. He wondered idly if he should be scared. He pictured Samir as he had sat in this very bathroom a few mornings earlier. David had interrupted something—he had seen the expression on Samir's face when he had cut short the conversation with Will. But hey, it was David's bathroom, and Samir, David had decided, could go fuck himself. Except that Samir was dead now, which was about as fucked as anyone could get.

The hot water settled around his chest. In his heart of hearts, he couldn't really say that he was all that sorry Samir was dead. There hadn't really been any love lost between the two of them. David himself was pretty enough or, if not exactly pretty, at least making the most of a blue-eyed aura of rakishness. But who needed to share the pick of the senior class with someone who had skin like antique ivory and a perfectly molded chest? Besides, whatever drug David dispensed, Samir always had a story of something better, opium in Istanbul or mystical Sufi hash, or riding peyote through the Mexicali night to where the Old Ones held court beyond the moon. David had been annoyed, then resentful, then decided it was mostly crap. You had to be a fool to smoke opium in Turkey these days—hadn't everyone seen *Midnight Express*? And Samir hadn't struck David as a fool.

Whatever their history, Samir and Annie had been before David's time. Zach was the one who was newly on the scene, and Zach was in the hospital. Annie hadn't seemed all that kinky—if anything, she liked it clean and uncomplicated—but anything was possible. Maybe there was another side to all that life-affirming wholesomeness, a juxtaposition of the soul, or of the groin, the nymph turned harpy, the priestess turned maenad, and Dionysus dead and bleeding on the ground. He had certainly felt like a satyr that morning by the goat pen. Under the water, David felt himself begin to stiffen. Perhaps there was a poem in this after all.

Zach lay propped up on pillows staring at the oil painting on the wall opposite his bed. The painting bothered him. The whole room bothered him, with its television, its single hospital bed, its attempt at pleasing décor. The easy recovery the doctor had promised should not have earned him this relative luxury, a private room he knew his health insurance wouldn't pay for. They were isolating him, perhaps even protecting him. That was the only explanation for the room.

He rested against the pillows, considering the fact that, probably very soon now, he was going to have to talk with the police. Annie and her damn pickles. He passed a hand across his face and closed his eyes. She had bristled when he teased her about the Lower East Side, her eyes flaring and her small breasts loose inside her T-shirt. He simply didn't believe that her tough little come-on had been meant to mask some inexplicable attempt to murder him. Zach had grown up in a world of simple loyalties: to the Dodgers for Jackie Robinson, to the labor movement for the eight-hour workday. What was he to do now? Lie to the police about where the pickles had come from—a lie that would be easy to disprove and that might well get his parole revoked—or leave Annie open to the tender mercies of the American legal system?

When he opened his eyes again, Ford McDermott was standing over him. Zach was surprised. He'd expected Johns.

"Professor Lerner, do you feel up to a few questions? We've got some information we want to verify."

Zach tried to pull himself up higher on his pillows. Ford, noticing, leaned down and handed Zach the control button that hung over the side of the bed.

Zach raised the top half of the bed so that he was almost sitting up. Ford took the single chair and waited for Zach to finish arranging himself.

"First," Ford opened his notepad. "Could you tell me what you ate yesterday?"

Part of the Solution

Zach stared blankly back at him.

"I can come back later if you like."

Zach shook his head. "I had breakfast on campus, bought some coffee at The Bean, had some chocolate at one point, an apple, and then had a hamburger for dinner with ketchup. And a bun."

Ford appeared to consult the papers in his hand. "And a pickle."

"Oh, yeah. I suppose so."

"Where did you get the apple?"

"One of the farm stands." He waved vaguely.

"The chocolate?"

"The supermarket in Williamstown."

"The hamburger meat?"

"Also the supermarket."

"The pickle?"

"I don't remember."

"You don't remember?"

"No."

"There is a jar of them in your refrigerator."

"I think someone gave them to me."

"Who?"

Zach was silent. Ford put his notebook in his back pocket and deliberately closed his pen. "Please," he said, "don't make us conduct a full search of The Bean, the Williams faculty dining room, the supermarket suppliers, and every farm stand in the county. That would be so much trouble for everyone concerned." He watched Zach closely. "Besides, it isn't necessary. If Annie McGantry isn't guilty of trying to hurt you, she isn't in any danger."

Zach regarded him. Zach had no fondness for or belief in the cops, but he understood the distinction between the police as an instrument of oppression and a young guy with good intentions written all over his face. He acquiesced but refused Ford's attempt at easy comfort.

He looked across at Ford. "You can't promise that."

Graham took Annie's frantic phone call, dialed the number of the Law Collective, and spent fifteen minutes on the phone with the lawyer, Steve Davies. Then he left the church and walked across the street. He followed the path that led from the street, past the closed door of the café, to the side door of Jennifer, Wendy, and Will's house. A murderer in the neighborhood, but, he noted, someone had still left the door unlocked.

He shouted upstairs, identifying himself before they could hear his footsteps. He mounted the steps and entered the living room.

"Johns closed down the café," Jennifer greeted him. "I called Steve Davies this morning, and the bastard is within his so-called rights."

Graham sat down next to her on the couch. "It gets worse." He dreaded telling them. "I just got a call. Annie's been arrested."

"What?"

"Apparently, the pickles she gave Zach were laced with poison. That's all I know."

Jennifer hurled her needlepoint onto the coffee table. It slid across the polished surface and fell to the rug. "Johns knows the pickles came from Annie. I'm really sorry—he saw them, and he asked me straight out, and I couldn't say I didn't know. And Mark—Wendy, I told you Mark was a disaster—Mark was doing his best to say the wrong thing at every possible moment, including that Annie had it in for Samir."

"Steve will handle it," Graham advised. "He's on his way over there now. Hopefully, he'll get her out tonight, but basically, we shouldn't expect her for dinner."

"But how could they think Annie . . ." Wendy let the sentence trail off.

"Hey," Jennifer exclaimed, "any woman who puts her hands in dirt would have no ladylike scruples about murder. The whore of Babylon. The female spider devouring her discarded mates. They would figure that, those pigs! Anyone beside me need some coffee?" She stomped into the kitchen. "Annie, for crying out loud!"

In the kitchen, Jennifer put the kettle on to boil and scooped coffee beans from the bright red canister. She ground them and placed them in a filter over the Chemex next to the stove. Then she reached into one of the bright yellow cabinets for the accounts ledger in which she had begun taking notes. Sexism, she thought, settling herself at the table, couldn't be the whole explanation. What else did they know?

That Annie was in a virtual war against Samir. That of all of them, Annie was the only one without—she wished there was another word—an alibi. The story of Samir being at the co-op that evening was far-fetched, even if you believed in Annie's truthfulness. And then there were the pickles, which she had handed to Zach in front of multiple witnesses, including Jennifer herself. She made a few additional notes on a page she had titled "Miscellaneous Weirdness," listing the questions she couldn't answer about when and how Zach had been poisoned and Samir killed.

The water was boiling. She set down the pen and poured the water gradually through the filter. Who was she kidding? There had to be a way of proving Annie could not be guilty, but she was damned if she knew what it was. The cops must have all kinds of information, not to mention a crime lab. Not to mention the courts. Not to mention an axe to grind that might reduce them all to pieces before Johns was satisfied. Will's workroom cordoned off, and now the café and the co-op both closed. Johns wouldn't have to frame them all. He could simply close Flanders down.

So where was Inspector Parker now that she needed him, running up from Scotland Yard to Lord Peter Wimsey's Piccadilly digs to discuss the details of the case over hundred-year-old sherry? Or Inspector Japp, a policeman so dumb that, no matter how many times Sherlock Holmes outdid him, he never believed he would do it again and so shared the details of the crime out of a thoroughly misguided egotism. Miss Marple walked around looking fluffy and bewildered and asked questions so seemingly batty that the cops, just to humor her, told her everything they knew.

What the hell. It was worth a try.

The Berkshire County phone book was on the telephone table in the hall. She searched the Ms for McDermott, Ford. There it was: Maple Drive, North Adams. What a nice place to have a flat tire, she decided. He had to go home sometime. He had to stop for a lady in distress.

She carried the Chemex into the living room, returned with cups and a pitcher of milk, and reached under the couch for her sandals.

"Help yourself to the coffee."

"Where are you going?" Wendy looked up at her.

"Look," she said. "We can't leave this to the cops. We'll all be dead or in jail if we do that. But we can't figure anything out because we don't have enough information. One"—she counted off on her fingers—"we don't know whose fingerprints were on the andiron. Two, we don't know when Samir was killed. Three, we don't know what they found when they analyzed the pickles except that it's just as well Zach didn't eat more of them. Johns, on the other hand, knows all of these things, but he'll never solve this because he assumes that we are all crazed degenerates who would kill someone for the hell of it. So, I am about to combine his knowledge with my infallible genius by having a flat tire on Maple Drive. Our well-wishing friend Officer McDermott has to pass that way on his way home from work. I'm going to try to get him to talk to me."

The two of them stared at her.

"Jennifer," Graham managed. "You wouldn't!"

Wendy turned to him as Jennifer headed for the stairs.

"Don't be silly, Graham. Of course she would."

part four

nineteen

Allard Johns' tiny office was stifling. The old metal furniture crowded the space inside the dull green walls. How was it, Assistant DA Doug Tyringham asked himself, that the Commonwealth of Massachusetts could build a new $10 million facility and manage to recreate everything tawdry about the one it had replaced? He was dressed for court, his usual late-summer khaki and linen replaced by light Brooks Brothers wool. In the old police station, you could at least open the windows. Johns sat stolid at his desk, papers spread out in front of him. Ford McDermott occupied the folding chair next to the desk.

Doug eyed the photo of a proud Allard Johns shaking hands with the governor. It was easier than looking at Johns himself. Doug was uncomfortable, not only with the heat, but with the arrest of Annie McGantry. It was his clear duty to make the most of the evidence, to prosecute whatever case the police could build. It was also his duty, he decided, to avoid looking like a fool.

"So, Detective, if you could start from the beginning."

Johns' look said that he would start anywhere he goddamn pleased. He was a trained professional, and he'd show this preppy from the prosecutor's office that he knew how to keep a chain of evidence intact. The evidence against Annie McGantry was solid, though he still had his suspicions about Will Hampton—the two crimes were obviously related, and there had to be something behind Hampton's confession. But he'd show them that he knew how to build a case.

Johns had handled two murders in his time. One a domestic squabble that had spun out of control, the poor woman beaten and then stabbed with a kitchen knife. They'd found her husband in New Hampshire, driving his own car up Interstate 91. And the awful time Jack Rodwick had burned down the Clancy house, for spite as far as anyone could figure. He didn't think there was anybody home.

Life, Johns knew, could catch you unawares. There were strains that ran through these old North Adams families, and if you'd grown up here, you also knew why some folks grew up twisted. Johns remembered Jack Rodwick lashing out when they were kids, the broken bones, and the scared-looking mother. Around here, you knew what unemployment and alcohol did to a man's self-respect. But this Flanders bunch was something else. They contained a different kind of chaos. Life had been good to them.

"We got two crimes here," he began, his voice officious, "but I'm focusing for the moment on the poisoning. Zachary Lerner collapsed at around five last Friday evening, that's the evening of October 16. According to the path lab, the cause was"—Johns took a pair of reading glasses from his desk and picked up the report—"American gherkins pickled in a combination of apple cider vinegar, pickling spices, and sugar, along with a strychnine solution suspended in vinegar, hydrochloric acid, and various ingredients used in commercial rodent poisons." He looked up.

"Got it. Go ahead."

"There's no question about the poison. We tested what was left in the jar. In fact, the remaining pickles were in the brine for an extra fifteen hours or so, and they had absorbed even more of the poison. Lerner's lucky he didn't wait another few days to eat 'em. Not so clear he would have survived."

Johns tossed the report onto the desk and pushed his glasses onto his forehead.

"Three other things. One, Lerner admitted to McDermott over here that he'd got the pickles from Annie McGantry. Two, we've got witnesses that she gave Lerner the pickles last Monday afternoon, that would have been October 12, at the café they've got over in Flanders."

"Café Galadriel?"

"Yeah, that's it. Three, the only fingerprints are Lerner's and the McGantry woman's."

Johns paused to let the significance of the fingerprints hover in the room. Ford spoke into the silence.

"The jar may have been handled by someone else as well. There are a number of smudges on the jar and the rim. Someone could have handled it wearing gloves."

"Could have been, sure," Johns barked. "Could have been Lerner opened it with a dish towel. Could've been he smudged it on his sleeve."

"I asked him that. He doesn't remember whether he did or not," Ford said.

Johns sat back in his chair and folded his arms across his chest. "So he forgot. The point is, the pickles were the source of the poison. And what do you think we found in the storeroom of that what-do-you-call-it, that co-op that the McGantry woman runs? Containers of gopher bait containing strychnine hidden on the bottom shelf!"

Doug Tyringham nodded slowly, keeping his thoughts to himself. Johns glanced at his notes again and continued.

"Okay then. Now here's the next point. McGantry only put the strychnine in the jar she gave Lerner. There's jars of the same pickles on sale at the co-op and also at that café place. We tested them. They're clean."

Johns ended with a curt nod of the head.

"Any idea as to motive?" Doug pressed him.

"Not yet," Johns conceded. "But we got opportunity and weapon, and that should be enough for an indictment. We've got time to sort the rest of it out. But you know"—Johns shifted in his seat—"here's something interesting about motive. I don't think we've got enough to charge her yet, but the waiter at the café was very clear that McGantry was known to have a grudge against Samir Molchev. She fought with him in full view of numerous witnesses, and she's apparently been making threatening statements about him for a while. I know"—he waved away Ford and Doug's attempted interruptions. "Like I said, we're focusing on Lerner for the moment, but the two crimes are related. You're not going to tell me they're not. She's got no alibi for when Molchev was killed, just that story of him showing up at her co-op, and that's got holes all over it. Meantime, let's just keep her off the streets. We got a good case here. What time's the arraignment?"

Ford McDermott decided it was time to intervene. In his eagerness to make the case, Johns had been ignoring important evidence. Ford trusted Doug Tyringham to see through Johns' bluster, but the ADA might be inclined to follow the line of least resistance, which at the moment ran straight through Flanders. Jennifer, he winced remembering, had walked him step by step through the interaction between Annie McGantry and Zach Lerner. He was convinced that Annie was innocent.

Ford cleared his throat. Doug looked up at him.

"Officer?"

"There are a few other angles to this, and frankly, I think the case falls apart when they're considered."

Doug raised an eyebrow. "You've got my attention."

Ford ignored Johns' glare.

Part of the Solution

Steve Davies parked his 1968 Dodge next to Doug Tyringham's MG. He let the desk clerk sign him in and walk him past the closed door of Johns' office for a meeting with the prisoner.

"They're trying to give me cancer," Annie shouted when she saw him. "Get me the fuck out of here!"

Annie stood between the cot and the open toilet, barefoot, still wearing the blue work shirt and jeans in which she had been arrested. A pair of red cowboy boots lay on their sides in two separate corners of the cell. Her dark blonde hair hung on either side of her face.

"Look at this shit." She pointed to the eggs and bacon congealing on a tray at the foot of the cot. "Carcinogens! Get me out of here before I starve!"

Steve knew bravado when he heard it. He waited while the clerk opened the door of the cell. He entered quietly and set down his briefcase, keeping his voice steady. "I will get you out of here. You just need to be patient."

"I will not be patient!" Annie hollered. "Have you ever spent a night in jail? They turned off the light when the sun went down, and all I could hear was this jerk who does the night shift watching laugh-track television. And then I heard him snoring, and believe me, he snored all night because I sure as hell didn't sleep. I mean, apartment buildings make me claustrophobic, let alone a fucking jail."

Steve took the single chair and bent down to open his briefcase. He retrieved a pad of yellow paper from his briefcase and took a pen from his jacket pocket. "Look, as far as I can figure, they don't have a case."

Annie crouched next to him. "Yes, they have a case," she whispered fiercely. "They know I had it in for Samir, and they know I gave Zach the damn pickles. Johns keeps asking me about some poison or other and what I had against Zach."

"Did you answer him?"

"Hell, no, I didn't answer him. I just said I wanted a real

lawyer, and not that ghoul they sent in here last night. He looked like he worked his way through law school stealing corpses. He had these long fingers, and he kept rubbing his nose."

Steve attempted an apologetic smile, chagrined at the description of his colleague. Tom Graves, he knew, was a competent attorney, but neither his appearance nor his unfortunate name inspired confidence.

"Sorry. I was in Boston. Nobody knew how to reach me."

"Yeah, well." Annie jumped up and raised her voice to reach into the hall on the other side of the bars. "I told them they could all go screw themselves."

She pounded against the rough wall with both fists. The impact left a streak of blood, and when Steve looked more closely, he saw that there were abrasions along the side of her hands.

"Annie," he said sternly. "Don't do that. Don't hurt yourself."

"Jesus, Steve." She hugged her hands to her chest, smearing blood on the blue work shirt. "I didn't try to murder anyone. Tell me they can't keep me here."

"I don't think they can. I don't think they have enough evidence to charge you. But let's just do this a step at a time. You're being arraigned in two hours. I think we can avoid an indictment."

"What does that mean?"

"They have to bring you before a judge. At that point, they either have to drop the case or else convince the judge there is enough evidence to charge you. I don't think they've got the evidence."

Steve took a breath, not sure how she would respond to the next, necessary question. "Look, now that I'm here, they have a right to question you, so this is the time for honesty. Is there anything you should tell me that you don't want to have to tell them?"

"Aside from the fact that I thought Samir Molchev was a phony piece of dog shit and that I gave Zach the fucking pickles? No. And they already know that."

"So I'm going to ask you some questions, okay, and then we'll meet with the assistant district attorney. Are you ready?"

"No. But go ahead."

There was something in the give and take of Steve's questions that made Annie feel somewhat calmer. Yes, she'd given Zach the pickles, everybody in three counties had seen her do it, and that was the last bunch of pickles she'd ever make. No, of course she hadn't put poison in them. Nobody deserved such an awful death, for fuck's sake, although now that she had met that bastard Johns, there was an exception to everything.

Steve banged on the cell door and signaled to the clerk that they were ready. He watched Annie pull her boots on. As they waited by the cell door, she elbowed him. "I can't do prison, whatever happens. I swear to God, Steve, I'd rather be dead."

"I can't promise anything."

"Yeah, I know that. I'm not an idiot. And neither are you, right? I mean, I just spent the night in this shithole because I wanted to wait for you. Just do me a favor and live up to your goddamn reputation."

Steve leaned toward her and patted her arm.

"Well, for one thing," Ford McDermott was saying. "A very strong case can be made that the poison was added afterward. According to Jennifer Morgan, Miss McGantry arrived at the café with a whole barrel of pickles, which apparently she does every year. She hadn't brought any jars with her because, she said, the pickles weren't ready to be canned. To give Professor Lerner the pickles, she grabbed a mason jar from the café kitchen, where they were all lined up, newly cleaned—boiled, in fact. This time of year, the café gets a lot of homemade foods, jams and honey, and stuff like that, so they have to get the jars ready. She also took a ladle and a pair of tongs from the kitchen and filled the jar in front of Lerner, Jennifer Morgan, and a number of others. Second of all, giving him the pickles seems to have been spur of the moment. There's no indication she knew Lerner was going to be at the café. Look, if the poison had been injected directly into one of the pickles, I suppose she could have staged it all. But it wasn't. It was in the brine, and none of the samples that came from that same barrel had any trace of poison."

Ford kept his eyes steadily on Doug as Johns jumped to his feet.

"It's obvious," Johns spat out. "She dropped the powder into the jar, fast, when she was in the kitchen."

"She couldn't have just added powder. Strychnine is harder to dissolve than that. I don't see how she could have done it, that's all."

Doug Tyringham turned to Johns. "Detective?"

Johns exploded. "So she snuck into Lerner's house and added the poison afterwards! So what? She gave him the pickles. Her fingerprints were on the jar. The poison in her storage room."

"But once we say," Ford countered, "that the poison was added later, anyone could have done it. Plus, the co-op has close to one hundred members, and every one of them puts in four hours of work each month. That includes restocking the shelves in the storeroom, so the fact that the strychnine was found in there means nothing. People are always going in and out of there. As for fingerprints, of course her fingerprints were on the jar. As you've said, she handed Zach Lerner the pickles in full view of a dozen or so people. In the absence of motive, we really don't have a case."

There was a knock at the door; the clerk had come to tell

them the prisoner and her lawyer were waiting in the interrogation room.

Doug nodded, eager to get out of the airless office but not looking forward to the coming encounter. "I have to tell you, Detective, that I'm not happy with this. The case falls apart the minute you look at it sideways, and every arrest we make makes it harder to get a conviction when the time comes. You nearly arrested Zachary Lerner—"

"Who has a prison record."

"You arrested Will Hampton—"

"Who confessed, God damn it."

"And now you've arrested a young woman on evidence that will never hold up in court. You've made no effort to investigate possible suspects beyond the small circle of a village that, however much you don't like them, come across to the rest of the world as a postcard of bucolic New England. And Steve Davies knows how to scream harassment with the best of them."

The interrogation room was furnished with a grey metal table and a ring of varnished wooden chairs. Only a one-way mirror and a small, barred window broke the uniform green of the walls. Steve had seated himself below the mirror and placed Annie beside him, not wanting her to have the distraction of staring into the mirror and wondering, assuming she'd ever seen a TV cop show, if there was someone staring at her from the other side.

Steve watched carefully as the ADA entered the room, followed by Johns and Ford McDermott. It was just as well that Annie did not know how to read the nuances of Doug Tyringham's wardrobe. What Steve thought of as Doug's Wall Street get-up meant that he was taking the case seriously. But Steve could smell it in the room that the confab between Doug and Allard Johns had been something less than a meeting of minds. Johns took a seat with a belligerence that seemed directed at everyone equally. The younger cop sat on the other side of Doug, his face giving nothing away.

Steve Davies knew the law, but his greatest gift as an attorney was to know the opposition. He had both studied and worked with Doug Tyringham, and he knew the ways in which they were—and weren't—on the same side of things. Doug thought of himself as a new breed, a prosecutor who could combine a belief in the penal code with a respect for the rights of citizens. The presumption of innocence. Trial by jury. And if Doug talked at times as if his family had personally helped Alfred the Great formulate the principles of Anglo-Saxon jurisprudence, well, better that than some of the cowboys who were hell-bent on making it to the statehouse on the backs of the falsely accused.

"Hey, Doug. Good to see you." He stood and leaned across the table to shake the ADA's hand, then righted himself and placed his hands reassuringly on Annie's shoulders. "Doug, my client, Annie McGantry."

"How are you, Miss McGantry?" Doug asked.

Annie snorted. "How do you think I am?"

They settled in, Annie silent and motionless as Doug repeated the charges. Miss McGantry was being held on attempted murder. There were multiple witnesses that she had given Mr. Lerner the pickles. Only her fingerprints and his were on the jar. A packet of gopher bait containing strychnine had been found in the storage room of the co-op, and the chemical composition was consistent with what was in the remaining pickles in Lerner's jar.

Steve's ensuing outrage was more for Johns' sake than Doug Tyringham's, though Johns had no way of knowing that. How many people could have hidden the poison? Were Ms. McGantry's fingerprints on the package? Was there any proof that she had purchased the gopher bait? Was there any explanation for why she would conceivably have wanted to harm Zach Lerner? Was there, in fact, proof of anything other than her handing an acquaintance a perfectly innocent gift? Detective Johns, Steve pointed an accusatory finger, had been carting people in and out of jail like they were so many interchangeable parts, and enough was enough. There wasn't enough evidence to indict Ms. McGantry for jaywalking, let alone attempted murder, and why didn't they stop wasting the taxpayers' money and everybody's time?

Doug Tyringham had made a decision before Steve was finished. He was furious with Johns, furious with the travesty of a case that had been ripped to shreds by both McDermott and Steve Davies, but he wasn't willing to shame Johns directly, and he didn't want Steve to know he had already concluded that he didn't have a case. He yielded the floor to Johns, willing to listen as the detective questioned the prisoner. When were the pickles made? Why did she give them to Zach Lerner? What was their relationship? Where had the poison been obtained?

Annie, however, had recovered, and as far as she was concerned, this two-bit tub of lard, with his Marine haircut and his Elliot Ness antics, could just about go fuck himself.

"In my kitchen," she spat at him. "In a big vat on the stove—you ought to know, you hauled it off God knows where, and I want it back. You didn't find anything in it, did you? My relationship with Zach is none of your goddamn business. And I have no idea where the poison came from. I don't use poison, for your information. Ever heard of a have-a-heart trap?"

When she was finished, Doug said quietly, "We aren't going to move forward with an indictment at this time. Miss McGantry, you are free to go, but I'm asking you not to leave the county. We may well want you again for questioning."

"Hot damn." Annie jumped to her feet.

"You will still have to appear in court. But we aren't pressing charges."

"I don't care where I have to appear. Just get me out of here." She turned and headed for the door.

Johns helplessly watched her leave, trailed by both her lawyer and the ADA. "McDermott," he barked. "I want a list of every place in Western Mass that sells strychnine in any form. And while you're at it, I want any fingerprints we still don't have of all those weirdoes over there. Start with the fingerprints. Those café women. That Sullivan character. That phony minister. All of them."

Ford knew better than to protest. Yes, he promised. He'd do what he could. He'd be on his way to Flanders now.

twenty

"Oh, Jesus, Wendy. I just want to shoot myself. I am such an asshole."

They were in the kitchen, and the church clock was striking twice for nine-thirty in the morning. Jennifer sat at the table, a third cup of coffee beside her and her head in her hands. Bogey, she thought, would have had no trouble. Ingrid Bergman off on an airplane, Mary Astor on her way to jail, he'd have lit a cigarette and forgotten the whole thing by morning. Sean Connery would have carved another notch for the minister and politely misplaced the lady's name. And here she was, feeling totally wretched, wishing she had someplace to hide.

Wendy, wide-eyed and steadfast, sat down next to her.

"Tell me everything that happened."

"I can't."

Wendy adjusted her shoulders under her embroidered Persian robe and waited patiently for the story to begin.

Ford had come to the rescue, right on schedule, just as the coke bottle had served its purpose and the right front tire was seriously flat. He had seemed glad if somewhat surprised to see her and would have the tire changed in just a jiffy, she wasn't to worry about a thing. She had stopped at a farm stand and the supermarket in North Adams, and the back seat of the car was a carefully staged cornucopia of breads and autumn vegetables, a scene out of a Renaissance painting or a travel ad for Tuscany.

"I mean, I had everything but the live chickens for market and the dirt still on the onions. I wanted him to be hungry just looking in the car. So I made some vague remark about shopping in North Adams because the co-op was closed, mostly to give myself an excuse for being practically on his doorstep. And then I said, 'You've saved the day. I'm still such a city girl that I've never changed a tire. I insist on at least cooking you dinner.'" And so they had ended up in his scrupulously neat one-story rental, cooking pasta and feeling awkward until the wine she had provided began to take effect. Over dinner, he had told her about his love for 1950s rock and roll, and she had countered with her roots in folk music and 1960s protest songs. He said, "If you think young people's protest songs started in the sixties, you've never listened carefully to Eddie Cochran." Then he'd played her 45s of "Weekend" and Summertime Blues."

Jennifer paused. They sat for a moment in silence. "And then," Jennifer said, "I really messed it up."

"Oh, no," Wendy wailed.

"Yeah. I mean, I don't know what I had expected would happen. I suppose I thought I'd flirt the information out of him. I don't know, like the villainess of a B movie or something. But here we were, actually liking each other, and I realized that I didn't have a plan. So I said, 'I guess I've sort of put you in a compromising position,' and he said, 'Not really. That would only be true if you were a suspect, and as far as I'm concerned, you're not.' So I pretended that I had just remembered that Annie had been arrested and tried to ask a bunch of subtle questions, and he saw through me in a minute. He answered every single question, and I got more and more embarrassed and acted more and more businesslike, and the whole time he had these hurt eyes, and I just felt awful. Then when I couldn't think of any more questions, I tried to be sweet and flirtatious and nice, and man, he wasn't having any of it. He got up and sort of walked me out the door and to the car. Like, he essentially threw me out. And when I got into the car and turned on the ignition, he leaned down and said, 'Jennifer, you didn't have to make me dinner. I would have told you whatever I could,' and walked straight back into the house. God damn it, I could've cried. I could've fucking cried."

"Oh, Jen."

"Yeah. Oh, Jen. Oh Jen feels like she ought to crawl back to whatever scuzzy pit she came from. I guess now I have to be hard-hearted Hannah and get my trusty old notebook out and write down everything he told me. I just haven't been able to force myself to do it."

Wendy put out her arms, and Jennifer settled into them. "I think it's very romantic."

"Romantic? It's *pathetic*." She sighed, her head on Wendy's shoulder. "I never learn."

The streets seemed more depressing than usual as Ford McDermott drove through North Adams. Was he never going to get out of here? As a kid, he had fantasized about becoming a priest, going to Africa to work with starving children, and being someone played by Spencer Tracy in the movie. But when he took the civil service exam and was hired by the state police, he told himself that Western Massachusetts was big enough to hold him. There would be troubled kids to work with. There would be people preyed upon by crooks, and the helpless elderly, and DWIs to keep off the roads. He went to Berkshire County Community College at night and took courses in American history. He learned about racism. He read I. F. Stone.

Ford drove toward Flanders thinking hard about the previous

evening. He had been on his way home, trying to work through the logic in his head. He was tired of Johns' contempt, tired of being blocked from his own detective's shield, and he wanted to be the one to solve these crimes. There was a connection between the murder of Samir Molchev and the attempted murder of Zachary Lerner, and he wanted to know what it was.

The obvious connection, of course, was Café Galadriel. Annie had given Zach the pickles at the café. Samir lived above it. Zach had nearly died there. He hated to think of the café in that context, but there it was.

And then, as if she had jumped out of his thoughts, Jennifer Morgan had been standing on the corner of Route 2 and Maple, leaning against the door of an old yellow station wagon. He had pulled up behind her, helped her change what proved to be an extremely flat tire, and somehow found himself in his own kitchen with Jennifer cooking pasta while he chopped onions and worried that she would notice he didn't usually drink wine. He had, he told himself now, been a jerk. How did girls like her make their hair so perfectly haphazard, announcing to the world that they had opinions, and sexuality, and a brave and effortless defiance? How did they find sandals that looked like they'd come from the feet of a Greek goddess? How did they look so tough and yet throw such an unguarded shadow? In a word, she had charmed him, and if he had believed her innocent all along, their dinner had convinced him that she was wise and smart and could help him find the answers. And when, after dinner, she started asking him questions, he had felt like the biggest fool God ever made—a God who was too busy laughing at him to bother with fairness. Or honesty. Or the fact that he was on their side.

Well, at least he hadn't betrayed himself. He had given her only the facts that had been given to Steve Davies: that strychnine had been added to the pickles they'd confiscated from Zach's refrigerator and that the pickles in the co-op and the café were poison-free. He told her that strychnine had been found in the storage room of the co-op and that this was one of the reasons Annie had been arrested. But then he had shut his heart and kept from her his worry about the list of things the police did not yet know.

Jennifer pounded her fists together painfully. None of it made any sense. She had written down everything Ford had told her, rearranged the few facts on several pages of her notebook, but mostly, she told herself, she was chewing on the details in an ersatz imitation of coherent thought. Strychnine here and not there. In this jar, not in the others. In the brine and not in the pickles, or, rather, being absorbed from the brine into the pickles themselves. She threw down her pen. No café to run and her list abandoned on the kitchen table, she took down the canister that held the marijuana and rolled herself a joint. At the very least, it would stop her from spending the day in the company of her own palpitations. At best, it would ease the tears of self-reproach that kept rushing to her eyes.

She took the joint and a portable tape deck down the stairs and out into the back garden. Cultivated only in those corners that were visible from the café windows, the garden was a jumble of grasses and weeds, but the chrysanthemums and asters were still in bloom, and the Joe Pye weed was still bright against the remains of sunflowers. The herb garden was gone, now hanging on hooks in Wendy's kitchen. She thought of Wendy, sitting in this garden talking about the Empress card and the ten of pentacles, and of Annie, hopefully released from jail by now. Graham would let her know.

A solid hedge of forsythia hid the garden from the street. She eased herself onto the painted metal chaise lounge that served as garden furniture, lit the joint, and pressed the play button on the tape deck. She took the smoke into her lungs and held it there.

Leonard Cohen. His was the right music for this morning. She finished the joint, her eyes closed, and let the words of "Suzanne" run over her. Was that what she had pretended to offer Ford, some half-mad visionary dressed in thrift shop finery? Is that what she imagined he might want, a chance to peruse the riverbank for magic as he made himself comfy in her bed? She looked up as the song faded. Ford McDermott was standing on the path, staring at her.

For a moment, she thought she was hallucinating. But no, she couldn't be that stoned, and anyway, she wouldn't have imagined him in full cop regalia, a radio on one hip, a gun on the other. She would have imagined his badge pinned to sun-bleached Dodge City cotton, not some dark blue, pressed shirt that looked polyester, and the holster wouldn't be standard issue bureaucrat. Why, howdy, Miss Jennifer, and how's the little lady today? Oh, Sheriff, she is one sorry mess.

She watched his face retreat into impenetrability.

"Oh, Ford," she said. "You hate me. I've messed everything up."

It was the last straw. He had made his rounds, taking fingerprints. David Sullivan had refused point blank, appealing in his anxiety to Ford as a fellow Irishman. Did Ford know that James Connolly had been a poet as well as a patriot, that he'd been wounded in the Easter Uprising and, unable to walk to his own execution, had faced the firing squad in a chair? As if Ford cared, as if Ford in doing his job was betraying some kind of shared revolutionary heritage while David remained true to it because he wrote poetry and took drugs. It was bullshit, and Graham Marlow hadn't behaved any better. Ford had long admired Graham, but he had deeply resented it when Graham presented his hands with an aura of Christian fortitude as if he was going to be martyred instead of fingerprinted. And now here was Jennifer, lying in a chair, with her long legs bare and another appeal to him on her face. He had knocked on the door several times, his heart scrupulously quiet. Then he had heard the music and followed it to the garden. Hate her? He wished he did.

"No, I don't hate you. I'm just tired of this phony place."

Jennifer grimaced. "I deserved that."

"Look," he said. "We're asking for everybody's fingerprints."

She sat up, raising the back of the chaise lounge and tucking her legs under her. She gestured for him to sit next to her. He didn't move.

"Ford, please."

He shook his head. His mouth was twitching from everything he wasn't saying.

"You know," she ventured. "You're out of luck. You can't take my fingerprints if you won't touch me."

The provocation worked.

"I have no idea why all of you think you're so special. You have a couple of ideas that cost you nothing, but you're close-minded and bigoted and you don't trust anyone who isn't like you. You thought that I was just some sort of dumb country hick who you could twist around your little finger. Well, you were right. I am a dumb country hick. You did twist me around your finger. You had that flat tire on purpose, didn't you?" The realization came to him as he said it. It stopped him cold.

She nodded, miserable.

"And *I'm* the fuzz?" he spat out. *"I'm* the pig?"

Jennifer sat, daunted by his anger and wishing she wasn't stoned. The music droned on. *Yes, you who must leave everything that you cannot control.* Fuck you too, Leonard, she thought.

"No, you're not the fuzz." She leaned down and shut off the music. "You're the Cisco Kid, and you ride around saying, 'Look, Pancho, those people over there are in trouble. Let's go and see if we can help them.' And Pancho says, 'Oh, Cisco, you are such a brave man, and I don't know what we would do without you. I admire you mucho.'"

Ford steeled himself as he listened. This was the Jennifer who tempted him, with her free associations and the way she had of moving whenever she talked.

"So, that's why I went to your house last night," she went on. "You know, when I was a kid, I thought it was obviously much better to be Pancho than Cisco because Cisco would take you with him everywhere he went, but you didn't have to do anything hard, like be lonely and noble and make all the decisions. Don't you see? I'm tired of trying to be bigger than everyone else and having everyone say, 'Oh, Jennifer, we admire you mucho.' I mean, nobody here is any good to talk to. Will listens, but he doesn't talk and goes around looking like he's guarding state secrets. Wendy . . . well, Wendy's *my* Pancho, if you know what I mean. So I thought, I'll go hang out with Ford McDermott, and he'll tell me everything he's thinking, and it'll be much more fun than scribbling in a notebook trying to feel intelligent. And it *was* more fun. In fact, I've been lying here thinking about how nice it was."

"I don't believe you."

"Yes, you do. You're just mad at me and paying me back. Well, stop it. I'm already paid back. It was a lousy thing to do, and I'm sorry. Besides, I think I have a crush on you."

"That's not funny."

"Yes, it's funny. The whole thing's funny. It's like a goddamn Restoration comedy. There I go, thinking I'm absolutely the cleverest thing that ever came down the pike, and I end up with my ego bleeding. I really wouldn't have done it if I wasn't, you know . . . if I didn't think it would be very nice to get to know you."

There was something in the way her shoulders narrowed that made him suddenly see her again as vulnerable. He unbent enough to sit beside her.

"I was scared," she said. "I needed to do something."

"Yeah, well, you should be scared." He couldn't resist the chance to be unkind. "You're all suspected of being criminals when it's much more likely that one of you will be next."

"You think I don't know that?"

He felt a stab of shame at what he had allowed himself to say. Some of the anger drained away, and what he was left with was a kind of ruefulness. He had wanted to be part of them. He was tired of the world of North Adams and Williamstown. Flanders, at least, was colorful. They hung windsocks on their porches. They reminded him of harlequins. And she reminded him of the fairy queens in his grandmother's stories from County Cork, the ones who could lure you away for one night and ten years would have gone by.

It felt good to her to let him take her fingers. His hands were warm, and the fingerprinting tickled. When he was finished, she kissed him on the cheek.

"Friends?"

He wouldn't look at her. "I don't know yet. Maybe."

When he was gone, she wiped her inky fingers on the grass, readjusted the chaise lounge, and switched on the tape deck.

When you're not feeling holy, sang Leonard Cohen, *your loneliness says that you've sinned.*

twenty-one

Doug Tyringham drummed his fingers on the rutted tabletop. He badly wanted a beer. A murderer on the loose just as the leaves were turning didn't look good anywhere —not in the papers, not in the governor's mansion. Far worse, somebody else might be murdered before they had brought the killer to justice, and he'd wasted the day, dependent on a relic like Allard Johns. His conversation with the DA this afternoon had not made Doug feel any better, and he wasn't looking forward to this coming meeting with Steve.

Across from Doug, on Federalist blue stools along the bar, the Berkshire County government was unwinding from another day. Framed maps of Revolutionary War sites lined the walls, and a stuffed owl loomed dustily over all of them from its perch above the cigarette smoke. Doug removed his jacket and rolled up his sleeves. The hair that fell around his narrow, pretty face was streaked blond from the sun.

Steve Davies turned away from the bar and approached the booth, carrying two pints of Bass. He set them down, threw his jacket over the backrest, and slipped into his side of the booth.

He took a deep draw on his beer, grunted his relief, and allowed himself a thorough scratching of his thick black beard.

Doug both liked and respected Steve Davies. Steve wasn't one of those radical lawyers who viewed the law as a minor subset of politics, and he didn't waste people's time by posturing just for the hell of it. On the other hand, a guy like Allard Johns played straight into Steve's strong suit. It wasn't cynical; Steve would have an unshakable belief that both Will and Annie were innocent. But Doug needed help right now, and instead he had Steve breathing down his neck. Not that Steve breathed, exactly. He just grinned and let the DA's office fall on their own swords.

"So." Steve leaned back in the booth. "What's happening in the Tyringham world these days?"

"Not much except work. I barely got away all summer. Just weekends is all."

"How's Deb?"

"Busy practicing her backhand. She keeps promising to get a job."

"Which she'll be expected to resign from the first time you run for office."

Doug sipped his beer in lieu of a reply.

"Well, you'll have the votes of the flower-child contingent if I have anything to say about it. Thanks for not dragging things out this morning."

"Don't thank me. I would have cheerfully gone after your client if Johns had given me anything to work with."

"You know she's innocent."

"No, I don't know she's innocent. I know I couldn't have gotten an indictment, which isn't the same thing."

"Bullshit. She's no more capable of murder than I am." Steve set his forearms on the table and leaned in. "Can I just be honest here?"

"As opposed to lying through your teeth?"

"Look, aside from trying to avoid a miscarriage of justice, I gotta tell you, Doug, I'm worried. I'm scared that some maniac is out there running around killing people off because he thinks the smell of patchouli oil is un-American and doesn't like veggie burgers."

"Well, you have to admit," Doug drawled, "that tofu in sufficient quantities could make anyone feel murderous."

"You got a point there. But seriously, that Flanders bunch couldn't be more harmless. Hell, Doug, half of them sit around feeling guilty about being harmless. They'd much rather be a threat to the establishment. But someone who isn't the least bit harmless is running wild, and the cops should be guarding those folks, not investigating them."

Doug was silent, not wanting to let on how frustrated he felt. "Look," he said finally. "I'm as worried as you are, but I don't buy your version of these crimes any more than I buy Johns' version. The two are just mirror images of each other, the crazed, homicidal hippie versus the crazed, homicidal anti-hippie. They're both walking clichés that get us nowhere."

"I've been called a lot of things, but never a mirror image of Allard Johns."

"You're not being called that now. But you've got an equally hackneyed version of what's been going on in Flanders. It may be that's all you need—you've only got your clients to worry about."

"But you've got *the People* to protect, right? Spare me. When your crowd starts talking about the People, the rest of us start looking around for a place to hide our daughters."

"That's not the point. I need to put a murderer away, and for that, I need to start with some reality under my feet. Real people commit real crimes for real reasons. With motive. With opportunity. With a step-by-step series of events that I can convince a jury of, not just because it's plausible, but because it's true. You want to help your clients, help me do that."

"It's not my job."

"I've never known you to have conventional ideas about what your job is. Screw the adversarial system. The folks in Flanders must know something. Johns made the mistake of throwing arrests and accusations around instead of calming everyone down and asking them about whatever strange stuff they've noticed lately. Now I have to start all over again, with their memories days older and everyone more scared of the police than the killer."

"When you and I agree is when I start getting nervous. So much for equal protection under the law." He drained his glass and grabbed his jacket.

"You got time for another beer?"

"No, I've got to go." Steve slipped out of the booth and picked up his briefcase. "Truth, justice, and the American way. But hey"—he peered down at Doug—"I suspect we understand each other. Say hi to Deb for me."

Doug sat alone, finishing his beer. He glanced at his watch. Six thirty. He could make a phone call. He fished in his pocket for a dime.

Ford McDermott had been off duty for an hour, but he was still in the office when the phone rang. His steno pad was on the table, and he found himself flipping through the pages over and over, looking for patterns, looking for contradictions. Johns was hopeless on this case because he couldn't get beyond his own assumptions. Ford could, but first he would have to figure out which assumptions were supported by logic and which had to be abandoned if anyone was to solve these crimes.

He was, for the moment, willing to assume that the murder of Samir Molchev and the attempted murder of Zach Lerner were connected. He was willing to play with the assumption, at least provisionally, that the same person had committed both.

He made a note: contradiction number one. But that also led to another assumption: if you were in the clear for one crime, you were in the clear for both of them.

He threw down his pen. Talk about seeing through your own assumptions! Jennifer and her housemates had been in each other's presence from before Samir left the co-op until after the time of his death. Was that why he was sitting there, still at his desk at six thirty? So that he could convince himself that Jennifer Morgan had not committed murder? That she was guilty of nothing but fear and curiosity and, if he wanted to be hard on her, a bit of bad faith?

Face it, he told himself. She got to you. She fascinated you and attracted you and, more than that, she made you happy. Yes, that was the word. Happy. He had drunk her wine and talked about music, and before she let on that all she wanted was information, he had been so glad. She's trouble, he thought. But he'd believed her today when she'd tried to explain. That was the bottom line. He believed her.

With a sigh, he picked up his pen and bent to the logic of the crimes. Ford wasn't convinced that even Johns believed that Annie McGantry had added strychnine to the pickles through some sleight of hand. There was no indication that she had even known Zach would be at the café. It was far more likely that the pickles had been laced with poison after they were in Lerner's refrigerator. Someone had walked in and done it when he wasn't home. Zach's house was open—folks like him seemed to consider it a badge of honor that they never locked their doors. Ford hoped that people were thinking better of that now. It was a coincidence that he had taken ill at the café, and the pickles were likely a coincidence as well. No, he stopped himself. That assumption didn't hold. There were very few foods strong enough to mask the taste of strychnine even a little bit. Whoever had tried to kill Zach, he reasoned, would have to have known that a solution such as vinegar and pickling spices was waiting in the fridge.

He turned to the murder of Samir Molchev. Samir was either killed in the workroom or else brought to the workroom afterward. To do that without detection meant that the killer had to know not only where the key was but also Will Hampton's likely movements and when the craft shop was closed. All of that implied local knowledge. But the killer had gone after Samir and Zach. Another contradiction. He made a note. He was still taking notes when the phone rang and was surprised to hear Doug Tyringham. Yes, he could meet him. In half an hour. The Spring Street Café in Williamstown would be fine.

The Spring Street Café was filled with undergraduates. Students sat with heads bent over textbooks, ignoring the Eagle's *Hotel California* blasting from the stereo. Ford found a table, ordered a coffee, and picked up a copy of the *Williams Record*. An a cappella group called the Springstreeters holding a concert. A performance of *Marat/Sade*. A fight over whether or not the campus should have co-ed dormitories. A campaign to divest from South Africa.

Ford looked up as Doug Tyringham slipped into the chair across from him.

"Glad I caught you. Thanks for coming to meet me."

"Sure thing."

"I expect you're wondering why I wanted to talk with you."

Ford blinked, suddenly wary. If he was being patronized, he didn't want to play along. "Detective Johns is batting zero," he said bluntly. "The crimes in Flanders are not getting solved, and you want to know what I think about it."

"Exactly."

Ford hoped the point had been made.

"So, then," Doug prompted him. "What do you think?"

"Well, for one thing, I think that the available evidence points in contradictory directions. I'm trying to figure out the logic behind that. If we can solve the contradictions, maybe we can solve the crimes."

"Say more."

"Well, the first contradiction is that, on the one hand, these two crimes are likely related, but the MOs couldn't be more different. The murder of Samir Molchev looks like an impulsive act. Molchev's movements that night were erratic. It doesn't seem to be a crime that could have been carefully planned. But the attempted murder of Zachary Lerner is the opposite of impulsive—all kinds of careful planning went into it. It required the careful gathering of material. It had required the watchfulness to know when Zach would not be home and the meticulousness to leave behind no evidence of entry. So, that's the first contradiction, that this is a killer who is both impulsive and methodical."

Ford paused. Doug gestured for him to continue.

"The other contradiction is that these are both local crimes, and they aren't."

"I don't understand."

"Well, on the one hand, whoever did them needed local knowledge. He had to know where the key to the workroom was kept, but more than that, he had to know when nobody would be in Will Hampton's workroom, when Lerner was reliably away from home, and even that there were pickles or something very like that in Lerner's fridge. On the other hand, the two victims, Molchev and Lerner, are the only two newcomers, and I'm not willing to think *that* is a coincidence."

"We don't know that for sure."

"No, of course we don't. But there's another thing about the localness." Ford groped for a way to explain. "The people we've been focusing on, in their own ways, live very public lives. They work on the same street, in full view of each other: Graham

Marlow at the church, Will Hampton at the craft shop, Annie McGantry at the co-op, and Wendy Scholes and Jennifer Morgan at the café. David Sullivan works at home. Samir Molchev, Jennifer Morgan, Wendy Scholes, and Will Hampton all lived in the same house. Zach Lerner is the only one whose job takes him away from Flanders every day."

"Yes," Doug said tentatively.

"Well then, why didn't they see it coming? Why didn't they know something was going wrong?"

Ford stopped and waited for a response. When none came, he looked down at his hands. "Anyway, that was what I was thinking. You've probably figured all that out by now."

But if there was one thing Doug Tyringham knew, it was intelligence and drive masquerading as modesty.

"Tell me something, Ford. May I call you that?"

"Sure."

"And I'm Doug. Have you taken the exam for detective?"

"Yes."

"Passed it?"

"Yes."

Doug waited.

"There are," Ford offered, "several possible explanations as to why my promotion has never come through."

Doug regarded Ford McDermott's good-natured face. The expression gave very little away, though Doug guessed, accurately, that the thick mustache was a conscious act of rebellion. The guy was smarter than he looked and no doubt less pliable than he acted. Doug had given him an opening a mile wide, but McDermott wasn't taking him up on it.

"Would you object," Doug asked carefully, "if I made a few phone calls?"

Doug Tyringham's contacts reputedly included senators, governors, ambassadors, and the odd cabinet member. Ford's promotion to detective in the state police would be fifteen minutes' work. It wasn't the way Ford had wanted it to happen; he was not in the habit of asking for things, and his parents' example had taught him to play by the rules. But Johns had already interfered with what should have been the progress of his career. Besides, maybe these were the rules.

Ford shifted in his chair and offered Doug the slightest bow of his head. It was as close to a thank you as his self-respect would allow.

twenty-two

Graham had lost the argument. Nobody could say whether Samir had ever been baptized, and those at the diocese who cared about such things determined he could not be buried in hallowed ground. Even Graham's appeal to the ecumenical spirit had been met with tight-lipped resistance; Samir's soul might have been that of a seeker after Truth, but his body would go wherever bodies go that had not been freed from sin as infants and who leave behind no kin or money for burial. In the old days, they called them potter's fields. Graham had no idea what they called them now.

But they couldn't stop him from holding the memorial service he had scheduled for the morning. It was unthinkable not to have one. It would be like stringing a banner across Main Street announcing that, as Samir had been a follower of Eastern traditions, there would be no sanctified ritual marking his death. Graham was loathe to let any soul go into the great beyond without at least a small human farewell, and what did the difference among traditions mean, unless you were one of the spiritual bureaucrats with the gall to think you had cornered the market on certainty? Besides, he didn't mind the excuse to get people to the church on a Sunday morning. It happened so few times in any given year.

At the moment, however, he was heartily sorry he had ever scheduled the service. The church bell had just rung for eight forty-five in the morning, it was little more than an hour until the memorial service, and Graham was in his office, staring down at a blank piece of paper and still not knowing what to say. These days, it was never easy to write a sermon. His neighbors could be called a lot of things, but "congregation" wasn't one of them; David was a lapsed Catholic, Will an equally lapsed Baptist, Jennifer—and Zach, he figured—very secular Jews, and if Annie and Wendy had ever been Episcopalians, it was not something they'd mentioned to Graham. Still, every soul was in need of keeping. There was a wound to the heart of the communal body, and Graham ought to be able to help heal it. The question was, how?

He picked up his pen, positioned his hand over the paper, and laid the pen down again. He had barely known Samir, and what he had known had confused him. Samir had seemed well-read in his way, able to glide in and out of the Absolute with a confident step that Graham had, more than once, found himself envying. But in the end, that was the problem. Samir had been too polished. Too sure-footed. There was no modesty in his faith.

Graham considered the idea of taking a leaf from the Quakers and having everyone sit in silence until they were moved to speak. That guy who sold incense at all the street fairs —Brother Vishnu, he called himself—would no doubt say something. And Jason. And what's-her-name from the craft collective who was always hanging around. But no, that was just a cop-out, and he knew it. If only he knew the Vedas well enough to find something suitable.

He heard the side door open, and he followed the sound of the footsteps as they approached his office, bracing himself. An hour until the service, he had nothing written, and now he was going to have to respond to whoever owned those footsteps. He turned and was relieved to see that his visitor was Jennifer.

She leaned against the door frame. "Hey," she said. "How's it coming?"

"It isn't."

"The God of deathless prose is a jealous God."

Jennifer seated herself cross-legged on the floor. Graham was an activist, a philanthropist, and, as far as she could figure, a sincerely religious man, but he was no preacher—if by preacher one meant someone who could spin conviction into words. She had decided over her second cup of coffee that he might need the help of an ex-teaching assistant in freshman composition, and so here she was, having left Will and Wendy to their own unfathomable preparations for the day.

Graham leaned back in his chair and interlocked his fingers on top of his head. "Jen, I've got nothing to say about this guy."

"So don't talk about him. Talk about us. Isn't that what funerals are for? For the living?"

"Yeah, but I can't just leave him out of the sermon."

"Gag me, Graham. We hardly need a sermon."

"But I have to say something."

"Okay, then. What do you want to say?"

Graham thought for a moment. "I want to tell the truth."

"Oh, is that all? I can't imagine why you're having a problem."

"Look, Samir was a complicated guy."

"To say the least."

"There will be people here who really liked him, or were awed by him, and other people who found him a total cipher."

"Not to mention all the women who had the hots for him and those of us who thought he was a pompous ass."

"I don't want to get in the middle of what everybody thought about him. What I want to say is that, whatever our relationship to him, we need to mourn because he died terribly and because, until proved otherwise, every human being deserves that."

"Sounds right to me."

"Sure, it sounds right to you, but how will Wendy feel?"

"Well," Jennifer said demurely, "you could tell her that, according to Samir, celebrating a discrete, individual life would be the opposite of enlightened."

Graham grunted.

Jennifer screwed up her face to indicate she was thinking. "Conrad Aiken," she said finally.

Graham blinked at her.

"Conrad Aiken," she repeated. "He has a poem called 'Tetelestai.' It goes on for pages about how we should blow the burial horn just as loudly for all us poor schmucks who lived imperfect little lives, but who still deserve our fanfare of glory. It's perfect." She pulled herself to her feet and turned to go. "I'm sure I've got a copy."

"Jen?"

"Yeah?" She glanced over her shoulder.

He blew her a kiss. "Thank you."

"You're welcome. I'll be right back."

The phone rang before Jennifer's footsteps faded.

"Graham?" He recognized Annie's voice.

"Yes. Hi. What's up?"

"What's up? It's the fucking harvest, and they won't let me open the co-op, that's what's up. Can you believe it? Emma Krouse has bushels of corn rotting in a truck, there are still tomatoes coming in, and I'm not even talking about the fruit trees. If we don't get a market going, we're going to have to support all of the growers this winter because they won't have money for food, let alone fuel. Sam. Tina. All of them."

"Including you."

"Me? I'm already fucked. Asshole Johns has made it clear

that everything going from my fields to anyone's plate will go by the way of the pathology lab."

"Does Steve Davies know that?"

"What's he gonna do?"

"Nothing if he doesn't even know."

"I mean, I can't believe this," Annie exclaimed. "Keeping the co-op closed during the harvest? Where's everyone supposed to shop in the meantime?"

"The supermarket."

"Shit. And they think strychnine is poison? Graham, you gotta help me. Can I use the church parking lot as a farmers' market?"

"Yeah. I guess so."

"Far out."

"Not on Sundays, but any three days of the week. Saturday can be one of them."

"Thanks, man."

"So, are you coming to the memorial service for Samir?"

"Are you fucking kidding?"

"You want a farmer's market?"

"Goddamn it, Graham."

Annie slammed down the phone.

Jennifer returned with a dog-eared Signet paperback entitled *Contemporary American Poetry*. "It's all here." She leaned against the door frame again and flipped open the book. "*Say that I have no name, no gifts, no power,*" she read aloud, "*Am only one of millions, mostly silent.* Blah, blah, blah," she skipped down the page. "*Well, what then? Should I not hear, as I lie down in dust, the horns of glory blowing above my burial?*"

She looked up from the book, leaned across him, and set the book, page down, on his desk. "Here you go. Just intone it in that fabulous Protestant baritone of yours, and you can ad-lib from there."

"It doesn't make me feel good that you're a better sermonizer than I am."

"Nonsense. I just have the *Norton Anthology* plastered to my brain. So how are you? I haven't talked to you in days."

"Feeling completely ineffectual. I just had Annie on the phone, on a tear about making sure the organic farmers don't starve because the co-op is closed. The only thing I could offer was a parking lot. That's not exactly what I had in mind when I went to seminary."

"Guilt and powerlessness. Your two favorite food groups. What else is new?"

"Don't be glib with me, Jen, okay? I'm having a hard enough time. I know what I should be doing, and I haven't a clue how to do it."

"What should you be doing?"

"You'll laugh."

"No, I won't. I promise."

He took the risk. "I'm supposed," he said, "to be a keeper of souls."

Jennifer was only marginally inclined to laugh. "And which of our souls need keeping?" she asked gently.

"Everybody's soul needs keeping. But it's okay, Jen. I know this isn't your vocabulary."

"Don't worry about it." She slid her back down the door frame until she was again seated on the floor. She looked at him expectantly.

"Well, then, Annie, for one."

"Annie? Annie's too pagan to have a soul. It's more like she has a direct line to the Goddess."

"You should have heard her just now. From her voice, you'd think nothing had happened to her personally, but I can't imagine what it did to her to be locked up for all those hours."

"C'mon, Graham, give yourself some credit. What she needed this week wasn't a minister. She needed a lawyer, and you got her one, and if you want to do some God stuff today, give some thanks for Steve Davies. Look, I realize that if you want to torture yourself, I'm not going to be able to talk you out of it, but . . ."

"How's Wendy?"

Jennifer groaned. "In truth? She's a mess. I think she's getting littler by the hour. Her clothes don't fit, and it's not about getting thinner. It's about getting smaller. You know how she always looks like the good witch in a children's story, you know, the scarves and medieval sleeves and stuff? Well, now she just looks like a little girl dressing up as Eleanor of Aquitaine. But hey, I'm the one who's supposed to be the keeper of Wendy's soul, not you, and I'm blowing the job completely. She's trying to mourn for Samir behind Will's back, and you can imagine how well that's working. She gives us this artificial smile and goes upstairs and cries. I went upstairs to her once, and she was sitting there with her Tarot cards, looking down at, I think it was the Moon card, with the Wheel of Fortune on one side and the Burning Tower on the other. It doesn't take a Tarot reader to figure out what that means."

"And Will? How's he doing?"

The question stopped her. "I have no idea. Now, there's a soul that needs keeping, if you really want to know."

Zach turned another page of *The Impeachment of Richard M. Nixon: The Final Report of the Committee on the Judiciary, U.S. House of Representatives*. Ordinarily he would have found it gripping, but now that he was out of the hospital and back home, it was harder to lie in bed pretending to read. Someone had tried to kill him, hard as he found it to believe.

Who could possibly hate him that much? Zach had searched

his mind. A few right-wingers back in California. That Maoist from Ann Arbor whom Zach had outargued one too many times. But those hatreds, if they could be called that, were political, not personal. This had been a clear, specific, personal attempt to kill him. What was he supposed to do?

It was the first of October. He had met twice with his freshman Survey of American History and twice with his senior seminar on the origins of American foreign policy. The academic year had begun, and he was stuck. There would be no more jobs in the offing until spring. And even then, he would have to explain that he'd walked away from a prestigious gig at Williams because someone had tried to kill him. Aside from the fact that it sounded insane, what college would want to hire an ex-con who was being stalked by a killer? It couldn't possibly be worth it, even for the honor of having a faculty member who had gone to North Vietnam with Hanoi Jane.

Of course, he could sit back and trust the cops to find the killer. The irony didn't appeal to him. He didn't like the idea of having to be grateful or of passively waiting until they solved the crime. And how would he keep safe in the meantime? Perhaps he should, under the circumstances, eat all his meals from the communal hotplates in the faculty dining room. They couldn't poison the entire faculty of Williams, although, given how easily they could all be replaced, he wasn't entirely sure why not.

Zach eased his legs onto the floor and tentatively held himself upright. Not great, but if he was careful, he could probably even drive. The least he could do, he told himself, was to attend the memorial service for Samir Molchev. It had come so close to being his.

It was a slow morning at David's house, the two weekend occupants nursing hangovers as David, standing naked in the kitchen, mixed a remedy of Tabasco sauce, pepper, and raw eggs. He had been up most of the night with his weekend guest, Charles MacCloud, a Canadian poet with roots in Alberta and tenure at McGill. Charles was a large, bearded man with an unlit pipe usually clamped in his teeth. They had met on a panel entitled "Up-and-Coming" at a poetry conference at the University of Iowa, squared off as rivals at the opening reception, and outdone each other trading sexual innuendos concerning the title of the panel. By the next day, they were fast friends, having agreed that Surrealism was overrated and that the northeast quadrant of North America was large enough to hold them both.

Charles had driven down for the weekend to appear as a guest poet at the regular Sunday night poetry reading at the café. David, nonplussed by recent events and thinking he could use a friend, had neglected to tell Charles that the café had been closed down by the police, that there seemed to be a killer on the loose, and that the poetry reading might not happen. Once informed, Charles didn't seem to care. Saturday evening had ended in a heated argument about whether or not T. S. Eliot was a repressed homosexual who would have swapped "The Love Song of J. Alfred Prufrock" for a roll in the hay with Ezra Pound. Charles felt himself something of an expert, having as a teenager visited the City Lights bookstore in the Ginsberg-Orlofsky days, but David was having none of it. Unless Charles had actually slept with Ginsberg—the fact that David referred to him as Allen only served to raise the stakes—he didn't know whereof he spoke, and anyway, mentioning "Howl" in the same breath as "Prufrock" was a crime against humanity. Charles, lying prone on David's rug, had knocked over the bottle of Chianti at his side, denounced David as an ignorant popinjay, and promptly fallen asleep.

It was now a quarter to ten on Sunday morning, and the memorial service for Samir Molchev was about to start. David had to be there, and if Charles wanted to come along, well, there was a sociology of death that even a poet might profitably observe. Charles declined, pleading his own half-dead state and a compelling need for a shower. David, swearing fondly at him, threw on the clothes he had worn the day before and headed down the street.

Wendy was at the mirror in the bedroom, brushing her hair and willing her eyes to stop crying. She did not want to go to the memorial service looking like the grieving widow, and she was tired of everyone thinking she was fragile because she was the only one who seemed to get it that Samir was really dead.

She had to admit, though, that she did look fragile. There were circles around her hazel eyes, and her rich red hair, as she brushed it out across her shoulders, seemed to overwhelm her face. She reached up and gathered her hair into a braid, but the starkness around her face made her skin look even paler and the dark circles more prominent.

Wendy did not experience herself as fragile. She experienced herself as watchful in the face of other people's fragility. One angry moment, and someone could be dead, and life would not be long enough for repentance. All you could do was let your heart break at other people's sorrows, trying to prop them up in their inadequacies by loving them and being kind. Samir, her knight of wands, recipient of her kindnesses, was dead. She hadn't saved him. She had failed.

She turned away from the mirror and returned to the Tarot spread laid out on the bed. Of course she didn't believe that the Tarot spoke to her directly. What a simple-minded, childish belief that would be, like the magic thinking she used to have that she could open the Bible at random and whatever sentence she came upon was God talking to her. But she could go very quiet inside, and if she opened her heart, the cards gave her access to her higher self, giving that self shape, giving it focus. Giving her support for what she already knew.

And what she knew was that it was all her fault. The cards could not be clearer: the page of swords crossed with the five of cups. Somehow, she had caused this. If it weren't for her, Samir would be alive. She didn't know how, or why, but she knew in her bones that it was true.

Will stood at the kitchen counter, squeezing oranges. His fingers were slightly raw from sanding wood, but the brief sting of citrus was a kind of comfort this morning. He poured the orange juice into a glass and carried it to the table, lowering his big-boned body onto a chair. He sipped the juice and waited for it to be time to walk to the church.

He could hear Wendy moving in their bedroom upstairs, and he forced himself not to go to her, to give her space to grieve without having to confront him. He had been avoiding opportunities to be alone with her, staying away during the day and, at night, holding her in silence as she wept. He hoped that she experienced his silence, not as anger and withdrawal, but as his best attempt at sympathy.

Because he knew, of course he knew, what had transpired the weekend of the craft fair. Wendy had met him at the door when he returned Sunday night with a plate of hash brownies in her hand and a dab of patchouli oil between her breasts. She was endearingly solicitous, and it made him wonder if she had played Lady Bountiful overnight to Samir's itinerant wandering. If so, he told himself, he didn't really mind. He liked to think of her as the Empress card; he was charmed by her beneficence, and if that beneficence overflowed sometimes in wayward directions, he liked to think he didn't care. But the next morning he had glanced across the kitchen table and caught Samir looking at him. Samir had quickly shifted his expression back to its usual masked placidity, but while Will forgave Wendy the infidelity, he had not quite forgiven her for the momentary look of gloating in Samir's eyes.

If he could help it, she would never know that. He didn't blame her exactly for having fallen into infatuation with Samir; it was the other side of the haplessness that he loved, the impulse to good that meant she would always be tripping over other people's games. But he was desperately glad that the memorial service was this morning and that it would all soon be over. Samir would be gone. The memory would fade. Even now, Wendy rested her head in the crook of his arm each night, trusting in his reliability. The horror would close slowly over itself, and life would go on as before.

As for the rest, Zach was recovering, and if Will was correct in his surmise, he would not be attacked again. For Will knew, or thought he knew, who had tried to kill Zach. He would not say anything about it—that would only hurt people. And anyway, it didn't matter. If he was right, it wouldn't happen again.

The church bells began tolling for ten o'clock. He walked up the stairs quietly. Wendy was sitting on their bed, knees to her chin, each hand and forearm curled into the opposite sleeve. He walked into the room and sat next to her on the bed. "It's time for the service."

He felt the sob well up in her before she turned to him and threw her arms around him. "It's my fault he's dead," she blurted.

"No, baby. It's not." Will stroked her head. "It's not. It's not." There was nothing more to say.

twenty-three

As far as Jennifer was concerned, handing over the Conrad Aiken poem had exhausted her obligations to the memorial service. She wished she were in a position to skip it altogether, but having insisted publicly, on more than one occasion, that ceremony was the foundation of both art and community, she knew she had to be there. Besides, Wendy would never forgive her. Having done her bit to make the event happen, she was going to have to sit through it.

Graham was already at the pulpit when she made her way through the tall pine doors and down the wide center aisle of the church. Deep-set oak paneling framed the walls on either side between the tall, narrow windows, their eighteenth-century panes decorously free of stained glass, so that the sky and the venerable old trees of the churchyard were visible through the glass. The deep sheen of the oak pews had hardly dulled in the years since the long-defunct women's committee had last lovingly polished them. Only the artwork was different.

The church building itself had national landmark status and a long list of prohibitions against change, but the guidelines concerned the permanent structure only, and Graham had been allowed to deck his halls with a Jesus-was-a-peacenik brand of Christianity. A peace sign crafted of this year's autumn leaves, made by the local Friends Academy day school, hung below the marble plaque commemorating Berkshire County's World War I dead. The framed sampler opposite it read, *They shall beat their swords into plowshares and their spears into pruning hooks.* The words of the long banner above the altar—*If you're not part of the solution, you are part of the problem*—might not be exactly a Christian adage, but not even the outraged great-great-great-grandson of the church's first pastor had been able to force Graham to take it down.

Jennifer, whose religious upbringing had consisted largely of singing "Go Down, Moses" at Passover seders, was always surprised to find how uncomfortable she felt in this room. It was too pat, too self-satisfied, and she wondered if Graham knew how little his ardent ecumenicalism changed its essential entitlement. This room had been built for the God-fearing Protestant elite, a population that did not include agnostics, Jews, New Yorkers, or the aspiring middle classes. Jennifer was four for four.

She seated herself at the far end of the front row and turned her head to study the crowd. Not a crowd, really, just small clusters of people dwarfed by the big room. She knew everyone at least by sight, from the co-op, from the café, from film festivals and concerts at Williams. Zach was sitting by himself in the back looking as uncomfortable as she felt. He, she realized, had more reason than any of them to find the memorial service for Samir unsettling, if not downright macabre, and Jennifer wasn't sorry to see Steve Davies come through the door and slip into the pew next to Zach. David sat with an arm extended across the top of the opposite pew. The Poet, his body language announced, observing the vicissitudes of life and death, and Jennifer would have bet the ranch that he was already choosing the details that would make their way into a poem. An evocation of this hoary clapboard and its deep New England roots, perhaps. A juxtaposition—David's favorite word—between its Episcopalian founders and the people who now occupied its rows, between youth and death, between Hawthorne and Whitman, between the current solemn occasion and a sense that the scene in front of them was slightly ridiculous.

Will and Wendy sat several rows behind her, Wendy's small face hidden in her hair and Will's arm around her. Jennifer felt a sudden stab of anger: Wendy looked like a ragamuffin pieta, and it was, she decided, simply unfair that Wendy was receiving all the comfort when Will was so obviously suffering. You don't appreciate him, she found herself thinking, taken aback at the annoyance she felt toward her friend and the love and pain she felt for Will. There was a set quality to the habitually gentle cast of his face, and even the beard he was growing for the winter didn't mask his clenched jaw and the tic playing along his cheek. She could not bear how alone he looked. On impulse, she eased herself out of the pew, moved up the aisle, and slipped in beside him. She took the hand that wasn't wrapped around Wendy's shoulder and squeezed it. He squeezed her hand in reply.

From her new vantage point, she spotted Annie on the other side of the room, surrounded by members of the co-op. She took note of Vishnu—Jennifer had known him when his name was Marvin—and of Betsy and Jill, two weavers from the women's craft collective. Betsy was crying. Jennifer shook her head and turned her attention to Graham.

As she had expected, the Conrad Aiken poem served its purpose.

"*Tell me, as I lie down, that I was courageous,*" Graham was intoning.

"*Blow horns of victory now, as I reel and am vanquished. Shatter the sky with trumpets above my grave.*"

Fair enough, she decided. Not that the sky beyond the tall windows was anything other than bright autumn blue against the yellow crowns of the sugar maples. Far from pausing to pay tribute to the dead, the world was exulting in autumn, and Jennifer felt a sudden urge to stand up, march out the center aisle, and stand in the bright, crisp air. She wanted her town back. She wanted her life. She had fought for this idyll between uninspired graduate school and sober adulthood. Well, there was nothing more sobering than murder, and it was time for this invasion of death to pass on and for Flanders to revert to being her own personal Never Never Land.

At the altar, Graham was talking about Samir as a man of peace and the injustice of his violent death. Then a prayer and one last "amen," and finally, the service was over. People stood up, stretched, and began to make their way into the aisles. Jennifer slipped out quickly and stood on the porch of the church, blinking into the light.

There was a tap on her shoulder, and Steve Davies stood next to her.

"Hey, Steve. Thanks for coming."

"I wasn't planning to. But I got a call. Apparently, you can open the café."

"What? You're kidding."

"Nope."

"When?"

"Any time after noon today. You won't get the jars of pickles back, but I expect you'll settle for the café."

"Hell, yes. Steve, thank you so much."

"Don't thank me." He shrugged. "I did my best Clarence Darrow imitation in front of the judge, but that's not what did it."

"What did, then?"

"Truth is, I haven't any idea. Something's shifted, I'm not sure what. But I've been at this job for five years, and it's the first time I've been phoned at home on a Sunday morning."

"All I want"—she breathed, hugging him—"is for life to go back to normal."

"Well, here's one piece back."

From over Steve's shoulder, she saw David exiting the church. "David," she called. "We can reopen the café. Are you still up for a poetry reading tonight?"

David sauntered over. "After being forced to listen to that unutterable swill from Conrad Aiken?"

"Hey, that poem was perfect for today." She released Steve and raised her chin in protest. "I picked it, if you don't mind."

"Obviously you picked it. Left to his own devices, Graham would have given us something from the Beatitudes."

"Which would have been better?"

"Marvel Comics would have been better."

Jennifer flashed him a brilliant smile. If she wanted life to go back to normal, she decided, David insulting her taste in poetry wasn't a bad start.

The chairs and lectern were set for the poetry reading long before the church bells chimed at seven. David sat in his usual corner by the bookcase in a black turtleneck and jacket and, inexplicably, on an October evening, shades. Charles, the visiting Canadian poet, sat next to him, and Sally, David's new Bennington conquest, sat on his other side. Sally had arrived accompanied by a second Bennington student, a tall, too-thin brunette named Margot in a hand-crocheted vest and leg warmers. Jennifer, helping to fill orders before the reading began, passed their table in time to hear her gush, "Yes, but the cold is so primal." Charles stretched his arms out, making himself even larger in a wooden chair that Jennifer had bought for a dollar and that now, she noted with concern, did not look strong enough to hold him.

"It's not the cold," he said gruffly. "It's the alternation

between fighting the cold and surrendering to it. With the cold as a synecdoche for nature."

Yeah right, thought Jennifer. Gotta go wrestle me a grizzly bear in between dinner parties in Westmont. Keep the T-bone rare, little lady, and the bourbon on ice. What was happening to her, she wondered. A few years back, she'd have been the first one flirting with Charles. Still, the café was open, the tables were full, and it was nice to feel relaxed enough for feminist outrage. She delivered two more bean burritos to a group of interns from the Clark and dropped into a seat at her own table where Graham was halfway through a veggie burger and Annie was sipping hot cider and flipping through the pages of *Mother Jones*.

"Look at that," Jennifer snorted. "Hasn't the women's movement hit Bennington yet? I mean, there they are, vestal virgins begging for their moment of reflected glory, bowing down to the gods of poetry. Damn, it pisses me off."

Annie followed her gaze and eyed the poets and their companions. "Leave them alone," she shrugged. "They're still babies."

"Yeah, right. *He for God only. She for God in him.*"

"You know," put in Graham, who, unlike Annie, had caught Jennifer's reference to *Paradise Lost*, "I suspect that Joan only married me because it was as close as she could get to giving Jesus a tumble. And now she's off in a seminary reading articles about whatever became of God the Mother."

"A very good question. Meanwhile, until they find Her, I will have a menu item on Sunday nights called Baudelaire's Muse. Ingredients: estrogen, humble pie, and crow."

"Hell, Jen." Annie waved away Jennifer's indignation. "I mean, I once fucked this guy because he said he was walking across the country following what he said was Johnny Appleseed's route."

"That's the point, Annie. I thought you wanted to *be* Johnny Appleseed, not sleep with him."

"Yeah. But don't tell me you don't understand it."

"Oh, I understand it. I told Ford McDermott the other morning that I wanted to play Pancho to his Cisco Kid because it was so much easier to be someone's sidekick. Except that I didn't mean it. *They*," she said, indicating David's table, "still mean it."

"Well, whether or not you meant it"—Annie was staring past her—"don't look now, but the, uh, Cisco Kid just walked through the door."

Jennifer spun around.

She had never seen him out of uniform. He was wearing jeans, a flannel shirt, and high tops, and with his longish sandy hair and mustache, she had to admit he didn't look out of place. She watched him seat himself at a small table set and sit back in his chair, one ankle on the opposite knee.

Jennifer found herself caught between wariness and delight. What the hell was he doing there? Spying on them? Investigating their outlandish behavior? Was it possible that he had come to see her? I should feed him, she decided. Get him something to eat on the house. A person might think it was a bribe, but she would insist it was just a way to make a stranger feel welcome. Tough old world out there, filled with rustlers, and you gotta put your feet up every little while. She took a deep breath and tried to calm her mind. Beware the rustler, she counseled herself. The horse he steals may be your own.

She walked over. "Hey, Cisco," she greeted him.

They blinked at each other in silence.

"Look," she said finally. "I'm totally flummoxed to see you here. Are you here about the case? I mean, is this an official call?"

"No. This is the start of my weekend. I'm off duty. I just thought I'd come by."

"To see me?" slipped out before she could hold it back.

He nodded.

She was embarrassed to find she was blinking back tears. "Ford, truly, I'm so sorry. I should never have—"

"It's okay."

She hesitated. "I expect that I owe you a thank you. I bet it was you who got the café re-opened. It wasn't Johns. I know that much."

He nodded, unsmiling. "Well, then, you're welcome."

"How'd you manage? How'd you get around him?"

"I didn't have to. He's been taken off the case."

It took her a minute to get it. "Whoa! Does that mean you're in charge of it?"

"Yes. I've been promoted. I'm a detective."

She didn't know him well enough to read his face. He took the hand she held out in congratulations, and a quick throb ran up her arm and headed straight for her groin. What was it about him? she asked herself. Had she read too much Raymond Chandler at an impressionable age? But it wasn't that, she knew. It was how he held himself each time they met, how unwaveringly he occupied his own space whatever was whirling around him. The result was that she had told the truth in the backyard the previous morning: she had a crush on him.

"So," she stuttered, "can I get you something?"

"Sure. A Coke."

"You want to go native, Cisco"—she smiled at him—"you're going to have to do better than that. Herbal tea. An espresso. This time of year, hot cider with cinnamon. But trust me, not a coke."

"Some herbal tea then."

She made a dash into the kitchen toward the thermoses of hot water. She could hear her English department friends now. Jennifer's dating a cop? You're kidding! I mean, it's one thing to turn her back on the Victorian novel, but does that mean she has to turn into one? Who does she think this guy is? Heathcliff? And their banter would have nothing on the sheer incredulity of her more earnest political friends, who wouldn't say anything. They'd just stare.

Then she'd stare back, she decided. No, she hadn't gone crazy or over to the other side. She'd stumbled across a man who thought things through before he spoke, which is more than she could say for the English department. She took a deep breath and returned to Ford's table with a cup of rose hip tea and a crock of honey. She set the tea down and pulled a chair to sit beside him.

"Well, then, Detective. Any chance you found a fingerprint that traces back to the FBI's ten-most-wanted list?"

"'Fraid not. But I couldn't tell you if I had."

"Then just tell me you ran the bastard to ground at a truck stop, so we can all go back to what passes around here for ordinary life."

Ford's eyes briefly surveyed the room. David was standing at the microphone tap-dancing and laughing to himself as Ginger circled the tables, shaking a cowbell to bring the poetry reading to order. Annie, ignoring Ginger, was regaling Graham as to why the country needed another Johnny Appleseed. "Apple seeds are anarchists," she was exclaiming loudly. "They *never* run true to type. They're the mote in the eye of standardized fucking agriculture!"

"I don't know," Ford said. "Whatever else it is around here, it's hard to believe it's ordinary."

"Oh, it's ordinary, all right. Mid-century motley is a total cliché, and I assure you, boysenberry-carob mousse is about as exotic as a donut."

He regarded her, deadpan. "What's a carob?"

"Jesus, Ford. I don't even know if you're kidding."

Ford sipped his tea and looked around. He liked how the light fell on the salmon walls and the way the unmatched tables and chairs managed to blend. He liked the smell of apple cider and the slightly sour taste of the tea. He recognized a few of the people at the tables: Graham Marlow and Annie McGantry, but also an assistant librarian from North Adams, whose stolen car he had returned, and a social worker from the Bureau of Child Welfare. Strange that he should find them here at the café. Librarians and social workers seemed so pedestrian, and here he was hoping to embark on something new. On a magic carpet. In a yellow submarine.

He took another sip of the tea. Well, what did you expect? he asked himself. He had learned from 1950s rock and roll that freedom and light-heartedness had something to do with each other and that neither of them came easy. He had learned from his parents that life passed quickly and that joy came with no warranty.

And now Jennifer Morgan was watching him drink the tea. Her nipples stood out under her embroidered peasant blouse. She smelled of incense and shampoo. She was visibly curious and attentive, so he took another sip as a gesture of goodwill.

"Are you hungry?" she asked.

"No, thanks. I had dinner."

"Yeah, but I bet you didn't have baked eggplant with feta cheese and watercress, topped with tahini dressing."

"Next time," he promised.

Ginger passed by the table and pointedly shook the cowbell at them. Jennifer leaned forward and brought her mouth close to Ford's ear. "Look," she whispered. "A poetry reading is the last thing I'm in the mood for. Let's go hang out upstairs."

He drained his cup, then looked away from her as they got to their feet, trying, and failing, to mask a smile.

twenty-four

Ford lay naked on the bed and studied the room. The ceiling sloped sharply between two dormer windows, and the candlelight flickered on the ceiling and against the deep rose-colored walls. An antique dresser occupied the far wall, an oil lamp and additional candles resting on its top beneath a gold-leaf mirror. On the near wall, a record player and speakers were mounted on a plank between two orange crates. Closest to the bed, a matched set of Penguin paperbacks in orange and black stretched across the top shelf of a bookcase. He'd read a few of them in high school. He squinted to read the titles along the second shelf: *Bound for Glory. The Female Eunuch. One Hundred Years of Solitude.*

Jennifer lay curled beside him, her head on his stomach. He was ticklish, and there was a layer of softness under his skin that belied the hard muscles of his arms and back. Making love with him had been passionate and intense. She had expected boyish eagerness. She had found a skilled playfulness that had teased her to orgasm and then turned rhythmic and serious as he buried himself inside of her. He had held himself up on his arms and kept his eyes on hers as he came. She played with the soft hairs that circled his belly while Carol King's *Tapestry* played on the stereo.

Above the music and the sound of the wind, she could hear the top branches of the maple tree brush against the windowpanes. She pulled herself to her feet and crossed the room, threw open the window, and reached out. She returned to the bed with a handful of yellow leaves and laid them on Ford's body. "I bedeck you in autumn," she said.

He smiled lethargically. "Adam and Eve, only with maple leaves?"

"Not a chance," she laughed. "Some Celtic goddess and her paramour, maybe. We don't do Adam and Eve around here."

He raised a questioning eyebrow.

"Adam and Eve is just a bunch of propaganda about bad-assed women getting the world into trouble."

"Got it."

"And anyway, I don't believe that knowledge is a bad thing, not of good and evil or even of life and death. But that stuff is your business, not mine."

He grimaced, not quite sure if he was being accused of something. "I always meant to be a priest," he said defensively, "and go off to some African country and rescue babies."

"From what?" she demanded. "Paganism? Were you going to rescue them from being black?" She started to say that it was all racist crap, that what African babies needed wasn't Christianity but a change in the maldistribution of wealth. But she stopped. Put a sock in it, she told herself. He's being honest and sincere, and the last thing he needs right now is the benefit of your entirely unsolicited opinions. Besides, it occurred to her, if he was actually going to stick around, she had all the time in the world to lecture him.

She swung herself around, sat up, and crossed her legs. "So, then. Why did you decide to be a cop?"

Ford looked past her at the ceiling. "I don't know if you can understand. I mean, you could have gone anywhere, and you came here. I started here, and I didn't really have anyplace else to go." She could see it from his point of view as she listened—parents growing prematurely old in a town with more bars than employers, and of the options, well, at least the police department was a form of public service. Besides, there weren't a whole lot of jobs around, and what was the point of moving to some crowded city where you didn't know anyone and they didn't know you? He had gone to New York City once, he said, and he knew there were places where people read books and talked about ideas. But he couldn't find them. He had stood on a street corner and asked someone the way to Greenwich Village, and the person had said, this *is* Greenwich Village. So he had bought himself some Middle Eastern lunch in a kind of bread with pockets.

"Falafel," she interjected and immediately wished she hadn't.

Then he had taken a subway up to the Met, but he couldn't figure out why looking at Greek statues was supposed to make him a better person. At least in North Adams, people knew him. There were guys to drink with and gripe about the Red Sox, and no, he didn't want to talk about the Red Sox, especially not with a New Yorker, especially not *this year*. But there was so much sorrow in the world, people baffled by life, baffled by—he groped for the word—unfairness, and at least as a cop, he could help them.

"You know," she admitted. "I think I have a totally schizophrenic view of the police."

He waited, knowing that if he was quiet, she would explain.

"I mean, on the one hand, they're the pigs—they make war on people for being black, or against the government, or different. They have no moral scruples, they don't care about minor details like guilt and innocence, and they would be even more dangerous if they weren't so inept. But on the other hand, I am perfectly well aware that I have this totally idealized view of you.

I mean, I see you as some bizarre combination of gumshoe, cowboy, and altar boy."

She stopped, hoping she hadn't gone too far.

I'm just a guy, he wanted to tell her, who is curious, and horny, and a little bit dazzled, and maybe even a little bit in love, but I can't be here if you don't take my life seriously. But she had already gotten up from the bed and was digging around in a blue glass box on the dresser. She returned to the bed and straddled him, placed a sheet of rolling paper on his chest, and began tapping out marijuana from a plastic bag.

"Uh, I'm not sure I'm ready for this," he said hurriedly. "I mean—"

"Oh, right," she protested. "Let me get this now. You walk in here—and this time you came to *me*, let's remember, not the reverse—and you think you are going to sit around and, oh, I don't know, burn incense and listen to *Magical Mystery Tour* and read *Siddhartha* by the light of a lava lamp. But of course, there won't be any marijuana around."

"I guess I didn't think about it."

"Uh-huh. And did you think about how we were likely to have some very outré political opinions?"

"I'm a Democrat," he said, again feeling defensive.

"Well, I suppose that's the good news. I'm not. I mean, I vote for the Democrats because they are usually the lesser of two evils, but I believe down to my socks that private property is theft, that women hold up half the sky, that the answer, my friend, is blowing in the wind, and that philosophers have only tried to interpret the world in various ways but that the point, however, is to change it." She casually went back to rolling the joint. "My parents pushed my carriage in Ban the Bomb demonstrations in the fifties and woke me up at four in the morning to take me to the March on Washington."

"Well, my parents raised me on tales of Michael Collins and Éamon de Valera."

"The point is that hanging out with me is probably not a smart career move."

"Does that mean that I may as well get stoned because I'm going to be dead in the water professionally whether I do or not?"

"Something like that. Anyway, what else are you doing here?"

He raised his hips and ground himself against her.

"Okay," she acknowledged. "I supposed that's one answer. But now that you're here, you gotta *be* here."

"Are you sure the door's locked?"

"Who are you afraid of getting busted by? Wendy?"

The last thing he remembered from the evening when he woke up the next morning was sitting on her bed in the candlelight, listening to Jimi Hendrix, and eating peanut butter with a spoon.

Jennifer was gone when he opened his eyes to the daylight. Ford squinted into the dappled sunlight on the walls, then slipped out of bed to explore the room.

The dimensions seemed larger in the daytime, the décor more improvised and haphazard. A Mickey Mouse clock stood on the dresser next to a porcelain bowl and pitcher. Sets of earrings had been strung along a piece of black lace inside a silver picture frame. A puppet in the form of a witch sat on a miniature antique chair, her lamb's wool hair hanging down from a pitched hat and her legs covered in black and orange stripes. A button had been pinned to her glossy purple dress. *If I can't dance, I don't want to be part of your revolution: Emma Goldman.* He wondered who that was.

He reached across the bed for the quilt and moved to the window, wrapping the quilt around him. Graham Marlow's church was visible through the yellow leaves, and, on the other side of the churchyard, Ford could see the small green building that held Will's craft shop and the workroom where Samir had been found. The wooden window frames of the shop were painted robin's egg blue. He could not see the café two stories beneath him, but he could smell the morning's baking, and he could see Wendy sweeping leaves from the flagstone path to the front door.

Here he was, then, seeing Flanders from the inside, from a bedroom on the third floor above Café Galadriel, from Jennifer's bed, from his own longing, but he was still in the middle of a crime scene and staring straight across the street to where a murdered man had been found. Three days a detective, and he was naked under a handmade cotton quilt, wondering where he belonged.

There were footsteps on the stairs, and he turned to see Jennifer nudge the door open with her shoulder. She was barefoot, and one breast was visible inside the collar of her red flannel robe. She held a cup of coffee in each hand.

"I made a guess," she greeted him. "Milk and two sugars."

"Just milk."

"I underestimated you."

Apparently, it was a good thing not to like sugar. Ford made a mental note.

She crossed the room toward him and set one cup on the dresser, then reached her face up and kissed him. Her mouth tasted of toothpaste and coffee. Her skin smelled of sleep.

"We can share this one." She handed him the remaining cup, then glanced at the Mickey Mouse clock as a single church bell chimed across the street.

"Seven forty-five. I told Wendy I was taking the morning off."

"Did you tell her why?"

"Yeah."

"What did she say?"

"She said, 'Oh, Jen. Are you really sure about this?'"

"And are you?"

"I haven't been sure of anything since Bob Dylan went electric. But I'm scared, I'm sad, and all I want to do is bury my face in your neck and hide."

They sipped the coffee, handing it back and forth between them.

"You don't look scared, you know," he observed. "You keep saying you're scared, but you don't look scared."

"Yeah, well, don't buy my mock-epic routine. It's how I make myself feel better. In the meantime, I keep finding reasons not to go out alone after dark, and every time I open a home-canned jar of something, I listen for the little ping sound that says it hasn't already been opened. I've become totally paranoid."

"That doesn't sound paranoid to me. It sounds sensible."

"Maybe. But then, I didn't come here to be sensible. Sensible was back in graduate school planning an academic career. Sensible was a rent-controlled apartment. Sensible was being in therapy to get over my own craziness. I've been here for almost five years now, and I wake up in this room, and the first thing I do is come look out this window. The air is fresh, the wind chimes are going, and I feel like picking this town up by its ears like a teddy bear because it's so goddamn cute."

"Nothing wrong with that."

"I'm not so sure. It's like I've been playing Galadriel, being nice to the hobbits and dispensing granola cookies in Rivendell, when I'm actually much more complicated than that. I mean, my real inner life doesn't come in lighthearted, or simple, and here I've been hiding out pretending it does while the rest of the world goes down the tubes. Well, now the world has caught up with me, and with a vengeance. People being poisoned, not to mention bludgeoned to death. How did this happen? I want my artificial little life back, selfish bitch that I am."

Jennifer left the window, got back into bed, and stretched her legs out under the sheet. She patted the mattress, gesturing for him to join her.

"You know," he said, settling in beside her. "It's funny you use the word 'artificial'. It's a word I thought of the first time I was here."

"Hey," she yelped. "That's okay for *me* to say."

"No, I don't mean about you. I mean about Samir. Remember when I searched his room?"

"Uh, you mean while I was weeping hysterically in the living room? Or while I was retching my guts out in the bathroom?"

He squeezed her arm in sympathy. "Well, there was nothing in the room. Oh, there were clothes and blankets and towels, and books, but we were looking for insight into Samir since nobody seemed to know much about him, and there was nothing there. No address book. No social security card. No checkbook. There was a wallet with some cash and a fake California driver's license, but we cross-checked and couldn't find anything. Whoever Samir Molchev was, or Charles Blair, which is what the driver's license said, there was no record of his existence. We even checked his fingerprints, and they weren't on file anywhere in the US. That's what I mean by saying that he was artificial."

"Well, his corpse was pretty damn real." She shivered, then continued in a small voice, "How did he actually die? Nobody ever told us."

"A single blow to the brain stem."

"Was it the andiron?"

Ford was silent.

"Oh, Jesus, Ford. You can't seriously think that at this point I'm seducing you in return for information!"

"I wouldn't be here if I did. But I'm still a cop, Jen. Look, I can tell you what we've told Steve Davies, and that's that we don't have the murder weapon and that the fingerprints tell us almost nothing."

Jennifer shook herself, sat up, and pulled the robe closer around her.

"So, then, talk to me about murder weapons and fingerprints. I would much rather feel like your intrepid aide-de-camp than the piteous bystander who lost her breakfast at the sight of a dead body."

"Okay," he sighed. "No, it wasn't the andiron. Bob McBride—he's the medical examiner—says that none of the edges fit the wound. Actually, there wasn't much of a wound, and the blow wasn't even particularly hard. It just happened to land in exactly the wrong place."

"Why do the fingerprints tell you nothing?"

"Because all of them have a simple explanation, and as much"—he reached under the blanket and pinched her thigh—"as you would like it all to be puzzling and exciting, good police practice says that the simplest explanation is almost always the right one. I went over Will's workroom so carefully, and I ended up with nothing. Will's fingerprints are all over everything except a trunk, which shouldn't have any fingerprints—and doesn't—because he'd just finished varnishing it. There are various other fingerprints, some of which are local and some not, but they are where you would expect from casual visitors: tabletops, the backs of chairs, the door, that kind of thing. The spare key had been wiped clean, which could mean anything or nothing but probably just means that whoever killed Samir wasn't a total idiot." He paused.

"Go ahead," she prompted.

"Well, then there are the fingerprints associated with the poisoning. Only Zach and Annie's prints were on the jar of pickles, but there are smudges that could have come from a dish towel—Zach doesn't remember exactly how he opened it. Only Zach's fingerprints are on the refrigerator itself, and only his are in the house, except for Will's, who seems to be the only one who had visited him. Zach just moved in, and the whole place had just been repainted, so it makes sense that nobody else's fingerprints were there, but someone could have been wearing gloves. Other than that, the packet of gopher bait containing the strychnine had been wiped clean. And there is nothing to be learned from fingerprints in the co-op—"

"Where I can personally attest to the fact that all hundred members both shop and work."

"Not to mention all the tourists who would have stopped by. The bottom line is that the fingerprints don't tell us much except to verify everyone's usual routine."

Jennifer watched his face register his frustration. This was a Ford she didn't yet know: the working cop who bore little relation to her own fantasies about him, or her own fear.

She needed to change the mood, if not the subject.

"So," she exclaimed. "Let me see. You now know for a certainty that Annie works in the co-op, that Will spends time in his workroom, that Wendy uses the oven in the café, that Mark and Ginger work the cash register, and that Zach has at some point been in his own house."

"That pretty much covers it."

She lowered her voice suggestively. "And have you figured out exactly where I've been?"

His expression softened.

"You've been in the café. You've been in Will's workroom. You've been in the co-op. As far as I can tell, you haven't been to Zach's house yet."

"And what if they dust you for prints and discover my fingerprints all over you?"

She was relieved to hear him laugh.

"Then I will have some explaining to do."

She eased herself back down and curled up against his chest. "What time do you have to be at work?"

"Not until ten-thirty."

"Excellent." She reached her hands under the quilt.

part five

twenty-five

"I don't know, Cisco," Jennifer was saying. "I mean, half the tourists who eat breakfast here have 'Alice's Restaurant' plastered to their brains. I'm not sure they want to see a cop in uniform sneaking out the back."

"What's Alice's Restaurant?"

"Oh, my God. The point is, you know how these folks see the police."

"Yes, I do. You weren't even particularly glad to see us when you had a body on your hands."

"I, for one, was very glad to see you."

"Yeah, right. You told Graham I was a pig."

Jennifer ran her fingers through her hair, cursing herself for having put the issue of Ford's clothing into words. Ford had been spending most nights with her and stopping at home in the morning to change into his uniform before reporting to work. He would slip out of bed in the autumnal dawn, kiss her good-bye, and whisper, "Don't wake up. I'll see you soon." This morning, she had followed him downstairs and told Will, who was brewing coffee at the stove, that Ford was leaving early to change into his disguise. She had meant only to tease Ford about their unspoken agreement, to invoke the sense of playful conspiracy. But Ford, not at all certain which, if any, of his clothes were the disguise, had not been amused.

Around them, the café was buzzing. Two weeks had passed since Samir's memorial service, and fears about the autumn tourist trade notwithstanding, it appeared that, at least on the surface, Flanders had emerged unscathed. The New England leaves were drawing the usual throngs, and Jennifer was spending her days serving lunches to retired mid-westerners who left their RVs at the campsite and bicycled over to what *Off-the-Beaten Track in the Berkshires* had called "a charming combination of whimsy and domesticity." On this evening, the whimsy was represented by Wendy conducting her Monday night Tarot readings at the corner table. The samovar of mulled cider on the counter and the aroma of baked apples and vegetarian moussaka offered the evening's domesticity.

As for Jennifer, the domesticity was trumping the whimsy. She had forgotten, she thought, how nice it felt to wake up in the night and feel warm arms around you. She felt protected and indulgent in equal measure, picked Ford's brains on the history of Western Massachusetts, and used the café stereo to put him on a regimen she referred to as remedial Bob Dylan. She had started with *Freewheeling* and thus far had worked her way up to *Highway 61*. Ford usually arrived at some point in the evening, invariably in dungarees and a flannel shirt, and sat at her table holding his own with whichever of her friends happened by. Zach had been guarded, Will friendly, and Wendy transparently relieved that someone was taking Jennifer in hand. David had rolled his eyes on first ascertaining the situation. "Human affections make strange bedfellows," he had said grandly, adding, "And I thought Annie's thing for Lerner was weird."

Ford found he liked Zach Lerner on the subject of politics more than he liked David on the subject of love. Zach, he thought, went too far at times—Ford just didn't believe that the law always put property before people—but it was certainly true that too many people lacked basic food and shelter and that, if the meek were ever to inherit the earth, it wasn't likely to happen anytime soon. This evening, Annie and Zach had arrived together, and Ford found himself rooting for Zach's indifference to the nutritional worthlessness of junk food.

"Have you any idea what they put in those things?" Annie glowered at Zach's plate, on which a slice of broccoli and mushroom quiche had been garnished with potato chips.

"Can't say I do."

"Then don't eat that shit around me. Ford over here"—she gestured in his direction—"already thinks I tried to poison you."

Ford shifted uncomfortably in his seat. Perhaps it was simply difficult to socialize with someone he had locked in jail, but he occasionally found Annie's tenacity as troubling as David's posturing. As for the others, Ford admired Graham too much ever really to befriend him. He was far more drawn to Will, who was steady and who kept his own counsel. Ford could see Will as a small-town boy, coaching the little league team. And Will was the one who, when the subject had been brought up that morning, had been adamant that Ford could show up dressed any way he liked, that if people didn't feel comfortable with a policeman around, they could just find somewhere else to hang out. Jennifer had winced when Will said it, noting, not for the first time, that Will could make her feel small and second-rate on the subject of loyalty.

"I tell you what," Zach was currently negotiating with Annie across the table. "I actually approve of the rebellion against the American packaged food industry. So you don't lecture me on the ill effects of junk food, and I won't lecture you on the inaccessibility of healthy food for the poor."

"I can't believe you don't care about this! Half the world is dying of starvation, and the other half is dying of hardening of the arteries."

"The deal is I won't lecture you, and you won't lecture me. Woody Guthrie was talking about migrant farm workers, not about potato chips."

"The saturated fats alone are enough to kill you."

Zach sat unmoved, his arms crossed, having a much better time than he was willing to concede. "Is it a deal?" he demanded.

"Is what a deal?" Jennifer glanced over at them, seeking the relief of somebody else's argument.

"That I am supposed to tolerate this man's disgusting eating habits," Annie growled.

"You mean he talks with his mouth full? Of course he does. He's a New Yorker."

"No, that's not what I mean. It's what's *in* his mouth that's the problem. Anyway, Jen, why do you serve potato chips?"

"Because not everyone likes sweet potato fries." Jennifer smiled innocently. Then she turned back to Ford, knowing she was at least as guilty as Annie was of not leaving well enough alone.

She rubbed the top of Ford's hand in apology. "Okay, I'm sorry I called your uniform a disguise. I guess I think masquerades are sexy and mysterious. I didn't mean to make you feel like a hypocrite."

"How would you feel if the reverse were happening?"

"You mean if I had to change clothes in order to arrive at your doorstep?"

"Yes."

"Stockings and heels? That sort of thing?"

"Yes."

"It's not to my credit that I can't even imagine it. I'd probably be loudly quoting Emerson: *Beware any enterprise that requires a new set of clothes.*"

"Actually, Thoreau said that."

Being corrected only added to Jennifer's chagrin. "Well,

then," she offered in conciliation, "let's just say that we're all in costume. Everyone's playing a part of some kind."

Ford glanced around the room and raised his eyebrows. Ginger was waiting tables in a leopard-spotted mini-skirt and red-and-yellow striped legwarmers. Mark was in his invariable Grateful Dead T-shirt and tie-dyed carpenter pants. At her table, Wendy bent over her Tarot cards, her red curls falling over the shoulders of a gold velvet gown.

Jennifer followed his gaze, saw his meaning, and laughed. "I rest my case." She leaned forward and put her cheek against his, then turned her face to kiss him. "Look, I have to go deal with the register. Mark screwed it up last night. I'll be back. Don't be mad at me, okay? I'm really sorry."

Left alone, Ford sipped his beer and tried to take Jennifer's apology at face value: she understood that she had hurt his feelings and was sorry. He couldn't expect her to understand how hard he had worked for the gold detective shield that had finally arrived the previous week. She had greeted the arrival of the shield with candles, *coq au vin*, and his first bottle of champagne, which they drank sitting cross-legged on her bed. He had not had the heart to express his discomfort. There he was, marking a solemn achievement in law enforcement in a rose-colored bedroom above a hippie café, Edith Piaf on the stereo, and Jennifer's copper jewelry flickering in the candlelight. How, when he thought about it, could she know what the badge really meant to him? And how could he even blame her? He had reached into her world, wanting to be part of it, curious and open and bored with his own limits. And now he wanted to sit, perfectly poised, on the fence of his own ambivalence.

In the days that followed the arrival of the shield, he and Jennifer had talked intermittently about the crimes. She knew that the driver's license found in Samir's room under the name of Charles Blair had proved to be phony and that the national call for information pertaining to a "Charles Blair" had come to naught. She knew that poison containing strychnine was found in most hardware stores and many of the supermarkets in Berkshire County. She had written it all down in the accounts ledger she was using for a notebook, which amused him and annoyed him by turns. Here he was, finally with his chance to solve a major crime and prove that his promotion had been deserved. And he was getting nowhere.

They had talked instead about the other cases occupying his time. The ring of car thefts in Clarksburg. Two kids who had been caught robbing gas stations and grocery stores. Talking about the other cases helped him ignore the fact that the crimes in Flanders had not been solved and that, as the days went on without additional information, it was getting less and less likely that they ever would be. Other than that, he heard about the time she had sat on the high school principal's desk and announced, "The Human Relations Club demands the immediate withdrawal of all American troops from Vietnam." She heard about the time he got thrown out of Boy Scout camp for saying that the pledge was stupid and that they didn't spend their time helping people, they just ran around sleeping in tents. He heard about what cretins all her ex-lovers had been until he wondered what was wrong with him—the woman clearly having no taste—and she pumped him for all the details of American teenage romance, circa nineteen sixty-eight, wanting the inside story of all the classmates she had despised at the time for being apolitical.

Bored with his own thoughts, Ford looked around the café. Wendy sat at her table in earnest conversation with a thin, dark-haired woman in a long brown skirt. The two sat across from each other, staring down at a spread of Tarot cards. He saw Wendy reach across the table and pat the woman's hand, saw the woman nod and stretch, and then watched as the woman stood, grabbed a suede jacket from the back of her chair, and made her way to the door. Wendy waved to the woman as she left, and as she glanced around, Ford caught her eye. They smiled at each other. Wendy raised her arm and gestured for him to join her.

The small table on which Wendy held her Tarot readings was covered with a dark purple scarf. Gold thread, sequins, and fake pearls adorned its velvet surface. Wendy was shuffling the cards as Ford approached, their deep blue backs covered with gold eight-pointed stars.

"Hi," she greeted him. "How about having your cards read?"

"I don't know. I've never done it."

"You can ask a specific question, or I can do a general reading."

"It's a little intimidating."

Wendy blinked modestly.

At her direction, he held the deck of cards and tried to wait until they got used to his presence. He took that to mean he should wait until they warmed in his hands. Then he mixed them, laid them out in three piles, and tried his best when she instructed him to hold his palm over each pile and select the one that spoke to him. Finally, just when he was feeling too foolish to go on with it, she took them back into her hands.

Silently, she turned over a first card, positioned a second card across it, and placed four additional cards in a larger cross around the first two. She looked up at him with concern in her eyes.

"What?" he demanded.

"Hang on."

She laid down four more cards on the table, in a column on the right. Then she set down the deck, placed each of her hands in the opposite sleeve, and studied the cards.

"Okay," she said finally. "Well, the first thing is, this is a pretty heavy reading. The most important cards in Tarot are the Major Arcana—they're like a permanent trump suit—and the next most important cards are the aces and face cards. Well, you've got four of the Major Arcana, the Judgment card in the middle, Temperance, the Hermit, and the High Priestess, plus the prince of cups. That's, like, heavy." She stared down at the cards again.

Ford waited, feeling apprehensive and a bit ridiculous. "Well," he prompted, "what do they say?"

"Well, the main issue I see here," she said slowly, "is about whether or not there is justice in the world."

"Really?" Ford was startled.

"Yeah. Like I said, the central card is the Judgment card, which is about how the ultimate cosmic justice plays in our own lives. The foundational card of the row is Temperance, which is about balance, and that's closely related to justice. You know, like with the scales. And the top card of the row is the two of swords, again about balance. See—she's got these two heavy swords, and the only way she can stay upright is to balance them. But there's no clear answer here. The top card is supposed to indicate the outcome, but see," Wendy pointed, "she's blindfolded. Like Justice, again."

Wendy stopped. He waited for her to continue.

"So," he said finally. "Is there?"

"Is there what?"

"Justice in the world?"

Wendy sighed. "You have to understand, this reading isn't about the world. It's about you, and there's a lot of contradiction here."

"I'm beginning to think I should have asked something simple, like if the Red Sox will ever win the World Series."

Wendy looked at him in distress.

"Okay, then. How's my love life?"

She remained silent.

"I'm a loser, right?"

"Oh, no," Wendy hurried to reassure him. "In fact, one of the funny things about this spread is that it's the Tarot equivalent of Jennifer's astrological chart. Jen has a Libra moon and a Libra rising sign. But look." She pointed to the top card in the larger cross. "Again, it's contradicted. That's the prince of cups, and cups are for love and passion. The prince of cups is, like, Lancelot."

He smiled at the image. "Okay, then, what's the problem?"

"Well, the bottom card, your unconscious, is the Hermit. Of course"—she reached out and touched his hand to reassure him—"that doesn't mean you have to be alone, only that you have to acknowledge the solitude inside you. And look here. This card"—she pointed to the left arm of the cross—"represents the past. It's the eight of cups, which usually means loss, but I don't think it does here. I think it means loneliness. And then this card, the third one in the row, which represents your hopes and fears, is the High Priestess. Well, it's almost a joke around here that the High Priestess is Jennifer."

"Okay, what does that mean? That we live happily ever after?"

"I don't know. The cards won't say. This card"—she pointed to the right arm of the cross—"is the future, and it's the seven of cups. In effect, another blindfold. For the unknown. And this second card in the row, for the general environment, is the nine of pentacles, which is about waiting patiently."

Ford squinted down at the cards. "All that, and basically they refuse to tell me anything."

Wendy dropped her eyes. "Oh, Ford," she said sadly. "They're telling you one thing. Judgment in the center is crossed with the five of swords." She looked up at him. "They're telling you you're not going to figure out who killed Samir. The five of swords means defeat."

twenty-six

"May I speak to Detective McDermott, please," Jennifer said primly.

"Who is calling, please?"

"Jennifer Morgan."

Jennifer waited to hear Ford's voice on the line.

"Cisco? Hey, listen. I've got to come into North Adams—tonight's special is spinach pie, and we just ran out of phyllo dough. Can you meet for coffee?"

Jennifer heard the silence on the other end of the phone. "What?" she demanded.

"What do you mean, 'what?'"

"I mean, what? Come on, Cisco. I know that silence. Something's up."

"Look, I can't really talk about it."

"It's something about the case!"

"Not *that* case."

"I'll meet you at the diner in twenty minutes."

"I can't."

"Yes, you can. Please, Cisco? You're scaring me."

Jennifer put the phone down without giving him a chance to

answer. She ran a brush through her hair, thought briefly of digging out pantyhose and high heels, and headed for her old Country Squire station wagon, keys in hand.

He was already at the diner when Jennifer arrived. She squeezed through the plastic chairs and Formica-topped tables and slipped into the booth across from him.

"Okay. Tell me. What's going on?"

Ford signaled for two cups of coffee before answering her. "You know the stretch of road on Route 2 that loops around the back of the Saunders farm?"

"Vaguely."

"It's mostly woods, but there's a clearing that's hidden from the road when the leaves are up. Phil Saunders maintains the road to it so he can leave a tractor out there when he needs to. The last time he'd been out there was two weeks ago. Well, he was driving past this morning, and with the leaves down, he noticed there was a car parked in the clearing. He phoned the office to come deal with it."

"I'm already hating this."

Ford pressed his lips together as the coffees arrived, nodded a thank you to the waitress, and added milk to his cup before looking back at Jennifer. "An abandoned 1970 Pontiac. No license plate. No registration or insurance card. The VIN number had been scratched off. Just about two pounds of what looks like pure cocaine in an unlocked glove compartment."

"Yikes! Who the hell would leave that much cocaine in an unlocked, abandoned car?"

"That's the point. Nobody would."

Jennifer wasn't sure if she had heard or imagined the accusation in his voice. "And you think we had something to do with that? Ford, you can't be serious."

"Well, somebody did."

"Who? You mean somebody in Flanders? Ford, it isn't true. Okay, so we're floating in pot and hash—"

"Shhh! Keep your voice down."

"And we've all done our share of acid and mushrooms and mescaline," she whispered across the table. "Truth is, we might do cocaine in a minute if we could afford it. But we can't. And *two pounds?*"

Ford regarded her in silence, visibly unhappy, his broad, gentle features tight. "Wendy read my Tarot cards last night," he offered.

"I know. I saw. I meant to ask you about it."

"She told me I cared more about justice than anything—"

"I believe *that* a lot more than I believe Tarot cards."

"And that I was never going to find out who killed Samir Molchev."

"She said that?" Jennifer's voice rose again. "That's so unlike her!"

"Why?"

"Because she's always going on about how the Tarot isn't fortune-telling, that all it can do is read a situation and indicate the—what does she call them—tendencies currently in effect. They are always subject to human will. They can always be changed. I mean, I don't buy any of it, so it doesn't make a difference to me. But what she told you goes against all of her entirely bizarre convictions."

Jennifer drained her coffee cup and replaced it, too loudly, on the table. "This coffee sucks."

"If you don't buy any of it, why are you so angry?"

"Because she upset you, and now you're upset with *me.*"

"I'm not upset with you. But I have a glove compartment full of cocaine, a town of potheads who are becoming my friends, and a murder I can't solve. This is starting to feel like something out of 'Tom Thumb's Blues.'"

"Well, at least you're learning Bob Dylan songs," she tried to joke.

"Which means a lot more to you than it will ever mean to me."

"Oh, Ford." She felt her eyes fill with tears. "Are we breaking up already?"

He was astonished. "Of course not. I mean, at least I hope not. Just keep your ears open, okay, Jen? If there is cocaine moving through here, and it's pretty clear there is, you are much more likely to hear about it than I am."

He watched her move uncomfortably in her chair. It occurred to him that he had never seen her sulk before.

"Look, I've got to go," she said finally. "Wendy's waiting for the phyllo dough. There will be just enough time to get the spinach pies in the oven before I chop her into little pieces and add her to tonight's chili. Can we talk about this later?"

"Sure."

She stood, looked around to see if anyone was watching, and leaned down to kiss him on the cheek.

Wendy was in the café kitchen, chopping onions on the butcher block. Cubes of feta cheese sat in a large bowl at her side. The baking pans, already floured and buttered, were lined up on the counter next to the oven. The kitchen was filled with the odor of the chopped spinach steaming on the stove.

Jennifer stormed into the room and flung the packages of phyllo dough onto the counter. "I can't believe you did that."

"Did what?" Wendy glanced up from the onions.

"Told Ford he wasn't going to solve Samir's murder."

Wendy set the knife down carefully and reached for a dish towel. She turned around and leaned against the counter. "Oh."

"What were you *thinking*? Don't you think he's torn enough between being a cop and hanging out with us? You know, I don't believe in Tarot cards, but I usually think of them as harmless. I even get your point that they can be helpful because, hey, we all need a mirror, right? It can be tea leaves, or chicken bones, or bird droppings—they're all just a way to read our own minds. But this wasn't harmless! I just can't believe you did it!"

Wendy stood, biting her lip and looking down at the floor.

"It's so not like you," Jennifer continued. "I mean, you talk about how the cards give suggestions, not predictions, and how you must always end a reading with something hopeful, and then you make the flat-out negative statement that Ford will never find out who killed Samir? Meanwhile, I'm trying not to lose this guy—who I like a lot, in case you haven't noticed. Not to mention all the other stuff he's trying to balance."

"Balance was a big thing in his reading. I told him that."

"And that's supposed to make it *better*?"

"And that justice mattered to him more than anything." A small anger of her own crept into Wendy's voice. "Even you."

"Did you tell him that?"

"No. But I saw it."

With a groan, Jennifer hoisted herself up onto a clear section of countertop and buried her face in her hands.

"Don't be mad at me, okay?" Wendy cajoled.

Jennifer forced herself to look up, hearing the tears in Wendy's voice. She tried to drain the anger from her tone. "I'll get over it. But just tell me. Why did you say that to him?"

"I didn't mean to. I'd never really talked to him before. I mean, not one-on-one, just things like, 'Hey, Ford, want some more carrot cake?' He scares me."

"*Ford* scares you?"

"Yeah. At first, I thought he was shy. But he's not shy, he's just thinking all the time, and when he decides something, there isn't any flexibility."

"A Massachusetts state police detective who's sleeping with

me can be called a lot of things, but inflexible isn't one of them."

"Yes, it *is*. That's where you're wrong. That part of him just lives deeper down. I saw it. It's in the Hermit card."

"Fuck the Hermit card!"

"No, it's true. And the Judgment card. And Temperance."

"But you broke your own rule."

"It just slipped out."

"But *why*?"

"Because," Wendy sputtered. "Samir hasn't even been dead a month, and nobody even talks about him anymore. It's like, everyone breathed a big sigh of relief that he was finally buried —and don't say you didn't, Jen. You did it louder than anyone. Will refuses to talk about it, and everyone else pretends it never happened. Ford is the only one who is trying to figure out who killed him."

"So am I, if you remember."

"No, you aren't. You said you would, and you did for a while, but then you just started hoping that life would go back to normal. You've even stopped writing in your notebook."

Jennifer grimaced an acknowledgment that what Wendy had said was true.

"So then last night," Wendy continued, "I saw Ford sitting there, and I figured maybe if I read his cards that I'd see something that he could connect with something else, and suddenly he'd figure it out. But it didn't happen. Instead, it was Justice crossed with the five of swords. And I knew he wasn't going to solve it, and I didn't want him to have to look anymore."

"He's the state detective in charge of the case," Jennifer told her. "He has to keep looking."

"But he doesn't have to keep hoping."

Jennifer slid off the counter, rounded the butcher block to Wendy's side, and put her arms around her.

"No, sweetie," she corrected softly. "*You* don't have to keep hoping. Let the dead bury the dead."

"I can't."

"Yes, you can."

Wendy eased her forehead into the warm spot on Jennifer's neck. "You know what the funny thing is, Jen?"

"What?"

"That I read my own cards before I came down here this morning. Like I always do. And it was the first day for months that everything was fine. The six of swords, the four of wands, and the Empress card."

"What does that mean? You're not scared anymore?"

"Not *as* scared. Something has shifted. We've been through a passage, but now things are solid and we can breathe again." Wendy sighed. "It's been so long since I turned up the Empress card."

Jennifer drew her head back to study her friend. Wendy's face had sadness in it, but it was true: the frightened, scattered look was gone. Wendy looked solid, at least, Jennifer thought, as solid as she ever did.

"You know what I'm scared of?" Jen asked impulsively.

"What?"

"That our little rural idyll is winding down. That none of us will be here in a year or two. What happened to Samir and Zach was just the noise of the world crashing in."

"But I think everything's okay now."

"It doesn't matter. This place was stuck together with bubble gum to begin with. We've got no roots here. We didn't grow up together. We don't think of growing old together. We got no parents in the graveyard or kids in the school. Do you know what a *luftmensch* is?"

"No."

"Someone who lives off air. And in the air. And what you got here is your classic group of *luftmenschen*. We'll all float away in the slightest breeze."

"I don't see anyone moving."

"No. But one of these days, Annie will announce that the growing season is better in North Georgia. Will will take it into his head to go study art someplace, and, for all I know, he'll drag you along with him. Then when Joan finishes the seminary, she and Graham will move to some church in a poor urban community. And everyone will be very nice to each other on the way out."

"You have to make sure that doesn't happen."

"Oh, right. The High Priestess to the rescue."

Wendy turned back to the onions. "Well," she said, her back to Jennifer, "you can always go back to graduate school."

Graham turned off the motor and reached into the back seat to retrieve his book bag. The meeting had been a good one. Sid Blumenthal, the reform rabbi from Pittsfield, and Father Joe Scanlon, the Catholic chaplain at Williams, had agreed with him that the theme of their ecumenical Christmas/Hanukkah service would concern the redistribution of wealth. The oil for the lamps that had lasted for eight days would be connected with the parable of the loaves and fishes. The three of them would each give a short sermon on the relationship between plentitude and righteousness. "And none of that Protestant crap about God rewarding rectitude with wealth," Joe Scanlon had insisted. Typical Jesuit irreverence. As if Graham ever would. Meanwhile, they would observe Thanksgiving as usual, with a vegetarian feast and ceremony with the Chaubunagungamang Band of the Nipmuc Council, who were preparing to petition the federal government for recognition.

He was walking up the steps of the church when he heard,

"Hey, Graham, wait up," and turned to see Jennifer coming toward him.

"Got a minute?"

"Uh-huh."

She followed him into the office.

"What can I do for you?"

"You can help me throw a Halloween party."

Graham seated himself at his desk and gestured for her to take the other chair.

"I'm about to be swamped with preparations for Thanksgiving and Christmas. Don't you usually do Halloween at the café?"

"More or less. We light jack-o'-lanterns and tell people to wear costumes. But I mean a *real* Halloween party, here in the community room of the church."

"All Soul's Day white-washing aside," Graham said warily. "Halloween is about as pagan as it gets."

"I know. The temporary reemergence of chaos, right? The blurring of distinctions between life and death. The breakdown of identity and order. For one night, everyone gets their various anti-social rocks off, and the dead get a night on the town so they let you alone the rest of the year."

"That about sums it up."

"Well, this year, I want to invite every witch in Salem. I want Nathaniel Hawthorne and Herman Melville swapping stories in the corner. I want Wendy to summon all twelve houses of the Zodiac. If I can't have that, I at least want a couple of gallons of witches' brew in a pitcher and you reading 'The Devil and Daniel Webster' aloud to the assembled multitudes."

Graham frowned. "Really, Jen. Haven't we been through enough in the past month?"

"Yes. That's the point. We've just been through the wringer, all of us, and doesn't it feel strange to you that everything seems to have gone back to normal? Even Wendy is saying that nothing else is going to happen. What I'm afraid of is that the more things calm down, the more we are going to notice the gaping hole in the middle of town where mutual trust used to be. I think we need one hell of a purgation, not to mention having a ghost to appease."

"How many people?"

"I don't know. Around fifty?"

"Nothing that will get me in trouble with the diocese?"

"We'll all be very discrete."

"And I don't have to do anything?" Graham paused. "Why am I letting you talk me into this?"

"Maybe because you agree with me. Look, you've been unhappy here for a long time, and my guess is that recent events have made it easier to think about leaving. If that's true of you, why shouldn't it be true of other folks?"

Graham pondered the question. "Jen," he blurted. "Do you think that someone we know is guilty?"

"Are you really asking me?"

"Yes, I am."

"When I'm being really honest with myself," she said slowly, "I think that one of us must have killed Samir and that none of us could have."

"Explain."

"I think that Allard Johns was right about one thing, that whoever killed Samir knew where Will kept the extra key to the workroom. But then, who did it? Annie says that Samir left the co-op at a quarter to seven, right? And the medical examiner says that Samir died shortly after that. Well, Wendy, Will, and I were all in each other's presence during that hour and a quarter. That leaves only Annie, Zach, and David without alibis."

"And me."

"And you, which is no more or less ridiculous than Annie, Zach, or David. I mean, I don't think you liked Samir. I think you saw through his peace-and-love guru act—although my guess is you've seen worse versions of spiritual hypocrisy—but I don't think you killed him! And I can't imagine you, David, or Annie walking into Zach's house intent on poisoning him with strychnine. Or Zach poisoning himself."

"Well, you're right that I didn't do it."

"So, then. Somebody must have, and nobody could have. I don't know what to think except to hope Wendy's right and that we can put this behind us. A blow-out on Halloween just might help that along."

"Okay, then."

Jennifer got to her feet and leaned forward to give Graham a quick hug. "I love that you let me push you around without ever letting me think I've gotten away with something."

"Is that what I do?"

"Something like that. But it's a gift that I know better than to take for granted. So, thank you. I promise, if we can't appease this ghost, it won't be because I didn't try."

twenty-seven

"Who's coming to this thing?" Annie demanded.

"The usual. Betsy and Jill from the women's craft collective are both coming, and I told them to bring the others with them. I said the same thing to Steve Davies about inviting the rest of the law collective. I've been slipping invitations to all the café regulars. Graham has invited the people he works with from Friends of the Earth and the Committee for Economic Justice."

"Graham's crowd at a party, Jen? Are you fucking putting me on?"

"I know. Not one of them has cracked a smile since Woodstock. But I invited some folks from the Williams English department."

"Do they know how to party?"

"If nothing else, they know how to drink. I'm bringing the booze, and I've got David in charge of the music and the drugs, so we'll get everyone high on something or other, and with a little bit of luck, people will lighten up and dance."

They were in the co-op, Jennifer having stopped by to

discuss the menu and post an invitation on the bulletin board. She stepped carefully around a crate of Brussels sprouts and placed the invitation between a photograph of Scott and Helen Nearing and a poster showing a Granny Smith apple and the words *Boycott South Africa*.

Annie eyed the invitation. "Vishnu and company will show up with cymbals and Hari Krishna drums."

"At least they'll be in costume."

"Well, I'm going to wear beige, put some greenery in my hair, and come as a turnip. And you?"

"I haven't decided yet. Probably something obvious, like Galadriel. Wendy's coming as the Empress."

"Of course."

"And she's dressing Will up as the eight of pentacles. Don't ask—it's got something to do with craftsmanship. Ford has flatly refused to come as the Cisco Kid."

"Can you blame him?"

"You mean, after I told him during that stupid fight the other day that everyone was in some kind of uniform?"

"Zach is coming as a Wobbly."

"Didn't you tell him it's a costume party?"

Annie laughed.

"At least it'll be interesting. We are not a group," Jennifer observed, "that is inclined to take symbolic identities lightly."

It was with no small measure of calculation that Jennifer put Wendy in charge of decorations. The kitchen appliances and plain white walls of the church's community room did not encourage revelry, and transforming its utilitarian shabbiness would, Jennifer hoped, distract Wendy from her thoughts. She was relieved to note that Wendy was carrying out her task with something approaching enthusiasm, using the party as an occasion to raid her bolts of old fabric and get out her sewing machine.

The result, when Jennifer surveyed the room on the afternoon of October 31, reminded her more of *A Midsummer Night's Dream* than Halloween: a Victorian *Midsummer Night's Dream* of tinkling bells and fairy dust. Tiny white lights hung from the ceiling on swatches of deep maroon velvet. Clusters of maple leaves and dried cranberries decorated the walls between wreaths of brocaded ribbon, autumn clematis, and witch hazel. The back door leading out into the churchyard had been framed in miniature wind chimes and Wendy's own collection of small brass bells. Graham had refused to allow Wendy to decorate the graveyard, but his insistence that no illegal substances be consumed inside the church made it likely that it, too, would have its share of visitors. Graham had also drawn the line at pagan decorations on the altar—really, Graham, Jennifer had protested, Christianity would never have gotten anywhere without paganism to add some spice. But Wendy had obediently limited herself to an autumnal border for the banner over the altar, which was now edged in grasses and dried herbs.

By nightfall, the food was being set on tables covered in red satin and lined with jack-o'-lanterns. Huge bowls of candy kisses and roasted chestnuts stood between baked apples, ginger cookies, and homemade peanut brittle. Salads and tahini spreads sat on trays, and a large pot of faux-meat balls and spaghetti was being kept warm on the stove. The wine and beer would arrive over the course of the evening—each guest had been told to bring a bottle or a six-pack—but Jennifer had contributed several half-gallons of tequila, which were surrounded by saltshakers and slices of lime and a sign reading *Witches' Brew*.

The church bell had rung for seven-fifteen by the time Jennifer headed across the road to change into her costume. Galadriel, she had decided, was too obvious a choice, and besides, she wasn't feeling like an elfin princess ruling over her paradise in the woods. Peter Pan or Robin Hood was more like it, she thought. Someone who lived by a more singular set of rules, unabashed and damned well getting away with it. Someone who tried to defy the laws of time, powerlessness, and change. I'll be a sorceress, she decided as she mounted the steps to her bedroom, mixing the magic potions to protect us all. She slipped her long, red velour robe over her head, covered it with a black woolen cape, and improvised a hat from cardboard and a purple scarf. Galadriel would have been exactly wrong. Galadriel had known her time was passing away. And if Jennifer's time was passing away, her future lay—she winced at the thought—not in the Grey Havens beyond the seas of Middle Earth, but with the half-written dissertation she had left back in New York.

David was climbing the steps of the church when Jennifer made her way back across the road. He was in a long brown robe, monk-like in its outlines, with moccasins on his feet and a rounded velvet hat on his head.

"Machiavelli?" she greeted him.

"Dante."

"I like it."

"And you are . . . ?" He regarded her. "Let me see. Wendy convinced you to be the High Priestess."

"Nope. Just your run-of-the-mill sorceress. Love potions, banishing spells. Y'know, the easy stuff."

"Eye of newt, horn of toad?"

"Only you better have brought along some decent grass because I am in need of a banishing spell, and eye of newt is not going to cut it."

"Not to worry," he assured her. "Columbian gold. And here" —he handed her a paper bag—"are tapes of music suitable for Halloween. The Grateful Dead. Black Sabbath. Get it?"

"Graham will have a fit if he figures it out."

"Graham doesn't know Jerry Garcia from Dmitri Shostakovich. But just in case, I prepared a pious alternative. There's a tape of songs entirely about saints."

"Just what I always wanted, a chance to boogie to Gregorian chants."

"You are a terminal literalist. I've got Billy Holiday singing 'St. Louis Blues,' Joan Baez singing 'I Dreamed I Saw St. Augustine,' Tom Rush singing 'San Francisco Bay Blues.' The best is an old cut of Cab Calloway singing 'St. James Infirmary.'"

"Clever."

"Purely selfish. At least we won't have to listen to whatever half-baked James Taylor imitations Graham has around this place."

"Amen. How about a detour around back before we go in?"

"Ah, yes. The old churchyard. The designated smoking section. That sounds good to me."

Jennifer had never been sure if one got more stoned or drunk on tequila, but with David's Colombian Gold in her lungs, tonight was not the night for a scientific self-diagnosis. It was easier just to nibble on ginger cookies and use the tequila to wash them down. She stood on the side watching the room fill. Steve Davies in a straw hat and suspenders. Annie, as promised, with turnip greens in her hair. She watched Will and Wendy dancing to "Friend of the Devil," Wendy in gold and sequins, Will in a carpenter's apron and leggings. She watched Mark arrive in an unrecognizable combination of nylon, cellophane, and aluminum foil.

She was downing her third shot of tequila when she saw Ford come in the door in a Red Sox shirt and baseball cap. He looked around for her, acknowledged her wave, and came across the room.

"Carlton Fisk?" she greeted him.

"Carl Yastrzemski. Hey, you look good in that."

"Thanks. How about some witches' brew, courtesy of *la bruja*?"

"I think I want a beer."

Beer fetched and opened, Ford came back to her side and leaned forward to speak into her ear. "There was an arrest this afternoon in the cocaine case."

"Really? Hey, congratulations."

"Don't congratulate me. It wasn't my collar. It's federal. They'd been keeping an eye on the car where we found the cocaine. Two guys came to get it, thinking it was still there."

"Not from around here?"

"Nope. And I can't say I'm sorry it's done with."

She studied his face carefully. "Okay, then. I won't say I told you so."

"Jen . . ."

"Forget it." She set down her shot glass as "High Time" came on the stereo. "I just want the whole thing to go away. I want to pretend none of it ever happened. I want"—she held out her arms—"to breathe you in with the party. Dance with me."

Graham reading "The Devil and Daniel Webster" aloud had been Jennifer's idea in the first place, but when the time came, she wasn't in the mood to listen. Graham had turned the music off and was flipping through the book as people settled themselves onto chairs and took places on the floor around him. She wondered guiltily if her absence would be noticed and then meandered out back to the churchyard to find Wendy sitting cross-legged on an iron bench under a maple tree, quietly smoking a joint. David was there as well, standing by himself among the gravestones. She sat down next to Wendy as David, catching her eye, struck a pose.

"*Nel mezzo del cammin di nostra vita,*" he chanted.

Wendy held out the reefer. "Want some?"

"I'm not sure I need any more. But hey, it's Halloween, right?" Jen accepted the offered joint.

"*Mi ritrovai per una selva oscura ché la diritta via era smarrita . . .*"

"I think he's speaking Italian," Wendy whispered as Jennifer took a drag. "I didn't know he spoke Italian."

Jennifer exhaled and passed the joint back to Wendy. "He doesn't. Those are the opening lines of the Divine Comedy. *In the middle of the journey of our life, I found myself in a dark forest where the straight path had been lost.*"

"Cool."

"He's Dante, remember?"

"I think he looks like the Magician. Here."

Jennifer laughed. "Don't we have enough Tarot cards at this party?"

"Yeah, but don't you think he looks like the Magician?"

Jennifer took a final toke on the reefer and glanced over again at David. He was standing with his arms extended in the darkness, the maple trees behind him. The light from the church windows fell over him in the Gothic pattern of the window frames. *In the middle of the journey of our life,* she thought. "I think I've had it with being the High Priestess," she said. "I think I'll be the Magician for a while."

Wendy nodded. "Thrice-Great Hermes."

"The god of journeys, if I remember correctly. And the god of thieves."

Jennifer squeezed Wendy's hand, stood up, and walked back into the church. Yes, she thought. I'll be the Magician. Mountebank, juggler, manipulator of the elements—isn't that me all over. Damn, that grass was good. She passed through the empty main room of the church and breathed its smell of dust and pine cleaning fluid. Above the altar, the banner hung with its framing of grasses and herbs. *If you're not part of the problem, you're part of the solution.* No, wait. She hadn't read that right.

Ford had said that the problem was that the evidence didn't add up to anything. All the fingerprints were where they should be. The times all fell into place. The obvious murder weapon—David's andiron—wasn't the murder weapon at all. Even the victim—Ford had called Samir artificial. Even the victim didn't seem to exist.

"*It's kindly thought of,*" Graham was reading when she returned to the party. "*But there's a jug on the table and a case in hand. And I never left a jug or a case half finished in my life.*" She sat down at Ford's side. If you're not part of the solution, you're part of the problem. No. That still wasn't right. The problem *was* the solution. The problem was that it seemed the crime had never taken place. The solution was that it never had.

Pleased with her logic, she raised her right hand before her face. She was the sorceress casting banishing spells. She was the Magician. She would make all the death and worry go away. She would make the crime disappear.

It was two o'clock in the morning. The co-op members, the law collective, and the café patrons had all departed. The room had been tidied. The trash stood in bags by the back door. She sat with her friends in a small circle on the floor, all of them slowly marshaling the energy to go home. They were quiet, tired, purged.

Jennifer felt too contented even for gratitude. The last weeks seemed a foggy memory, or a mild collective hallucination. A murdered man who never existed, crimes with no motive, no purpose, and a killer who had passed through their lives with no clues, no presence, and disappeared. She looked around the circle of her friends, torn between relief and pity. For Wendy, who had been so convinced that Samir's death had been her fault. For Annie, with her fear of enclosures and her night in jail. For Will, with the small hidden space in his blue eyes, who thought kindness a matter of principle. Would she ever know why his odd sense of honor had led him to say that he had killed Samir? On the stereo, Joan Baez was singing Dylan. She folded her arms and, in her mind, embraced them all—embraced the room, the town, her life, her places and times.

twenty-eight

Jennifer never quite remembered stumbling home from the party, although she did recall giggling as Ford coaxed her into bed and mumbling, "Don't go," when he kissed her goodbye at seven the next morning. In her dream, they were at a drive-in movie, and Ford was upset because someone had been killed. At first, she protested, "But it's only a movie," but Ford kept trying to find the killer, so Jennifer insisted that they must find Daniel Webster, for only he could try a non-existent murderer. When they found him, he was driving the devil away from the café, and the devil looked like Samir.

She came back to consciousness slowly. The party floated through her head and, with it, her stoned determination that the crime had never taken place. It had all, she thought again, been an illusion. Then suddenly, she opened her eyes, knowing that she was on the edge of seeing the crime that had never been.

The accounts ledger that had served as her notebook was still on the top shelf in the kitchen. She read it over quickly, nodding to herself, noting all the small details that had made no sense at the time. Samir, who hated Annie, stopping by the co-op, and Annie, for the first and last time in her life, being sure of the time. Samir being part of the Berkeley anti-war movement, and Zach never having heard of him. She closed her eyes and pictured the workroom: the big old table beside which Samir had lain, the high shelves, the doors and windows, the newly varnished pine chest. It was all there: the crime that had never taken place.

Far out, was her first reaction. I did it! I got it! Then she realized what it was that she had actually gotten, and, with a groan of horror, buried her face in her hands.

Will was alone in the craft shop when she entered. She walked up to him and put her arms around him. "My poor Will," she said. "You weren't lying after all."

They walked together without speaking through the field behind the craft shop, their footsteps crunchy in the tall brown grass. She forced herself into patience, letting him get used to her knowing, letting him decide what to say. Finally, Will threw himself down on a log at the edge of the field. She wrapped her jacket more tightly around herself, settled in beside him, and let him talk himself out.

He had closed up the craft shop that evening and gone to the workroom. He had a date to help Zach build bookshelves, and he needed his tools. As he walked in, he heard a sound, and when he turned toward the sound, Samir was there, holding what Will later saw was an andiron over his head. Will moved instinctively, his arms lashed out, and the shove knocked Samir off balance. Samir fell, and the back of his head struck the corner of the pine chest.

There was no doubt in Will's mind that Samir was dead. There was no pulse, no heartbeat. Samir's open eyes were fixed in a stare. Will crouched beside the body and, in his panic, thought, Go on as if it never happened. Wait until later, when you can think. It didn't feel right to leave Samir where he had fallen, so he had arranged Samir's body in a more peaceful position and, just to be sure, had carefully retouched the surface of the chest. Then he had made sure all the doors were locked, wiped the key clean and replaced it under the window ledge, gone home, and stood in the shower until the first layer of horror washed away.

He decided that he would go to Zach's as planned and then "find" the body in the morning. He didn't know that Jennifer intended to paint the wood-burning stove in the café, and he never dreamed that anyone would enter the workroom before he did. He had lain awake most of the night, waiting for it to be morning, and then must have fallen into an early morning sleep because by the time he woke up, Jennifer had called the police and everyone was talking about homicide. He'd kept quiet and waited; it was only when Johns started threatening Zach that he knew he had to speak up. Annie's story of Samir at the co-op, which appeared to give Will an alibi, had surprised nobody more than Will himself.

He paused.

"Lying awake that night . . . Oh, Will, I can't imagine."

"No," he said. "You can't."

"I wish you'd just said what happened. You didn't need to go through all this. It was so obviously self-defense."

She saw him dismiss her with a wave of his hand. The sinews and veins stood out on his wrists, and she stared at them because she had always loved his hands and because she couldn't bear to watch his face.

When Zach was poisoned, he realized what must have happened. "Zach coming here was somehow a huge problem for Samir. I don't know what there was between them, and I was mad as hell that he thought I'd tell Zach what he had confided in me. But trying to kill me because of it? Weird as it sounds, Zach getting sick made me feel better because I figured, hell, Samir had tried to kill Zach and me both and had gotten what was coming to him. I told myself I didn't care anymore that he was dead. Since then, I've just been hoping that no one ever figured out the whole damn mess—not the cops, not anyone."

For the first time, he turned in her direction. "I'm sorry you did, Jen. I thought you'd stopped trying."

"I had. And last night, I decided, in a fit of stoned logic, that the crime had never even happened. The only trouble was, I was right."

"I don't get it."

"Neither did I, till this morning. Suddenly it all made sense because there actually *was* a crime that never took place. Namely, Samir killing *you!* That's why nothing was what it seemed to be and why all the leads just seemed to disappear."

"I still don't get it. Walk me through this."

"Sure. First, take the supposed murder weapon. David keeps his best drugs in his andirons and would never take one of them out of the house. It's found in your work room that morning. It seemed obvious that the andiron was used to kill Samir, except that the medical examiner established that it couldn't have been. The same thing is true of the fingerprints. They were all exactly where they should have been, on every surface except for the pine chest, which nobody expected to have fingerprints because you had just varnished it the day before. So that's the first bit—a murder weapon that isn't a murder weapon, and a crime scene with plenty of fingerprints, but none out of place.

"And then." She sighed. "There's the victim, who also appears to have been an illusion. There never was any such person as Samir Molchev. You knew all along that wasn't his real name, but his supposed real name, the one on his driver's license, was also a fake. And this guy, who is supposedly a serious fugitive, doesn't even have his fingerprints in the FBI's national data bank. Ford even used the word 'artificial' when he was talking about Samir."

She stopped suddenly, sensing Will shudder. Even in his

woolen jacket, he looked more than ever as if his frame was somehow too large for his body, the bones too pronounced in his craggy face. "Will, we don't have to do this."

"No." He reached over and squeezed her hand. "Go on."

"You'll stop me if you need to?"

"Yeah."

"Promise?"

"C'mon, Jen. Do you really think that talking about it can make it any worse?"

She glanced over at him. "Okay," she said, picking up the thread. "So then, of course, you have a bunch of suspects, namely, us. We know each other so well that we can all finish each other's sentences, but the night Samir was killed, there are a few odd details in which people behave in unpredictable ways. Samir and Annie hate each other, but all of a sudden Samir is hanging out at the co-op. Afterward, Annie is totally clear that Samir left the co-op at exactly a quarter to seven. Annie, of all people, who can hardly tell morning from afternoon! Put that all together, and what do you have? Nothing—except absolute proof that you, Will, were home and in the shower while Samir was supposedly still at the co-op, so that you couldn't have killed Samir.

"But what if you assume the whole thing is, in fact, an illusion, a set-up, pieces of a crime that was *supposed* to happen but didn't. Then you have a heavy metal object that was going to be used as a weapon, a murder that had been planned for six thirty, and an alibi, not for you, Will, but for Samir. It all fits, the whole thing, if you only realize that Samir intended to be the murderer, not the victim. Once you see it that way, it all falls into place. Samir turned his watch ahead half an hour, went to the co-op, and when the church bell rang pushed a watch saying a quarter to seven under Annie's nose. It was actually a quarter past six, but the church bell always rings once for the quarter hours, so it's the same for both. He knows you'll close the shop at six thirty, and he knows you'll need your tools to build Zach's bookshelves, so he goes to the workroom, picks up the andiron, and waits for you to come by. If he'd succeeded in killing you, he'd have come home and found some way of getting me or Wendy to note that it was just after a quarter to seven and therefore, he wouldn't have had time to do anything but leave the co-op and come directly home."

"You know, I was so crazed that night I forgot all about the damned andiron. I must have just left it lying there where he'd dropped it. Why the andiron, of all things?"

"I don't know. Because it was heavy and belonged to someone else, I suppose. I have no idea when he might have been at David's house."

"He was there with me that day," Will remembered. "He was telling me he was worried that Zach would figure out who he was."

"So, he saw the andiron and figured that David wouldn't miss it in that mess of a living room. He had no way of knowing that David stored drugs in the finial."

Will thought a moment. "Maybe he did know. I'd finished fixing David's plumbing, and David went into the living room because he wanted to give me a nickel bag as a thank-you. Samir might have seen him."

"And if the cops found the drugs, so much the better. It would just make them suspect David even more."

Will turned and looked back toward the main street of Flanders, where the church and the roofs of the café and craft shop could be seen behind the bare branches of the trees. Jennifer forced herself to wait until he was ready to talk again.

"But why?" he said finally. "Why would Samir try to kill Zach and then come after me? I wouldn't have told Zach any of his secrets. He knew that. And even if I had, he must have known Zach would never betray a pacifist who had been framed by the cops."

"You know something?" Jennifer mused. "My guess is that Samir was never framed by anyone. I'd bet that he wasn't even part of the anti-war movement at Berkeley. He couldn't have been. Zach would have come into contact with him at some point, and Zach had never met him. He told Ford he had never heard of a Samir Molchev or a Charles Blair.

"Samir's problem was that Zach could have figured out that his stories were bullshit. You wouldn't have had to mention Samir's name. If you'd even said, 'Hey, Zach, tell me about the time the Buddhists threw red paint on the selective service records,' and Zach had said something like, 'What Buddhists? It was the Quakers who did that. Or the Catholics. Or whomever.' Well, then you might have started wondering. Once Zach showed up, Samir had two people who were dangerous to him: you, who knew his phony story of what happened in Berkeley, and Zach, who would know that it was phony. And Samir would certainly have known who Zach was. Unlike Samir, Zach really was famous out there."

When Will was silent, Jennifer continued. "So, here's what I think happened. I was thinking back this morning to when Annie gave Zach the pickles. Zach and I were sitting at my table, and Samir was at the table right behind us. He saw Annie give Zach the pickles, and he also heard her tell Zach not to eat them for a week because they hadn't had time to steep. Remember later that same day? Annie came charging into the café, furious at how Samir was hanging out at the co-op, sort of lurking around the storage room when she was trying to close? My guess is that he went in to stash a package of poison on a lower shelf. From there, it was basic high school chemistry. Strychnine is soluble in hydrochloric acid, and the pickle brine is strong enough to sort of mask the taste of hydrochloric acid. All he had to do then was sneak into Zach's house, open the fridge, and dump in some poison."

"But why, Jen? Why did he decide to kill two people who

never did him any harm? He could have just split. There was nothing keeping him here."

"I think there was. That's the final piece, and nobody knew it until a week or so ago. He was about to make a huge score. Cocaine."

"What?"

"The cops found two pounds of cocaine in the glove compartment of a stolen car that someone had left in the Saunders field. Samir must have been expecting it—otherwise, he could have just split when Zach showed up. But then the coke just sat there because, unbeknownst to whoever left it there for him, Samir was already dead. That must have been what Samir was doing here all along. A big score in a college town, with his peace-and-love routine for cover."

"God damn."

"Hell, a few pounds of cocaine would have been nothing. Samir's probably been dealing drugs for years. I suspect, in fact, that he was the one person in the world whom Zach would happily turn over to the cops."

Will stared at her blankly.

"That drug dealer in Berkeley who sold Zach's sister the bad acid that killed her. Samir was at dinner the night that Zach told us about it. He must have totally freaked out."

"Damn." Will shook his head, trying to let it in. "I don't get it. Why the hell did he tell me those stories? About what a hero he was."

Jennifer shrugged. "Partly, I suppose, to give himself a history and an excuse for being so secretive. Partly to win the backing of someone—you—whose word everyone would trust. But I think he was the kind of guy who really dug thinking of himself as a desperado, lying, living on the edge, and having everyone fooled. He must have been much crazier than any of us could have known, conning us and loving every minute of it. It looks like the wild-eyed maniac theory was true, only we got the characters wrong."

Will hunched further into his jacket. "You know, from where I was sitting, what happened that night was all so obvious that I couldn't believe nobody figured it out. I've been trying to put it behind me, even trying to forgive myself." He snorted. "Fat chance, right? And I've been drinking beers with Ford and looking at him and thinking, You're a smart guy. How come you haven't figured this out yet?"

"You had an apparently unshakable alibi," Jennifer responded. "And anyway, who would believe that you'd ever kill anyone? What should have been obvious was that Samir was the one who tried to kill Zach. Samir was already dead at the time, but so what? There was no reason Samir couldn't have put the strychnine in the jar of pickles. I bet he got a real kick out of stashing the poison at the co-op to make it look as if Annie had poisoned Zach."

Will stood and raised his face to the sky. "You goddamned son of a bitch," he whispered. "You goddamned son of a bitch."

The sun had disappeared behind a cloud when Will turned back to Jennifer. They eyed each other.

"Why didn't you tell the cops right away, Will? Or else, at the church when you confessed? Why didn't you just explain what had happened? They couldn't have touched you. It was self-defense."

"Because," he said quietly, "it wasn't self-defense. At least, not completely. Or at least I'll never be sure that it was."

"But Samir attacked you."

"That's true. He did. But I'm still not sure. Let me ask you something. What do you know about what happened between Samir and Wendy?"

It took a moment before she could answer. Then, she said, "More than I think I should tell you."

"That's close enough. Well, I knew it, too, okay, and I was spitting mad by the end. God knows I wouldn't have tried to kill him, but when I saw him come at me, I gave that shove everything I had. I didn't mean for him to hit his head; I didn't even think of the possibility. But if it weren't for the thing with Wendy, I might have, you know, just pushed him away."

"Will, you can't think—"

"Yes, I can. I *do* think. And I didn't want her to know that. She can't ever know."

"She's got to."

"No. What the hell would I tell her? 'Listen, Wendy, by the way, I killed that guy you slept with because he came at me and I was glad to have an excuse'? You want to be around when I tell her that? She already thinks it's her fault, you know, in that way she has of being intuitively right about something. I don't want to watch her blame herself all her life for the fact that Samir is dead and I'm a murderer."

"Come on, Will. You're not a murderer! And all she has to know is that you pushed him in self-defense."

"Yeah, sure. 'I hate to be the one to tell you, babe, but remember that bastard you thought was so wonderful, who you thought was such an enlightened soul? Well, the guy wasn't above a little murder when the going got rough.' No way. I'd have rotted in jail if I had to, but I wouldn't stand for that."

"But . . ."

He walked back over to Jennifer and sat down, turning to look at her squarely. "Jen," he said, "my decision is already made. It was made the moment I re-varnished the corner of that trunk. You're the one who has to decide what to do. You can tell Ford and let him do what he has to do. Or you can *not* tell him and learn to live with this thing."

"The cops would believe it was obviously self-defense."

"What you mean is, Ford would believe it. Yeah, well, maybe he would. But then what? Do you think he would keep it to himself? Risk his career so that Wendy never finds out? Are you willing to ask him to do that?"

She sat staring at the ground. In the end, she said, "I can't tell him, can I?"

Will reached out a hand to stroke her back, then reached around to cover his eyes. She heard him start to weep.

"I'm so sorry." She leaned toward him and put her arm around him. "I wish I could help you."

"I feel so selfish. I'm so grateful somebody knows."

"Nobody should have to be alone with something like this."

"No. Alone was good," he managed between sobs. "The only thing that's kept me going is that at least I hadn't pushed the burden onto anyone else's shoulders. What do I do now?"

"Oh, Will."

She held his shoulders as he wept, remembering how frustrated she had been at his stubbornness. He must have been so desperately proud, she thought, of having hidden it so utterly. From Wendy. From everyone.

Well, she decided, if he could take it, so could she.

When he had cried himself out, he stood up and shook himself.

"Are you okay?" She looked up at him.

"Don't be stupid." He reached out a hand and pulled her to her feet. "Let's go. It's cold. I need to start moving."

They walked back in the direction of the craft shop.

"If you ever need to talk about it," she said. "I don't care where I am or how much time has passed or if I haven't seen you in twenty years. You'll always have my address."

"Thank you. But no. Now it's really over."

They passed out of the field and onto the road. Glancing over at him, Jennifer saw the big jaw clench and the determined, hidden space reappear in his eyes.

twenty-nine

Jennifer sat cross-legged on the floor, sifting through a pile of books and singing along to Bob Dylan. John Wesley Harding, friend of the downtrodden, traveling the country with his girlfriend and his gun. John Wesley Harding, who the cops couldn't catch or convict.

On the bed, Ford propped himself up on his elbow.

"So, do you know anything about the real John Wesley Harding?"

"No. Do I want to?" Jennifer interrupted her singing to ask.

"Probably not. The real guy was a monster. He started off killing former slaves, which didn't seem to bother a lot of people. Then he started bumping off state police and deputy sheriffs, and that pissed people off. The story is that he could always find a reason for killing someone—for snoring, once, or so the legend goes."

"Dylan makes him sound like another American Robin Hood. Robbing from the rich to give to the poor, like Jesse James or Pretty Boy Floyd."

"If I remember right, Pretty Boy Floyd wasn't much better."

"Well, according to Woody Guthrie, he'd beg a meal from a

poor family and when he left, they'd find a thousand-dollar bill under his napkin. Will you please stop disillusioning me?"

Ford lay back, listening to the album and remembering his first day in Flanders, Jennifer on a metal folding chair, quoting Dylan and telling Ford that to live outside the law you must be honest. Only two months had passed. It didn't seem possible.

"I was raised on that myth," Jennifer continued. "The so-called outlaw is the good guy, while the real sociopaths are the capitalists who send the Pinkertons out with machine guns to mow down striking workers. That's the mythic America I grew up with."

"Is that why you like Dylan so much?"

"What do you mean?"

"Because he's mythic?"

She thought about it.

"I suppose so. At least it's one reason. But *liking* Dylan isn't really the point. Dylan is the wallpaper inside my skull. He's the soundtrack of my life."

It was the third weekend in November. The leaf season was over, the ski season a month away. The late fall harvesting was done. The requisite arguments were taking place about whether Thanksgiving would be strictly vegetarian, although Annie's demand for nut loaf instead of turkey was muted this year by Zach's insistence that he'd head straight to his mother's house in Brooklyn if that was Annie's idea of a feast. Other than that, the usual consensus held. Making the holiday about the Indians, not the Pilgrims. Singing along to "Alice's Restaurant." No cut-outs of cute Pilgrims. No smiling cardboard turkeys. No store-bought cranberry sauce.

Jennifer found that she had been holding her breath about whether or not there would be a communal Thanksgiving this year. She was deeply relieved to notice that nobody was behaving very differently from any other year.

In the weeks since Halloween, Jennifer had watched for

occasions to be alone with Will. She lurked in the kitchen when she thought he might wander in and found excuses to come by the craft shop. In the odd moments when she managed to catch his eye, she saw him shake his head to warn her off before quickly looking away. She told herself that this was just a new version of the pride that allowed him to move forward. He would survive by asking no one to share his burden.

Except that she did.

Ford watched the shadow of the bare branches of the maple tree shift slightly on the ceiling.

"I wonder what mine is," he mused.

"What your what is?" She had been thinking about Will.

"My soundtrack."

She laughed. "Hell, I don't know. What was the Cisco Kid's theme music?"

"You know, the Cisco Kid in the original story was a vicious murderer who arranged to have his girlfriend killed when she fell in love with another guy."

"Should I take that as a warning?"

"Yeah. A warning not to believe everything you see on fifties television. You know how Wyatt Earp died?"

"With his boots on?"

"In his bed in Los Angeles, working as a consultant to movie Westerns. And Bat Masterson died in New York City employed as a sports reporter for the *Morning Telegraph*."

"Enough already! You're breaking my heart!"

"But hey, speaking of lawmen." Ford raised his head. "I've been meaning to tell you. We might have a new angle on the strychnine."

Jennifer froze.

"There was a stash of it found as part of a drug bust in Albany. It was being used to cut heroin, and apparently there was a—"

The phone rang in the hall downstairs. Jennifer jumped up a

little too quickly, with an expression that, to Ford's eye, looked a little too much like relief.

Left alone in the room, Ford turned his attention to the music. Something about Tom Paine, and then the song about St. Augustine he'd heard at the Halloween party. Dylan's images could get under one's skin, that was for sure. He listened to the words and to Jennifer's voice coming up the stairwell. She was saying something about the evening's poetry reading. It must be David on the phone.

Let us not talk falsely now, Dylan's gravel voice advised. Because we're through with the idea that life is a joke. Because this is not our fate. He had wanted so badly to solve the crimes that had brought him to Flanders. He had wanted to protect them all, even befriend them, but he could not have imagined, as he drove down the road that morning in September, that he would ever be lying on Jennifer Morgan's bed on a lazy weekend morning. Or that he would have been promoted to detective and given official charge of the case. He remembered the respect that had come into Doug Tyringham's eyes as he listened while Ford explained why Samir's murder and Zach's poisoning both were and weren't local crimes. Well, Ford was the one with the local knowledge now. He had searched Flanders more carefully than Jennifer had ever known, and while he had tried to separate his growing friendships from his role as a detective, his greater access to them all had given him the opportunity to study them. Aside from the locked door of Will Hampton's workroom, there was no evidence to implicate any of the residents of Flanders. And his wishes drew him to the same conclusion: none of them was a murderer.

So he had been glad to turn his official gaze beyond the small circle of the original suspects, to move beyond the apparent local knowledge and to try to solve the murder and the attempted murder out in the wider world. There were few clues and fewer leads, but at least the new focus allowed him to circumvent what had always been the weakness of the case against anyone in Flanders, specifically, the lack of any credible motive. The problem was, he wasn't getting anywhere. He was already anticipating the day when Samir Molchev's murder would disappear into the file cabinet of failures or be sent—it amounted to the same thing—to the police branch in charge of keeping unsolved cases open. He felt vexation, even a kind of shame, at not having presented the murderer to Jennifer, in triumph, like a dozen long-stemmed roses. But was that the point? The chance to impress or, even worse, deserve his girlfriend? Wendy was correct: what he most cared about wasn't love but justice. And someone was getting away with murder. That wasn't justice. That wasn't right.

In the downstairs hall, Jennifer grabbed the phone from its cradle.
"Hello."
"Jen?"
"Yeah. Hi, David."
"Listen, I know how last minute this is, but Charles isn't coming." Charles MacLeod was the featured poet in that evening's poetry reading.
"You have got to be kidding."
"No, I'm not. He's still in Montreal. He's in a snit because Margot dumped him for some Russian émigré who recites Esenin in the sack. In Russian, apparently."
"Okay, what do we do?"
"Cancel the reading."
"I can't. People will stop coming if we start canceling at the last minute. We need a substitute. How about one of your students?"
"My students don't write poetry. They masturbate with fountain pens."

"Doesn't self-absorption come with the territory?"

"Yes, but this bunch is not ready to be inflicted on the public."

She thought for a moment. "Who's the poet-in-residence at Williams this term?"

"Forget it. Talk about self-absorption."

"Well, there's got to be someone who can read tonight. Please," she begged. "I don't care if you have to do it yourself."

"None of my new poems is ready."

"Then get up on your hind legs and recite Robert Frost."

"I hate Robert Frost!"

"You can't hate Robert Frost, David. It's bad for the tourist trade." She paused. "You know, Graham told me he's been writing this fall since Joan took off for the seminary. He's just completed something in anticipation of Advent. I could," she offered slyly, "ask him to read."

"You wouldn't."

"I might."

She prepared to put the phone down, knowing that David would think of something and that the poetry reading would take place as planned.

"Hey, listen," David hurried to say. "I got my andiron back. The benighted fools didn't even bother to look inside the finial."

"Watch it, David. I'm very fond of one of those benighted fools."

"Ah, yes. North Adams' answer to Philip Marlow. Does he make love to you wearing his gun and holster?"

"Don't be vulgar."

"Or just stand in adoring guard over your slumbers?"

"And don't be ridiculous."

"Is he there now?"

"Yes, as a matter of fact."

"Well, tell him to get his ass out the door. It's about time he solved this thing."

"David," she said patiently. "It's Sunday."

David fell silent. Jennifer could hear his fingers tapping against the phone.

"Listen," she told him. "I've got to go. I'm in clean-up mode, and if I stop, I'll never get started again. But you should stop worrying."

"Why? Because Dudley Do-Right will protect us all? I don't mind telling you, I'm still looking over my shoulder, and it's getting pretty old."

She heard the quaver in his voice. "Hey, are you really frightened?"

"Hell, yes."

"Well, don't be. And call me if you think of someone better than Graham."

In the bedroom, Ford's attention wavered between Jennifer's voice and the music. She was talking to David, first about the poetry reading, then something about it being Sunday. Dylan was singing about two guys named Frankie Lee and Judas Priest. *The moral of this story, the moral of this song,* Dylan sang, *is simply that one should never be where one does not belong.* Jennifer's voice came at him, strong and sure, telling David not to be frightened. He heard her say, "But you should stop worrying," as if she knew that to be true.

Ford forced himself to think about her responses to him in the previous few weeks. She had stopped being eager to discuss the investigation. Her old half-appalled, half-fascinated interest in the details had dropped away. She looked away now when he talked about the case, and her relief just now when the phone rang had been palpable. He was running out of ways to fool himself into ignoring the obvious. She knew who had killed Samir Molchev. It was as simple, and as awful, as that.

He heard her say goodbye to David and then heard her

footsteps on the stairs. The song ended, and the automatic phonograph needle lifted as she entered the room and came over to him. She sat down next to him on the bed.

"That song," he said.

"'The Ballad of Frankie Lee and Judas Priest?'"

"Yeah. What's the thing he says at the end about the moral of the story?"

"*Don't go mistaking Paradise for that home across the road.* You know, when I was in graduate school, my dissertation was on Emily Brontë's novel, *Wuthering Heights*. The heroine falls into the trap of gender and class because she's charmed by the refinement of the neighbors' house. It's actually more complicated than that, but anyway, I was sitting there one day and listening to that song, and I thought, wow, that's also the moral of *Wuthering Heights*. It's what happened to Catherine Earnshaw."

Ford felt his heart break a little. "It's what happened to me."

Jennifer's first instinct was to pretend she hadn't heard him. She peered across the room at the half-sorted pile of books.

He tugged at her shirt to make her look at him. "Jen, if I ask you something, will you promise to tell me the truth?"

She looked down into his face and slowly shook her head.

"Just tell me this. You know who killed Samir, don't you?"

Her shoulders rose in a small, helpless shrug. Ford sat up, and they looked at each other across the bed.

"I can tell you this," she said finally. "It wasn't a crime."

"What do you mean, not a crime?" he demanded. "Shouldn't I be the one to decide that?"

"It was just"—she groped for the right words—"a complicated accident."

"Then there is no reason not to tell me."

"Yes, there is. They aren't my secrets to share."

"*Not your secrets?*" He threw his legs over the side of the bed and jumped to his feet. "This is a murder investigation! *My* murder investigation!"

She had never heard him raise his voice before. He stood there, glaring at her. "But that's it, isn't it? It's my investigation. I'm still the fuzz, even if I happen to be your boyfriend, and you're still making sure I don't hurt your pals by tromping all over their innocent little lives."

"Ford, please."

"I get it. As long as your friends aren't inconvenienced, you don't care whether this murder is ever put to rest or whether people who actually know something about law enforcement conclude that the public is safe. I could subpoena you, you know."

She stuck her chin out. "That wouldn't make me tell you."

"Then you'd be looking at contempt of court." He threw himself back down on the bed and sat with his head in his hands. "This is my career, Jen. This is my case. Don't you care about that?"

"Of course I care. It's what *else* I care about that's the problem."

"*To live outside the law, you must be honest?*" he spat at her.

"Oh, come on." She raised her arms in frustration, then reached out and touched his shoulder. "Please turn around. Look at me. I don't live outside the law. I'm a privileged little middle-class café owner who will do her thing in the Berkshires for a few more years and then go back to being a privileged little middle-class academic. But I can't tell you. I can't make you promise to keep it to yourself."

"You got that right."

"Look, Ford, you can believe me or not, but people knowing about it would do more harm than good. If it helps, I can promise you that there's no awful injustice hanging out there waiting to be rectified."

"What are you saying? That Molchev got what he deserved?"

"I suppose so. Yes."

"And Zach Lerner?"

She was silent. Ford forced himself to look at her and then forced himself not to care that there were tears in her eyes.

"Let me tell you something, Jen," he said. "To live *inside* the law you must be honest, and that's just as hard. And that's what my life is."

He leaned down under the bed and felt for his sneakers. She saw him pick up a sock.

"Where are you going?"

He lifted the sock in a vague gesture. "I don't know. But I can't do this. I can't wait around hoping I'll figure it out too, or, even worse, hoping that you let something slip, because you're the smart one, and I'm the dumb cop who's good enough to sleep with but not good enough to hear the truth."

"You're not a dumb cop!"

"Gee, thanks. Can I put that on my resume? Look, I've got to get out of here."

Just for a moment, he was tempted to relent as the tears spilled over and ran down her face. "Jen," he said more gently. "Can't you see this from my point of view?"

"I don't want to," she said in a small voice.

"Why?"

"Because you're right. Of course you're right! Of course you can't do this. And I don't want to lose you."

He smiled sadly across at her. "Maybe not. But you want other things more."

"And what do you want?" she came back at him.

"You know what I want. I want to solve this case. I want to be with you. But you know something? I want the Red Sox to win the World Series someday, and that's never going to happen either." He turned away, raised his foot onto the bed, and pushed it into the sock. He reached down and retrieved his other sock.

She watched him bend again for his sneakers, put them on, and tie the laces. If only she could think of the right thing to say. Maybe she could swear him to secrecy. Maybe she could beg Will to relent. There had to be some combination of words that would make Ford understand and change his mind. If she could only think of them, he'd stop tying up his laces, turn back to her, and stay.

But then he was standing and picking up his jacket.

"Are you really leaving?"

"Yeah."

"Will I ever see you?"

"I don't know. I can't think right now. But I don't think so, at least not like this."

He leaned down and briefly kissed her cheek.

"I wish you'd change your mind."

"I can't." She raised her arms in a gesture of helplessness.

"I'll never stop trying to crack these cases," he told her.

"I know."

He turned at the door and held up his hand.

"Goodbye, Cisco," she said. "I'll miss you."

"Adios," he replied.

epilogue

The hotel bar was noisy with CNN, cell phones, and conference-goers catching up on the latest gossip. Professor Jennifer Morgan sipped her Tanqueray martini and listened to Ford fill her in on his life. He had been married to the same woman for thirty-three years, a social worker named Bridget. The marriage had been in meltdown ever since the kids had gone.

It was hard to see him looking so much older, his skin thicker, his body stockier, although he clearly worked hard to keep it under control. She had seen the muscles under his shirt when he tossed his suit jacket over his chair. Hours at the gym, she guessed, and the odd weeks watching calories when things got out of hand.

Across the little table, Ford was nursing a beer.

"So," she said. "You've got three daughters."

"Aislin, Cassidy, and Megan."

"Proper Irish names." She smiled.

"My wife's idea."

"And you're director of what again for the Commonwealth of Massachusetts?"

"Community relations."

"That sounds earnest."

Seeing him laugh, she took a risk. She said, quietly, "Oh, Ford, you must have been so angry at me. You really disappeared. Did you ever forgive me?"

"No." He set his beer down. "Not really. But I've also never stopped being grateful."

She waited, hoping he would explain.

"You gave me words," he said. "To plug into what I knew."

"Which was?"

"That earnestness alone wouldn't make the world better."

"You knew that a lot better than any of us did."

He was touched to hear her say it. Somewhere between talking politics with Zach and listening to Wendy read his Tarot cards, he had wrapped his mind around the idea of social justice, and he had liked both parts of the term, social, because it wasn't selfish, and justice, which connected him to a bigger world.

"So why," she asked, picking up an earlier thread of the conversation, "are you looking to retire?"

"Not retire. Just give up my day job. I've hit forty years of service, and it's enough. Besides, the post focuses on making the state police forces more representative of the community, and my second-in-command is a young African American woman with a master's in diversity management. It's time to let her be in charge and for me to go off and be a senior statesman."

"Or a consultant."

Ford rolled his eyes. "That's been suggested. So, Jen, what about you?"

"The short version?" She rubbed her hands through her hair in a gesture he remembered. "I went back to New York and did the graduate school thing—I know, of course I did—and got hired to teach the next generation the sundry joys of the Victorian novel. I married another academic, a materialist historian of twentieth-century American popular culture who plays a mean bluegrass banjo. The divorce was very friendly."

"Sorry about that."

"Don't be. He was offered a job at UCLA. He'd just written a book on the movie version of *The Grapes of Wrath*, and there was a part of him that hungered for whatever was down the road from all those black-and-white frames of Henry Fonda. I, on the other hand, had just gotten tenure, we were fighting about whether or not to have kids, and I was in one of those intense periods where what I really wanted was to explore the quote-unquote mutability of sexual orientation, which translated into sleeping with my girlfriends. So he did California, I did the lesbian continuum, and at some point when he was back east, we gave each other a divorce for Chanukah. We still hook up again whenever both of us are unattached and he happens to be in New York."

"Who was the one who wanted kids?"

"He was. Believe me, I did not *forget* to have children. I write books instead. I spend too much time in the library, although these days being in the library often means sitting on the couch with my laptop. I am a household name in Cultural Studies departments that specialize in a very small branch of post-Foucauldian constructions of nationalism and gender."

"Could an ordinary guy like me understand your books?"

"I hope so."

"Are they feminist?"

"Of course."

"Post-modernist?" He smiled at her.

"Will I never stop underestimating you? How do you know about post-modernism, Cisco?"

"Cassidy, my middle daughter, went to graduate school."

She studied his face, still mustached, still open. He had jowls now, and there were wrinkles fanning out from his eyes. Once upon a time, she could have fallen into those eyes, curled up in them, and made herself a home.

"I didn't really, you know," she said. "I didn't underestimate you."

He nodded in acknowledgment. "So then, tell me," he said, changing the subject. "Why did you leave Flanders?"

She shrugged. "I was always going to leave. It was only a question of when. Can you see me still doling out boysenberry muffins to sophomores? You know, I thank the Universe every day that I was a sixties kid, but Flanders was already a tide pool when I got there. Teeming with life and drying up."

"And you had no idea," he noted, "what was riding in on the waves. You thought Nixon was as bad as it could get."

But what she had said was only part of the answer. Her life in Flanders might have been a masquerade, one long Halloween party in which she could be the High Priestess, the sweetheart of the zeitgeist, and the ghost in the espresso machine. But what had made it impossible to stay was the real ghost lurking in the house. And the ghost wasn't Samir. The ghost was Will.

Will, the small ache in the bottom of her heart for forty years now. She had gone on with her life. It was a good life, and the parts of it that hadn't been good had little to do with Flanders, Massachusetts. She took another sip of the martini. Ford reached his fingers into the bowl of peanuts between them and dropped a handful into his mouth.

"So," he said, his mouth full, "do you ever see the others?"

"Some of them. Let's see. Annie went to college and then law school and specialized in environmental law. She's the regional director of the Department of Environmental Conservation in western Pennsylvania. I'm not sure how she manages to deal with the bureaucracy, but apparently she has them eating out of her hand. I don't see her much, but Graham does—Graham is fine, just as convinced as ever that Good Works—capital G, capital W—will save his humorless Protestant soul, but Joan, his wife—you didn't know her, she was away at seminary that year—Joan is just like him, so at least he has company. They run an anti-poverty program in Appalachia, not far from Pittsburgh, which is why they see Annie from time to time."

"Do they have kids?"

"Two. One is working in a health clinic in Guatemala—at least, she was the last time I heard from them. The other became a Buddhist and teaches yoga."

"I bet that went over well."

"They didn't mind a bit. All roads lead to God, as it were. But the real *scandal*," she giggled, "is that David reverted to Catholicism. Not reverted, actually, since I think his parents were only religious in a sentimental kind of way. But David has gone totally over the edge—anti-choice, anti-gay, and convinced that the two worst things that ever happened to America were no-fault divorce laws and the women's movement. I try to keep tabs on him—he's a loud voice on the other side of the culture wars, and I can't resist shooting him provocative emails from time to time."

"Does he still write poetry?"

"Oh, yes. David has gone from modeling himself on W. B. Yeats to modeling himself on Gerard Manley Hopkins. I suppose it was inevitable. But you'll be glad to know that our warrior on the other side is still going strong."

"Zach Lerner?"

"Yup. Zach decided Williams was too rich for his blood and got himself a job at Brooklyn College. Even his most exacting friends told him he was nuts. He ended up marrying the head of the African American Studies department. I've run into them at demonstrations so often that it's become a kind of joke."

"And Wendy?"

"Wendy owns a bed and breakfast in New Hampshire. A few years after she and Will broke up, she married a puppeteer, a great guy named Sam who was a single father with three children. They have a slew of grandkids. She's gained about fifty pounds, has grey curls streaming down her back, and looks sort of like the good witch in *The Wizard of Oz*. But she designed her own Tarot deck about ten years ago, so she's a minor luminary in the world of the cyber-occult. You should google her sometime. Her deck is all over the web."

"I always liked Wendy."

"You still would. That scattered quality of hers has mellowed. She's the High Priestess as much as the Empress now."

They smiled at each other.

"You'll always be my High Priestess," he said softly.

"Thanks, Cisco."

There was one name left.

"And Will?" he asked finally.

Carefully, she reached into her glass and retrieved the olive. She placed it slowly in her mouth and chewed. "I have no idea where Will is," she said finally. "He left Flanders about six months after you and I stopped seeing each other. He said he'd keep in touch, but he never did."

She paused, feeling the familiar wave of guilt. There had been a series of moments in which Will could have gone to the police—when Samir first died, when Zach was poisoned, or when Ford took over the case. He could still have done so after their long talk in the field behind the craft shop. She should have insisted, should have known that otherwise his life was ruined. Instead, she had watched him grow steadily more unreachable. She had wanted to rage at him, to get him to unbend, to get him to tell Ford, to tell Wendy, and the rant inside her head must have been audible. He could hear it, and, in response to the unmentionable, he had closed the craft shop, told Wendy he was leaving, and gone away.

Ford reached an arm across the table and took her hand. "I

don't know where he is either," he said quietly. "But just between you and me, I haven't looked very hard."

She stared at him, astonished. "You told me you'd never stop trying to solve it."

He looked back at her steadily.

"But how . . . ?" she managed.

"*You* told me."

"*I* told you?"

"Sure you did. I was just too busy micromanaging my own hurt feelings to realize it at the time. Think of all the things you told me about your friends. You told me that Wendy needed protecting, even from herself, maybe especially from herself, and that Will was the most loyal person you'd ever known. You insisted that none of your friends was capable of cold-blooded murder, and while you might have been wrong about that, I ended up coming to the same conclusion. You also told me that you hadn't liked Samir, and I should have known all along that your dislike of him was itself a key piece of evidence."

"How so?"

"Think about it. Samir was some kind of fugitive—nobody lives under the bureaucratic radar as much as he did without a great deal of effort. He could have been a political fugitive—"

"He said he was."

"But then why weren't people protective of him? Nobody except Wendy was truly outraged that he was dead. And then, when I confronted you, you told me flat out that Samir deserved what he got. You also told me in so many words that you weren't afraid anymore, which could only have meant that you knew the spate of crimes was at an end."

"You knew me pretty well."

"I knew that you couldn't bring yourself to lie to me. You fudged a few things, but you didn't even really withhold information, at least not when it came to the murder—you just refused to help me connect the dots. So put them together.

Someone was dealing cocaine, and it wasn't any of you. Samir Molchev was underground doing something fishy, and in a town full of pacifists, nobody cared that he had died violently. At the time I thought you were just protecting each other because, whatever he was, he wasn't as bad as the police."

"The fuzz," she said ruefully.

"Yeah, the fuzz. But what was fuzzy was my thinking—my ego got in the way of what was staring me in the face. Samir must have been the one who tried to kill Zach, and his death must have been precipitated by something he did himself. That's the only explanation for your not caring whether I ever found out who had poisoned Zach and for your insistence that there was no injustice waiting to be avenged."

She sat, wordless.

"Okay, then," he said. "In police parlance, what you were telling me was that Samir's death was justifiable homicide, or self-defense, or something that wasn't actually a crime. Well, all indications were that Samir was killed in the workroom and that he had gone there under his own steam. What could he have been doing there? It was Will's workroom, and Samir went there at about the time Will usually shut the craft shop, so the likeliest explanation was that he had gone to meet Will. What I never did figure out was Samir's motive, and the truth of the matter is that I'd prefer you didn't tell me. The case is still open. There is no statute of limitations on murder."

"The specifics don't matter." She took a breath. "It was self-defense."

"That's what I figured. But even if it wasn't, the lack of evidence was such that we would never have gotten an indictment, let alone a conviction. It's all water under the bridge."

"Except that Will drowned in that water. And I'll never know what happened to him. I should have told you."

"Who knows if that's true?"

"You know something? To this day, I think of Samir the way

other people our age think of Altamont and the Hell's Angels. Suddenly it was clear that not everyone was dancing beneath the diamond sky with one hand waving free."

He smiled. "So, the fancy professor still quotes Bob Dylan."

Jennifer shook herself. Her guilt about Will was an old companion. "Bobby D. is now a Nobel laureate, and there's everything short of endowed chairs in Zimmerman studies. You should see the dissertation titles. 'Modalities of Innocence in Dylan's Middle Period.' 'The Mock-epic Voice in *Bringing It All Back Home*.' 'If You Meet the Devil on the Road, colon,'—and the colon is important—'Dylan, Sin, and the Nature of Evil.' I'm not kidding."

"I never hear a Dylan song without thinking of you."

She smiled. "And I never hear one particular song without thinking of you."

He waited.

"It's the version on the *Basement Tapes* of 'If You See Her, Say Hello.' I had to change the pronouns. *If you're making love to him,*" she sang softly, *"kiss him for the kid, who always has respected him for doing what he did."*

He reached across the table and took her hands. "Thank you. There was nothing else I could have done."

"I know."

"So, change the pronouns back. I could say the same thing about you."

She lifted one of his hands to her cheek and held it there, breathed him in.

"I have a meeting in a few minutes," he said. "What are you doing later?"

"Practicing the keynote I have to deliver in the morning. 'The Virtual African in the Works of Charlotte and Emily Brontë.' Class and gender as tropes of race."

"And after that?"

She paused, tempted. He had smelled so much like himself.

But no, she decided. "I'd never be able to keep my hands off you, and you have a marriage to resolve."

He nodded, accepting. "What time are you on tomorrow? I'll come listen."

"Please don't. I'd never be able to keep a straight face."

He reached up and touched her face. *"If you're passing by this way, I'm not that hard to find."*

"You got it."

She watched him stand, grab his jacket from the chair, and slip his arms back into it. Ford McDermott in a dark blue Italian wool suit. Well cut, she thought, and expensive. Like the heroine in a proper Victorian novel, she considered, she had learned what everything cost.

acknowledgments

It would be impossible to name all of the people who, over the years, contributed to the writing of this book. Some of the people in my life who, in various amalgams, came together as its characters are still beloved friends. Some, sadly, died much too young, and others have gone their various ways, and I have no idea where they are. But they've all stayed with me as the warp and woof of *Part of the Solution*, and I thank them.

Enormous thanks to the team at Torchflame: Teri for her enthusiasm and support, Jori for her knowledge and skill, and Chelsea for an eye that floors me and a knowledge of the Chicago Manual of Style that put this former English professor to shame. Bless you all.

How we tell the story of the 60s-70s counterculture is still an open question. Its foibles are clear enough at this juncture – it's all too clear that we didn't change the world. But idealism and the belief that the world could be better never really die, and I see that idealism reasserting itself today, in these troubled times. It is that for which I am most deeply grateful.

about the author

Elana Michelson is a New York City native who has encamped with her wife Penny to the Hudson Valley, where she writes, reads, gardens, and volunteers with local social justice organizations. After thirty-five years as a professor, she has put down a beloved career of academic writing (and student papers) in favor of writing murder mysteries. She earned a PhD in English from Columbia University, but gained her knowledge of the life and times of *Part of the Solution* from, well, having been there. Connect with her online at elanamichelsonauthor.com.

thank you!

Thank you for reading! If you enjoyed this book, please leave a review on Amazon, Goodreads, BookBub, The Story Graph, or anywhere else you like to track your recent reads. Alternatively, you could post online or tell a friend about it. This helps our authors more than you may know.
  - The Team at Torchflame Books